ADVANCE
ATHENA UNLEASHED

Any reader interested in the issues of sexism in the workplace, the "glass ceiling," and women in combat units, will find *Athena Unleashed* an entertaining and thought-provoking read. The authors have accurately recreated the challenges and struggles women in the 1970s and 1980s faced as they were forcibly integrated into previous male-only Army units. The main characters, each from different backgrounds, form bonds of friendship that help them navigate the nuances of a unique military culture not always open and receptive to women. Their professional and personal experiences with both success and failure, provide relevant lessons about the power of individuals to prompt change, persevere and provide opportunities for others. As a retired Army officer commissioned in the Women's Army Corps, in the early 1970s, I and other women of our generation had experiences similar to those captured in the pages of this book and the two that preceded *Athena Unleashed.* I have enjoyed all three volumes and look forward to future volumes.

Dr. Paula F. Furr, LTC, (RET) USA
Professor and Department Head
New Media, Journalism, and Communication Arts
Northwestern State University

"Athena Unleashed" is an excellent and entertaining read for anyone wanting to learn about and understand the opportunities and challenges young women faced during the early years of fully integrating women from the Women's Army Corps, into the All Volunteer Army. This historically based fiction series brought back a lot of memories. All three books in the series realistically portray the frustrations, joys and obstacles young women, (officers and enlisted) faced and are similar to situations I faced while on active duty in the '70's and '80's. I highly recommended the entire series to anyone interested in learning about the history of women in the Army, since the inception of the "All Volunteer Army" in the early seventies.

Cynthia Pritchett, CSM, (RET) USA

YVONNE DOLL | RUTH VANDYKE

a novel

ATHENA UNLEASHED

BOOK THREE *in the*

GUARDIANS OF PEACE SERIES

This book is a work of fiction. Names, characters, businesses, organizations, places, events, and incidents are either a product of the authors' imaginations or are used fictitiously. Any resemblance to actual persons, living or dead, events, or locales is entirely coincidental.

Published by Dog Ear Publishing
4011 Vincennes Rd
Indianapolis, IN 46268
www.dogearpublishing.net

This book is printed on acid-free paper.

Printed in the United States of America

Distributed by Dog Ear Publishing

Design and composition by Dog Ear Publishing

Cover design by Dog Ear Publishing

Cataloging-in-Publication data

Print ISBN: 978-1-4575-6077-4

First Edition

Other Edition(s):
eBook ISBN: 978-

1

I-59, ALABAMA, FRIDAY, 30 May 1980

UNSURE WHAT WOKE HER first—the jarring sound of metal on metal, brakes squealing, the smell of burning rubber, or her upper body violently pitching forward as she opened her eyes to the sight of a station wagon turned upside down, tires spinning inches from their front bumper, Anne exclaimed, "What the Hell!"

Maura's fingers were clenched so tightly around the steering wheel they were as white as her face as she tersely announced, "A car suddenly pulled into our lane and clipped the front of the station wagon as I turned onto the exit ramp."

The silence following the initial sound of the two vehicles impacting was suddenly broken by the piercing scream of a young child, "Mommy! Daddy!"

Unbuckling their seatbelts Anne and Maura ran quickly to the overturned vehicle. Seeing small licks of flame coming out of the station wagon hood, Maura yelled to Anne. "I've got a fire extinguisher in the trunk, you check on the kids!" Trying to avoid the shards of glass that littered the ground near the station wagon, Anne got down on her knees and stuck her head inside the overturned car. Seeing the terrified faces of a small boy and girl in the back seat, Anne quietly reassured them, "It's gonna be okay. I'll get you out."

The sudden whooshing of the fire extinguisher activating startled both children. The little girl screamed, "I want my mommy!"

"I know honey..." Anne murmured soothingly, "but mommy and daddy want me to get you and brother out of the car first." Anne locked eyes with the little boy. "I want you to grab my neck while I unbuckle your seat belt, so you don't fall out. Okay?" He nodded silently as he reached out and Anne released his belt. Still hanging on to Anne's neck as she pulled him out of the car, he turned his head and reached out for his sisters' hand. "It's gonna be okay sissy." Once Anne got the girl safely out of the car, she took both children by the hand and quickly walked away.

Having extinguished the flames coming out of the hood, Maura turned to the small group of motorists standing nearby. Pointing to a young, burly guy in front, she yelled, "You! Come over here and help me get these people out!" Kneeling down, she yelled at the still unconscious male driver. "Are you hurt?" Getting no response, she looked over to the passenger side of the car, where the bystander from the crowd Maura asked to help was trying to rouse the woman, who moaned slightly and upon opening her eyes screamed, "My babies! My babies!"

"Calm down ma'am, we have your children. They're safe and out of the car. Are you hurt?" Turning at the sound of Maura's voice, the woman saw her husband and screamed again. Maura calmly replied, "Ma'am, we're going to get all of you out safely, but I need you to calm down and tell me if anything hurts!"

Responding to Maura's calm but stern commands she mumbled, "I don't know."

"Okay ma'am, the gentleman outside is going to unbuckle your seatbelt. Please wrap your arms around his neck to keep you from falling and injuring yourself further." The woman nodded as the burly stranger reached in to help her out.

Turning her attention back to the unconscious driver, Maura stood up, carefully opened the door and gasped at the sight of blood pulsing out of the gash on his thigh. Turning her head towards the small group of onlookers she yelled, "I need two strong guys to help me get the driver out!" Maura returned with a tourniquet from the first aid kit in her car, as two of the men who had come forward to help, had the still unconscious driver out of the car and on the ground. Kneeling down, Maura applied a tourniquet and asked, "Do you know if anyone went to one of the roadside emergency phones to let the police know we need them and ambulances?"

One of the two men who had pulled the driver out of the car replied, "Dunno ma'am, but I have a ham radio in my rig and called it in just after it happened."

2

TUSCALOOSA, AL, SATURDAY, 31 MAY, 1980

MAURA GROANED AS SUNLIGHT streaming into the car woke her up. Before leaving Germany, Maura had splurged and bought a 450SL convertible. The bucket seats were great for driving, but even with an almost horizontal recline, they were not meant to sleep in. Looking over at Anne who was splayed out on the passenger seat sound asleep, Maura glanced at her watch. "*0600, too early to go to the front door,*" she thought, and immediately fell back asleep.

Started awake by pounding on her window, Maura opened her eyes to the face of an irritated Amelia. Fumbling for the door handle, Maura barely had it open when Amelia launched into a tirade. "What the Sam Hill are y'all doin'out here? I hardly slept a wink, worrying that you two had gotten into an accident and I had no way of contacting you!"

By now, Anne was awake and had gotten out of the car. "Sorry Amelia, we actually were in an accident," Anne said sardonically. Stunned, Amelia remained silent as Anne continued, "A car cut off the station wagon in front of us, clipped the front end and sent it flying into the air, landing upside down just inches in front of us. I was sound asleep and the first thing I saw was a smoking overturned station wagon. Scared the ever livin' shit outta me!"

Realizing Amelia's outburst was justified, Maura apologized. "We probably should have called you, but we were a bit rattled ourselves and just wanted to get the trip over with, so we just kept driving."

Amelia lamented, "I was just so worried about you guys. I waited up 'til almost two o'clock before giving up and going to bed. Did anyone get hurt?"

"Yeah, the driver was hurt pretty bad. The medics said he would'a died if Maura hadn't applied the tourniquet to his thigh to stop the bleeding. The mom and kids had some cuts and bruises, but they're fine."

Amelia blurted out, "Well that just beats all. I can't leave you two alone for six months, without you having some sort of crisis!"

"Amelia, you're as bad as my mom!" Maura scolded. Seeing the wounded look that only Amelia could summon in an instant, Maura hugged her friend. "We're sorry we worried you. Can we go inside, get some coffee and a nice long hot shower, before you berate us further for our lack of communication?"

Anne added jocularly, "And a hug and so glad to see you, would be nice too."

Amelia reached out to hug Maura and Anne. "Oh gosh, you're right. I'm just glad you're both okay and so glad you're here! C'mon, I'll put a pot of coffee on. I made sticky buns and fruit salad yesterday as a treat for breakfast."

★ ★ ★

"WELL LOOK WHO THE cat drug in." Recognizing Mr. Howard's distinctive drawl, Anne put down the homemade bun she was just about to bite into and turned around. "Yep, I'm back and eatin' ya outta house and home, just like the good ole days." Amelia's dad chuckled as he reached out to give Anne a huge bear hug. "It's good to have you home darlin', almost like the old days. Your room is ready and waiting for you." Extending his arms, he looked Anne up and down. "Looks like Army life, agrees with you."

Anne felt a lump in her throat as a host of emotions welled up inside her. "Thanks, it's good to be back. I didn't realize how much I missed being here until now." Amelia had invited Anne to spend Thanksgiving weekend with her family shortly after both of them had met while pledging to Kappa Delta during their freshman year at Alabama. Amelia had confided to her parents that Anne had lost her mom when she was a teenager and didn't want to go home for the holidays, because her alcoholic father would only berate her for abandoning him and beg her to transfer to Tulane and come back home. That was the first of many weekends Anne would spend with Amelia and her parents, who made her feel like she was part of a normal family.

Winking at Anne, he turned his attention to Maura. "Maura, I presume?"

Maura stood. "Yes sir, nice to meet you."

Mr. Howard walked over and gave Maura a hug. Surprised by this unexpected show of affection, Maura involuntarily stiffened. Mr. Howard pulled back and smiled. "Although we've never met, Amelia has talked about you a lot. She considers you as much of a sister as she does Anne and we're big huggers in this family, so you'll just have to get used to being hugged."

"Thanks Mr. Howard. You just took me by surprise. When I met Amelia for the first time, a bit over four years ago, she was a bit standoffish and I just didn't expect you to be so welcoming." Maura stopped and felt a flush of red fill her cheeks as she realized that her comments might be misunderstood.

Anne quickly came to her rescue. "What Maura means is that when she first met Amelia, she thought she was sorta stuck up."

Amelia interrupted in a slightly accusing tone. "Yes as I recall, Maura accused me of bein' uppity and called me Scarlett."

Mrs. Howard had been standing at the kitchen door listening to the women's banter and announced her presence as she walked in. "Yes, and we have your room set up as well Maura."

Walking over to the table she hugged Anne and then Maura, before giving her husband a peck on the cheek and sat down at the table with her daughter and friends. "Good mornin' everyone. Father, could you please get me a cup of coffee?" Mr. Howard just smirked and silently walked over to the percolator on the counter, to get both of them a cup of coffee as Amelia's mother drawled, "Well now, let's just all get caught up."

★ ★ ★

MAURA, ANNE, AND AMELIA walked into the dining room at the country club and were greeted by a tall, reed thin black man with close cropped white hair. "Good afternoon Miss Amelia, table for three?"

Amelia smiled at the elderly waiter who had known her since childhood and always seemed genuinely pleased to see her. "Afternoon Willie. We are just about starved from tryin' on dresses and getting final fittings for the weddin' on Saturday mornin'." Gesturing toward Anne and Maura, Amelia added, "D'ya remember Miss Anne? This is Miss Maura. They're my best friends and maid of honor and bridesmaid."

Leading them to a table, the waiter nodded first to Anne, "Nice to see ya again Miss Anne. It's been quite a spell since you been here ain't it?" Turning his gaze to Maura, he added, "Nice to meet ya ma'am."

"Yes Willie, it has been a good spell since we last saw each other," Anne replied. "But you haven't changed one bit."

"Thanks ma'am," Willie replied as he started pulling chairs away from the table for them to sit in. "I'll get three teas and menus right away, so we can get you ladies somethin' to eat." and promptly walked away.

"Thanks, I'd love nothing better than cold tea right now." Maura dryly muttered under her breath as Willie walked away.

"You've never had iced tea, have you?" Amelia asked.

Maura rolled her eyes upward. "Nope and never planned to. A gin and tonic would taste real good after three hours with the dressmaker, but I guess this is as good a time as any to try something new."

"Hey, what about all the different foods and drinks you convinced us to try in Europe?" Anne admonished. "Remember that restaurant in Goppingen when they brought a grilled trout, head and all on the plate, beady little eyes staring up at us and Amelia ran to the bathroom and threw up?"

"Yes, you even convinced *us* to drink *hot tea and gluhwein!*" Amelia retorted indignantly.

"Okay!" Maura raised her hands in mock surrender. "I'll try it."

"Well now, what's goin' on here?" A deep male voice with a heavy southern drawl inquired from behind Amelia.

"Charles, what a nice surprise!" Amelia responded gaily.

Charles bent over to give Amelia a welcoming kiss and indicating the open chair asked, "May I join you ladies?"

"I'll get up so you can sit between Amelia and Maura." Anne offered.

"Thank you Anne." Charles replied stiffly as he turned his attention to Maura and said in a much warmer tone of voice, "Nice to finally meet you Maura. I've heard a great deal about you." Maura pasted a smile on her face, not sure what to say. Anne had already prejudiced her against Charles because of the way he had treated Amelia when he broke off their engagement four years ago. Charles broke the awkward silence by asking, "How did the fittings go? Do you like the dresses Amelia chose for you?"

Relieved at finding some neutral, but common ground, Amelia chimed in, "Yes, the dresses look absolutely gorgeous on them and only required a bit of adjustment. We'll go back for their final fittings on Wednesday."

Willie arrived at that moment with three iced teas and menus. "Afternoon, Mr. Charles. Would you like your usual?"

Charles smiled. "No thanks Willie, I'm headed to the gentlemen's lounge." Looking back at Amelia, he asked, "How did they like their gifts?"

Struggling to hide her frustration at Charles for ruining her surprise, Amelia reached for the handbag hanging on the back of her chair. Pulling out two small rectangular boxes wrapped in silver paper with white bows, she handed one to Anne and then Maura. "I was going to wait until after dessert, but now is fine, I hope you like these."

Maura had hers open first and gasped, "Oh Amelia! They're beautiful, but you shouldn't have."

"Wow!" Anne whispered, transfixed by the pearl choker and earring set. Looking up at Amelia, she got out of her chair and hugged her. "It's absolutely fitting that you would give me the first piece of real jewelry I've ever owned. Thanks."

Maura added, "I couldn't have picked out a better set myself. This is so kind of you."

Charles stood up. "Well ladies, I'm sorry I spoiled the surprise. Nice to meet you Maura." Putting his hand on Amelia's shoulder, he added, "The guys are waiting for me in the lounge. We're gonna have a few drinks before heading out for my bachelor party." He kissed Amelia on the cheek and walked away, without acknowledging Anne.

All three women were uncomfortably aware of Charles neglecting to say good-bye to Anne. Trying to pretend she didn't notice the slight, Anne picked up the menu. "Is there anything you recommend we try Amelia?"

★ ★ ★

ANNE HAD JUST FINISHED her shower when there was a knock at her bedroom door, followed by Maura's voice. "It's me."

"C'mon in." As Maura opened the door, Anne asked, "Hi, what's up?"

"Just wanted to chat."

Anne pointed to the set of chairs by the window as they both walked over and sat down. "I can't believe how rude Charles was to you today." Maura blurted out.

Anne shrugged her shoulders dismissively. "I'm used to it. It doesn't bother me because I know it drives him crazy that I'm still very much a part of Amelia's life and he's been forced to accept that will never change."

Maura pursed her lips and replied musingly, "Given your account of the tongue lashing he gave you and Amelia just before graduation, I guess I should have given him a chance to prove he isn't as big a butt wipe as he appears to be. But when he walked away without saying anything to you today, that just made my blood boil!"

Realizing this wasn't going to be a short conversation, Anne pulled her legs up to the seat cushion lotus style and leaned back adding, "She's loved Charles since first grade and there's never been anyone else, except of course Mattias."

Maura shook her head in disbelief. "I just don't get what she sees in Charles. Even worse, she dumps Mattias, who is German royalty, a hunk, and crazy in love with her, for the guy who didn't come to her graduation, broke her heart and wouldn't answer any of her letters for almost a year." Pausing, Maura looked at Anne and asked pensively, "Do you think they'll be happy?"

Before Anne could respond, there was a quiet tap at the door. Not waiting for a reply, Amelia opened the door juggling a tray with three wine glasses, a bottle of white wine, and some sliced cheese and fruit. Seeing both of them there, she gasped in delight as closed the door behind her with her foot. "I don't know 'bout y'all, but I can't sleep a wink and I've missed both of you so much!" Setting the tray on the end table between the two chairs, Amelia pointed to the unopened bottle of wine as she sat down on the floor "Would one of you please open that?" then added, "We spent the entire day talking about wedding stuff. I'm dying to hear about airborne school, Lori and Trish's graduation at West Point, and the latest about Derek and Eric!"

Anne grinned wryly as she reached for the wine bottle and opener. "I think this is gonna be another one of those all-nighters. Maura, you give her the details on the graduation while I get all of us a glass of wine."

3

TUSCALOOSA, ALABAMA, FRIDAY, 6 JUNE 1980

AMELIA TURNED AWAY FROM the window overlooking the backyard as she heard the door to Mr. Howard's study open and smiled at the sight of Anne and Maura in their maid of honor and bridesmaid dresses. The emerald green, strapless, a-line dress with an empire waist and pearl studded bodice was the perfect color to bring out Anne's amazing green cat eyes, while complimenting her tawny colored skin and chestnut brown hair. Maura was equally striking in the very same dress in royal blue, which accentuated the beauty of her striking blue eyes and jet black, flowing long locks, against her flawless, alabaster white skin.

Amelia gasped with delight, "Oh my gosh, you guys are beautiful! All eyes are going to be on you as you come down the aisle."

Anne smiled, "Well, I'm glad you think so, because you are the only person who could ever get me to dress up in something like this AND agree to having my hair and make-up done!"

Maura interrupted, "Have you looked in the mirror Amelia? No one will even give us a second look once they get sight of you and that's how it should be." Maura took Amelia by the arm, walked her over to the large mirror that had been put in the study that morning and pointed to her reflection. "That is the sight of an angel."

"All brides look beautiful, it's no big deal." Amelia replied reflexively, as she turned back to the mirror to study her reflection a bit closer. She had chosen to wear her grandmothers wedding dress that had been handed down from her mother, who had worn it on her wedding day. She was really nervous when she'd asked her grandmother's permission to alter it; but was pleasantly surprised when her grandmother told her the dress was hers to do with as she pleased. The dress had a lace covered, heart shaped, satin, close fitting bodice, with two rows of hand sewn pearls as a waistband that framed the full satin skirt, which seemed to float, with the help of two gossamer crinolines underneath. The only alteration Amelia made was to remove the long lace sleeves, making the dress sleeveless. In lieu of a veil, Amelia had sprigs of baby's breath intertwined in the Gibson girl bun at the crown of her head. "Do I really look that beautiful?" Amelia asked quietly.

The sound of a deep male voice startled all three women. "More beautiful than even I could have imagined darlin'." All three women turned in unison to see Mr. and Mrs. Howard standing in the doorway. Mrs. Howard had covered her mouth with her hand as she tried to regain her composure at the sight of her daughter. Looking at all three of the young women as she walked over to give Amelia a hug and kiss, Mrs. Howard's voice cracked a bit, as she emotionally exclaimed, "All of you are just so beautiful!"

Aware that they only had an hour before guests would start arriving for the backyard wedding and reception, Mr. Howard announced, "I apologize for rushing you ladies, but we need to get a few pictures taken out front on the porch, before the groom and guests arrive."

★ ★ ★

AMELIA, MAURA, AND ANNE laughed as they entered the study, quickly shutting the door behind them. They had just finished taking one last picture of the three women standing together on the front porch, when Amelia shrieked, "Oh my gosh, that's Charles and his parents comin' down the driveway!" Followed immediately by Mrs. Howard yelling, "Get inside quick!"

"Whew, that was a close one!" Maura declared. Flopping down in the wing chair, Amelia looked at the clock on the wall. "What in the world are they thinkin'? They're fifteen minutes early!" Looking at Anne and Maura, she nervously asked, "D'ya think Charles saw me?"

Not really sure, but wanting to reassure Amelia, Anne immediately replied, "No, no way."

Maura walked over to the small snack and bar area that had been set up for them while they waited for the guests to arrive and the ceremony to begin. "I don't know 'bout you guys, but I need a glass of wine. You want one?"

Without even a second's hesitation both Amelia and Anne cried, "Yes!" Both women started walking toward Maura at the other end of the room. With wine glasses in hand, Maura lifted her glass. "To Amelia, we hope life brings you nothing but joy and happiness."

"Hear, hear," Anne added. They touched their glasses together in a toast and took a sip of the sauvignon blanc Amelia had chosen for the reception. Looking at Amelia, Anne pointed to the bar that had finger sandwiches, berries, cheese and crackers. "You need to eat a little of this Amelia. You haven't had a bite to eat since breakfast this morning and you didn't eat much then. You don't want to pass out before you say your vows do you?"

Amelia shook her head. "I know I should eat, but I'm just too nervous. I couldn't swallow a bite right now, to save my life."

Noticing that Amelia had downed almost half a glass in a single gulp, Maura pointed to Amelia's wine glass. "Well, just make sure you don't drink too much of that, otherwise you may not even make it down the aisle."

Amelia giggled as she took another sip. "Oh my gosh, can you imagine the twitter if I arrive at the ceremony inebriated?"

At the thought of Amelia staggering down the aisle, eyes glassy, cheeks flush, and a goofy grin on her face, the three women laughed hysterically. Amelia finished off her glass and said as she reached to refill it, "Aw hells bells, I've got a lifetime of impossible expectations ahead of me, and this may be the last time for a long time that it'll just be the three of us together. Let's just have some fun and relax!"

★ ★ ★

SWALLOWING THE LAST BITE of wedding cake on her plate, Anne stood up, took a large gulp of water, picked up her wine glass and whispered in Maura's ear. "Let's see if we can get the bride to sneak away for a few minutes." Maura nodded as she grabbed her wine glass and got up from her seat at the head table.

Amelia turned her head and smiled, as she saw both of them get up and approach her. "Hey gals, are you enjoying yourself?"

Charles turned and scowled at both of them as Anne blithely ignored him. "Can we spirit you away for just a few minutes?"

Sensing Charles' disapproval, Amelia hesitated for just a second, before responding, "Of course." As she stood up, she reached over to Charles who was glaring at her and gave him a peck on the cheek. "No one will miss me darlin' and this will be the last time I have to chat with the girls before we leave for the airport." Pausing, she looked over to her right at the best man. "Will, would you be a treasure and come over here to keep Charles in good humor while we ladies go off for a bit?" Not waiting for a response, Amelia picked up her wine glass and walked off with her friends.

Walking arm in arm back towards the house, the women were silent until they entered the study and sat down together on the sofa.

Maura turned to Amelia, "Maybe we shouldn't have asked to spirit you away, but if we didn't, we wouldn't have time to to thank you for a wonderful week together and remind you how much we love and will miss you." Looking at Anne, Maura added, "Plus, little miss sour puss is worried about you."

With a look of frustration on her face, Anne remarked, "All I want is for you to be happy and if being married to Charles makes you happy, then I'm all for it." Pausing Anne continued, "Charles says he's changed, but everything I've seen this week tells me he's still the same stick up his ass, bigoted asshole he's always been!"

In a quiet, but firm tone, Amelia rebuked Anne. "That's my husband you're talking about."

Appropriately chastised, Anne nodded as she took a drink of her wine. Amelia continued in a gentler tone. "I know this is coming from concern for me, but I've known Charles all my life and he has a special sweet spot for me. He and I have had some very long conversations about my not being the timid, acquiescing girl he knew four years ago. He's willing to change, but it's going to take time and patience."

Anne looked at Amelia and asked plaintively, "
Are you happy Amelia? I mean, like crazy in love, can't hardly stand it kind of happy?"

Amelia blushed. "I love Charles and am happy, but I'm also a little nervous."

Going into the protective mode again, Anne demanded, "Of what?"

"Well, remember how nervous, crazy and scared Maura was when she decided that whether or not Eric wanted to marry her, she wanted him to be the first?"

"Oh God," Maura groaned. "Please don't remind me. I was such a goof ball and totally out of control!"

Amelia laughed quietly as her cheeks turned red again. "Well, you know me, I'm never out of control, but I am scared. In about six hours we'll be at the hotel in Atlanta and I mean....what if I don't like it?"

Surprised by Amelia's admission that she was nervous about losing her virginity and worried what to do if she didn't enjoy it, Maura and Anne were stunned into a momentary silence that erupted into unbridled laughter.

"Oh my gosh Amelia!" Anne chortled. "You are a mess! He's an asshole, but he's a good looking asshole and my guess is, he's had lots of experience. His ego will depend on you wanting more, so don't worry, it'll be good…no it's gonna be amazing and the most fantastic thing you've ever experienced!" Emptying her wine glass in one gulp, Anne abruptly stood up. "Okay, enough. This is a done deal and we don't have much time. We'll follow you when you come in here to change before you guys leave and put your dress and shoes in the storage bag. Maura and I put your overnight bag for the hotel in Atlanta in the back seat, but the rest of your luggage is in the trunk."

Excited at the prospect of the flight to Hawaii tomorrow afternoon and a week at the Ilikai hotel on Waikiki beach Amelia said excitedly, "I just about fainted when Charles' parents told us they were sending us to Hawaii for a week as our wedding present from them! I promise to take pictures and mail some to both of you." Amelia hesitated and then continued in a mock stern voice, "You need to send me your address at Ft. Bragg as soon as you get it and I'll expect regular letters and some pictures too!"

Before anyone could say anything else, the door opened, Charles walked in and sternly announced, "Amelia, we have other guests to attend to and we'll be leaving for Atlanta soon, so I really need the three of you to finish your good-byes."

Not wanting Amelia to feel any angst, Anne reached out to give her a final hug and kiss. "Charles is right. You have responsibilities and we're keeping you from them. Standing up, she pushed Amelia over to Maura who hugged her and insisted, "Have the most amazing time in Hawaii. We love you, now go with Charles and for God's sake, have fun!"

4

TUSCALOOSA AL, SATURDAY, 7 JUNE 1980

"LET ME HELP YOU with that," Knowing better than to argue with Mr. Howard, Anne relinquished the suitcase he'd grabbed and continued down the porch steps to Maura's car. Mr. Howard looked inside the trunk and asked dubiously, "Is this gonna fit?"

Taking the suitcase from him, Maura wiggled it in. "It's a tight fit, but there's enough room for everything except our gowns, which I've laid out flat on the back seat."

Everyone turned at the sound of Mrs. Howards' voice, as she walked down the porch stairs with a red and white cooler. "Well, you'll have to make room for this." Maura started to say they didn't need any food, but before she could get the first word out, Mrs. Howard raised her hand. "Just shush young lady. I know how you young'uns are and ya'll just drive 'til you almost can't stand it and won't stop for a proper meal. There's a container of homemade chicken salad from yesterday's lunch, chips, a six pack of cold Tab, and two pieces of leftover red velvet groom's cake. Y'all can eat it in the car, like pack rats, or maybe ya'll just stop for a bit, have a picnic and enjoy yourselves."

"Thank you ma'am, this will be a wonderful treat later on today." Anne said as she took the cooler and put it on the floor behind the driver's seat. Anne gave Mr. and Mrs. Howard a long hug. "Thanks for everything, you two are just so wonderful."

Tears welling up in her eyes, Mrs. Howard smiled, "Okay, now you just get on down the road and call us when you get to…"

"Fort Bragg, North Carolina," Anne added. "It's gonna take about 12 hours to get there ma'am, so it'll be late. How 'bout I call you Sunday afternoon, after ya'll have had time to go to church and the country club for lunch? That way we can have a nice conversation."

Putting his arm around Mrs. Howard, who had started sniffling, Mr. Howard said, "That sounds fine Anne. We'll be lookin' forward to it and call collect, that way we don't have to worry about the operator tellin' ya, to put more money in the pay phone or disconnecting us, because you ran out of change."

"Yes sir," Anne said, as she gave each of them one last quick hug and got in the car. Closing the door, she turned to Maura, "Let's go, I hate good-byes."

★ ★ ★

AS THEY PULLED ONTO Main Street, Anne took one last glance down the driveway, before reaching behind her seat to pull out the road atlas. Anne pointed straight ahead, "About half a mile up the street, you'll see a sign with the university on it. Follow those signs 'til you get to University Boulevard. From there, just follow signs to Alabama 43 and I-59 North to Birmingham."

Sensing Anne wasn't really in a talkative mood, Maura concentrated on getting them out of Tuscaloosa and on I-59. Anne looked out the window as they made their way through downtown Tuscaloosa, suddenly realizing she might never return. It was not until they had reached the outskirts of Birmingham that Anne turned to Maura and broke the comfortable, but long silence, "You need anything?"

"A cold Tab and a navigator update would be nice," Maura replied.

Reaching behind Maura's seat to pull out two cold Tabs from the cooler, Anne said, "Just follow the signs for I-20 East. It's about two and half hours from here to Atlanta. We'll stop for gas, eat lunch, and I'll drive for a couple of hours. Sound good?"

"Yup," Maura said as she took a long gulp of the ice cold Tab and placed the half full can in the built-in cup holder behind the gearshift.

Anne put her can in the slot behind Maura's. "This is a real beauty Maura. You were smart to wait until it was almost time to leave Germany to buy your car and get all the latest gadgets."

Maura laughed. "Yeah, you should'a seen my dad playing with the power windows and cruise control. He was like a six year old kid! It reminded me of the time in the sixties when we flew out of LaGuardia. I'd never seen electric doors that opened and closed automatically. My parents were busy with our luggage and getting checked in; so I took my brother's hand and we walked around the corner to the terminal doors. I told him to jump on the black rubber pad with me. The doors flew open and we just yelled with glee. We did that for about a minute, before a cop came up to us and sternly asked where our parents were."

"Oh too funny Maura! What did the cop do?"

"He took us back to my parents, who had just finished checking in and realized we were gone. I lost a week's allowance over that prank, but it was worth it."

Anne sighed as she remarked in a plaintive and reflective tone, "Life was a lot simpler and happier when we were little…."

"You've been a lot quieter than usual, is something bothering you?" Maura asked gently.

"Not really, I guess I'm just feeling a bit unsure of what I really want out of life," Anne looked over at Maura, "What about you?"

"Hadn't really thought about it. You wanna talk about what's bothering you?"

"Dunno," Anne mused.

Maura knew that if she pressed her, Anne would shut up tight as a clam, so she reached down to take another drink of Tab and was quiet until Anne was ready to talk.

"I guess seeing Amelia with Charles got me to thinking about Derek a bit more."

"Well he's at Bragg, so you can look him up when we get there, right?"

Anne blushed. "Uh, actually, he's expecting me to call him when we get there."

"Okay," Maura replied haltingly, unsure what to say next, because Anne hadn't mentioned Derek, since her and Maura's discussion about him almost two years ago, when she got back from emergency leave for her dad's funeral.

Anne hurriedly added. "Derek's been calling me once a month and we've had some interesting conversations. One of the reasons I chose Ft. Bragg was to spend more time with him to see if what we have is strong enough to consider marriage."

Surprised by this admission, Maura momentarily took her eyes off the road to look at Anne before returning her gaze to the road.

Anne continued," I'm not sure why I didn't tell you. I guess I just forgot.... Seeing Charles and Amelia and the issues they have—and realizing we're on our way to Bragg and Derek's expecting me to show up all crazy happy to see him has me nervous. Derek and I are so different and I'm sorta looking forward to seeing him, but sorta dreading it, because I know I won't react well if he presses me to commit to marrying him."

"If he asked you right now, what would you say?"

Anne hesitated for a few seconds, before responding querulously. "I'd say I love him....but not sure I'm ready to commit to marriage. Derek and I are so different—I think we need to take some time to get to know each other better and revisit this about a year from now." An uncomfortable silence set in as both women tried to figure out what to say next. Suddenly Anne blurted out, "What would you say if Eric proposed to you now?"

Maura laughed heartily. "How the heck did we go from Derek and you, to Eric and I?"

"Well you're still crazy about him, you saw each other at least once a month while we were still in Germany and he's trying to get to Ft. Bragg now too. Right?"

"Yeah, but he's never even hinted at the possibility of marriage."

"Are you okay with that?"

"Yeah, I mean there's a big difference between seeing each other occasionally and deciding to get married. That's the main reason I'm glad he decided to ask for Bragg when I told him that was the assignment branch had offered me. It'll give us time to be a real couple and see where that leads."

"Does it bother you that he's a lot older than you?"

"Not really, even though he's 40 and I'm 27, I just never think of him as old; he's so energetic, smart…"

"And a real hunk," Anne added teasingly.

"That too…" Maura acknowledged with a lopsided grin. "But I just have so much fun with him. We like the same things…"

"And the sex is great!" Anne interjected again.

Blushing, Maura wryly admitted, "Yeah that too, but I'm content to enjoy what we have for now and not think about the future."

"I think that's great and I feel the same way; but Derek has taken it to a new level the past few months."

"How so?"

"When I told him I'd gotten assigned to Bragg, he said, 'Wonderful, I've got a great apartment off-base, you can move in with me!' Seeing the look on Maura's face, Anne hurriedly continued, "I know, I should'a talked to ya about this before, but I wasn't even ready to have this talk with myself or Derek, let alone anyone else!"

Maura replied sardonically, "Yeah, I'm sorta getting used to you dropping these bombshells on me and having to catch up."

Worried she'd upset Maura by not confiding in her earlier. Anne said dejectedly, "I'm sorry."

Maura waved her hand, dismissively. "Anne, I get it that you don't talk things through with other people; but it's just a little jarring the way you finally choose to open up to me and it takes me awhile to figure out how to respond."

"No offense meant Maura, but just listening helps. You're always wanting to respond and fix things when lots of times, I just want to talk and am not asking for advice."

"That's fair and no offense taken. I guess I was a bit irritated when you mentioned Derek expects you to move in with him; because I thought we were going to try to find a place to share and live together."

"We are. I never said yes or no, because I wanted to tell him in person that while I love him, I'm just not ready to commit to moving in together. I'm going to have to drop this on him in the next day or so and I'm worried about hurting him."

"Well," Maura mused, "if you explain that you're not saying no, you just need some space and want more time together before you commit to moving in with him, I think he'll be fine with it. I'm guessing he knows how guarded you are?"

Anne chuckled as she recalled a few incidents from the past. "Yeah, he does and he's never lost patience with not knowing what I'm thinking or going to do and pretty much just goes with the flow."

"I'm looking forward to meeting him."

"Yeah, he wants to meet you too. I've talked about how close we are and he knows you're coming to Bragg." Before Maura could respond, Anne added in an apologetic tone, "Oh by the way, when I told him both of us were coming to Bragg, he offered to set you up with one of his friends; so I told him about Eric, that it was serious and Eric was working on an assignment to Bragg."

Seeing a look of irritation momentarily cross Maura's face, Anne was relieved to see the tension drop from Maura's face as she responded. "We're good, glad you mentioned he knows about me and Eric."

Changing the subject Anne asked, "Are you excited about being assigned to the 82nd Airborne? Have you gotten any update on what position they're giving you?"

"Apparently, there's as much consternation about my coming to Bragg as there was about my going to the First IDF in Goeppingen. Branch said the G-1 at Corps wanted to assign me to the XVIII Airborne Corps Artillery; but branch pushed for me to be at a brigade again. It appears I'm going to the DISCOM, but I won't know for sure until I get there. What about you?"

"I got a nice letter just before I left Stuttgart from my sponsor at the JFK Warfare Center. She's an MI Captain. I'm apparently going to be assigned to the logistics support branch. I have her office phone number and she told me to call her when I get there."

"Wow, that's nice. I don't think they've assigned anyone to sponsor me, probably because they haven't figured out exactly where to put me. I can survive most anything, but I'm hoping it won't be as brutal as the first IDF."

Anne exhaled loudly, "Man, that was a nightmare. I don't know how you did it."

Maura wryly noted, "Well, to quote Nietzsche, 'What doesn't kill you, makes you stronger.' I don't mind challenges, but I feel like I'm part of a social experiment."

"Well I'm actually a bit envious of you. I still haven't served in a combat division yet."

"Yeah, but you did get to be a platoon leader and company XO. I wasn't allowed to do that, because of where the chemical platoons are deployed on the battlefield."

Anne ruefully replied, "Yeah, but the really sought after positions are in the division….

Having said that, the good news is I'm going to Bragg, so I might have the opportunity to transfer over to the division after a year or so."

"I'll be on the lookout for who might be rotating out of the DISCOM in a year or two. Maybe you can come over to my office in a few weeks and I'll introduce you to the '3' and whoever else is in a position to offer you a job somewhere along the way."

"Thanks Maura. That's a really good idea! Pausing for a second, Anne added, "It'd be really cool to both work together."

Maura smiled, "Yeah it would. Speaking of good ideas, I'm getting hungry. What about you?"

Craning her neck to look at the highway sign they were approaching, Anne responded, "The sign says we're 40 miles from Atlanta. I'll keep an eye out for a large truck stop. We can fill up, go the bathroom, and get a bite to eat."

"Sounds good, maybe they'll have some picnic tables nearby and we can eat the chicken salad and red velvet cake Mrs. Howard gave us."

5

FORT BRAGG, NC, MONDAY, 9 JUNE 1980

MAURA WALKED OUT OF the 82nd Airborne Division Support Command (DISCOM) headquarters company looking at a map of Ft. Bragg, to determine how to get to her new office, when she literally ran into the headquarters company commander. After apologizing, she asked him if he could tell her how to get to the DISCOM and he told her he was going there right now and she could follow him.

"What in Sam Hill took so long?" was the first thing Maura heard as she walked into the DISCOM operations shop behind the company commander.

The captain gave the manila folder in his hand to the tall, lanky lieutenant colonel bellowing at him, as he whined defensively, "Sorry sir, had to get some additional information from the XO."

With a look of disgust the lieutenant colonel grabbed the folder and yelled over his shoulder. "3, here's HHC's input. Add it to the report and I'll look it over before I bring it to the Old Man to review and sign."

Turning back to the HHC commander he demanded, "This is the second time in two months you've been late. I'm seeing a trend here that doesn't bode well for any of us. You know what the requirement is. Don't miss the suspense again." Without waiting for a response, the lieutenant colonel walked away to confer with the S-3 who was preparing the required monthly Unit Status Report (USR).

His face red with embarrassment, the captain turned to Maura. "That's the XO, your boss. I was going to introduce you, but all things considered, it might be better for you to just wait a minute and introduce yourself."

"Understood," Maura replied, feeling sorry for the young captain, who walked out the door they had just come through, but empathizing with the XO's frustration over recurrent late reporting. The USR provided commanders at all levels the ability to identify the number of equipment items and personnel currently available to accomplish core functions and assigned missions. The operations shop had to consolidate all subordinate unit reports, look for possible disconnects, and correct any errors before forwarding it up the leadership chain and ultimately to the Pentagon. Looking around, Maura was reminded of the first time she'd reported to the 1st Infantry Division forward, operations center. Commonly referred to as the 'S-3' or '3,' it was always noisy and insanely busy. Walking slowly, but deliberately toward the S-3's desk, Maura firmly announced, "Sir, Captain Collins reporting for duty."

Turning around, the XO looked her up and down, before extending his hand in greeting. "Our new ChemO, boy am I glad to see you!"

Walking out from behind his desk, the major who Maura would later learn was the DISCOM S-3, stood up cheerfully adding. "Not as happy as I am! Are you ready to get to work?"

Maura reached out to shake hands with the S-3, "I am sir, guess you're tired of doing the USR?"

"Damn right Captain! Your predecessor left two months ago. How familiar are you with the USR?"

"Airborne Sir!" Maura bellowed. The Ops NCOIC at my previous unit told me that in addition to being the NRAS custodian and ensuring the unit can pass any NBC readiness inspection, they depend on the ChemO to consolidate USR input and if I did a good job, they might let me do some NBC training once in a while."

That elicited laughter from both the XO and S-3. Addressing the S-3, the XO pointed to the USR report on his desk. "That's your baby this month. Captain Collins needs to get her feet on the ground and the old man and I have her the rest of today." Grinning, the S-3 jocularly addressed Maura. "Welcome to the 82nd."

The XO motioned Maura to follow him and walked toward the adjacent hallway that led to the command suite and his office. Stopping abruptly, he pointed to the far right corner of the ops center. "That's the Chem section where you'll work. Master Sergeant Primo is your NCOIC. He's at Division Chem right now; but you'll get to meet him later this afternoon."

Walking into the XO's office, he indicated a small round table with four chairs in front of his desk. "Let's sit down and go over a few things." Reaching for his coffee cup, he started pouring a cup of coffee from the percolator that was in the corner and asked, "You want a cup?"

"No thanks Sir."

Surprised, he asked, "You don't drink coffee?"

Maura smiled. "Yes Sir, but only one cup first thing in the morning. Me on too much caffeine is not a good thing."

Raising his eyebrows at Maura's attempt at humor, he sat down at the table opposite her and continued in a brusque manner, "The division ChemO sent us your Officer Record Brief a few months ago, along with the news that you wouldn't be here until the second or third week of June. Your predecessor left here at the end of April, but Master Sergeant Primo has been doing a great job on the NBC readiness stuff and will bring you up to speed. I know you Chem pukes like doing all this bugs and gas stuff and that's fine, but you mentioned you helped with the USR at your last assignment. My question is, are you familiar enough with it that you can do it on your own?"

"Yes sir. I may have a few questions here and there, but I know the process and forms."

Maura's response resulted in a visible relaxing of the XO's face and body. "Good. Quite frankly we were surprised to be getting a junior captain and a woman. Most of the chemical officers that come to us have several assignments under their belt before coming to the 82nd. As I recall, you've had one assignment and just graduated from the career course."

"That's correct Sir."

Taking a gulp of black coffee, the XO remarked brusquely, "Okay, you're at the 82nd now. When responding to a question you say, "Airborne Sir! Got it?"

"Airborne Sir!" Maura bellowed.

The XO grinned and nodded approvingly. "While I understand your primary responsibility is NBC readiness and training, your major duty requirement is the monthly USR. If you screw that up, nothing else matters. We provide all the logistical support for the division, which is a very different mission from the combat brigade you were assigned to in Germany. You'll need to learn our language and requirements quickly. No one has time to coddle anyone. You can ask questions, but quite frankly, we expect you to be able to figure out most things on your own. We also have real world contingency missions to support. You need to be ready to deploy at a moment's notice, twenty-four seven, three hundred sixty-five days of the year. Did you get your TA-50 issued yet?"

"Airborne sir, that's one of the first things they had me do this morning at HHC."

"What else do you need to do?"

"The typical finance, transportation, housing stuff sir."

"Okay, we'll add your name to the sign-out board. Whenever you leave here for more than five minutes, fill out the time you leave and the time you expect to return; because if anyone needs you and can't find you, the first place they'll look to determine your current status is this board. That's another thing you don't want to screw up. Any questions?"

"Not right now sir, but I do have an NBC readiness concern I need to discuss with you."

Frowning, the XO leaned forward, "Continue."

"Well Sir, when I reported to the NBC room for my protective overgarment and mask issue, I was told that there are no extra small masks; and because they're short small masks my only option is to be issued a medium mask. I need an extra small mask sir and until I get one, I can't deploy, because I can't get a seal on the medium mask I was issued this morning."

The XO growled, "I'll get with the S-4 on this. If you don't have an extra small mask by the end of the month, let me know. Anything else captain?"

Maura stood up and came to attention. "No sir!"

Motioning Maura to sit back down, the XO responded in a more relaxed tone, "This is the first I've heard we have a problem with masks. We'll get you squared away."

Maura was a bit nervous as she interjected, "I don't mean to create issues sir, but I'm really concerned about the DISCOM's readiness status. According to the NBC NCO, in addition to not having any extra small masks, he doesn't have enough small masks. I'm more concerned that you may have a readiness issue that extends beyond me not having the correct size mask. With your permission, I'll get with my NCOIC when he returns, dig into this a bit and let you know what I find out."

"Okay…" the XO replied thoughtfully, "I'll let the S-4 know your concerns and advise him that you'll get with him to determine the fix for whatever our mask shortfall is." Before Maura could respond, he asked in a lighter tone, "Do you make it a habit to stir up hornets nests everywhere you go?"

A bit upset by this comment, Maura tried to keep any emotion out of her voice as she responded, "Well sir, I prefer to look at it as being proactive and vigilant. My former brigade commander occasionally took the time to pass on a few *pearls of wisdom* as he called them and one of those pearls was: *If you see something wrong, fix it. If you walk past it and ignore it, you just established a new lower standard and that gets soldiers killed and puts mission accomplishment at risk.* If you call that stirring up a hornets nest, then guilty as charged sir."

The XO chuckled and stood up. "Noted captain. Let's go see the old man before he heads out for his meeting."

★ ★ ★

HER OFFICE CALL WITH the DISCOM commander was much more pleasant than her interview with the XO. He was an easy going sort who had spent a majority of his career supporting 1XVII Airborne Corps and Army Special Forces. He asked Maura if her sponsor had contacted her prior to her arrival and was surprised when Maura said she didn't know she'd been assigned a sponsor. The XO, who had remained for the duration of the office call, interjected quickly that he would get to the bottom of it and Maura's sponsor would contact her in the next day or two. She smiled, thanked him, and couldn't help recalling his half teasing, caustic remark about her liking to stir up hornets nests. The office call took less than 10 minutes and as she and the XO walked down the hall towards his office, he told her to go back to the '3' shop and see if her NCOIC had returned from his meeting at Division Chemical and if not, she should go to lunch and return around 1300 hours.

Fort Bragg was really spread out and the heavy lunch time traffic caused Maura to regret her decision to go to the post exchange for lunch once she'd confirmed that her NCOIC was still out of the building. Surveying the meager fast food options available, nothing really appealed to Maura as she fondly recalled the small kantina on the kaserne in Germany, where she would get a schnitzel sandwich and fries. She walked into the exchange to look around and decided to buy a package of peanut butter crackers and a Tab for lunch. Sitting in her car, she opened her crackers and soda to watch the never ending hustle and bustle of cars and people coming and going. She was intrigued by the similarity of Ft. Bragg's constant noise and motion to New York City, where she had grown up. She wasn't sure what she had expected Fort Bragg to be like, but she certainly had not expected it to resemble a major metropolitan area. Sure, there were lots of WWII era whitewashed wood buildings, but there were also large modern buildings like the new nine story hospital and the JFK Warfare Center, both of which were very recognizable from a distance.

Looking at her watch, she got out of her car, threw the empty peanut butter cracker wrapper and Tab in the nearby trashcan and walked back to her car.

★ ★ ★

RETURNING TO HER OFFICE Maura got her first glimpse of her NCOIC. This was Maura's first experience having a senior NCO assigned to her. He was so immersed in the document he was reading he didn't notice she'd walked up to his desk. After a few seconds Maura quietly inquired, "Master Sergeant Primo?"

Looking up at the mention of his name, he immediately stood up and came to attention bellowing, "Ma'am!"

Maura couldn't help noticing his sculpted arms that were as big as her legs and his slim waist and hips. Looking up at him, because he towered over her, she motioned him to sit down. "Master Sergeant Primo, we're going to be working together all the time, you don't need to stand up every time I talk to you. We're a team, please relax."

He gazed intently at her, sizing her up, just as she had instinctively done seconds ago. Sitting down, he pointed to a large dark blue binder on her desk with the 82nd patch emblazoned on the cover. "Sounds good ma'am. XO mentioned you'd be by sometime today, so I put the Chem Section SOP and reports binder on your desk. It has a copy of the latest reports we submitted to DISCOM Commander and Division Chem, along with report suspense dates and assigned duties for your and my positions." Pointing to the acetate covered manning board on the wall between the two windows to the right of both their desks, he added, "That's our current manning status at the HHC and battalions."

Maura sat down at her new desk. "Thanks, looks like I've got my work cut out for me. In addition to going through our SOP, I have to go through the DISCOM SOP and meet with the S-3, who is chomping at the bit to turn over the USR to me. Is there anything else?"

"Yes ma'am, when the XO told me you were on board, I called the division ChemO and told him you'd reported in. He wants to see you this afternoon."

Surprised by this Maura asked, "He specified it had to be this afternoon?" MSG Primo shook his head yes and Maura pursed her lips a bit. "Okay, I need his phone number and directions to Division Chem."

MSG Primo Pointed to the rolodex near her phone. "Phone and building numbers along with Division ChemO's name are behind the C tab ma'am. Once you call LTC Wise and arrange a time to meet, I'll take you there and talk to Sergeant Major about a few things while you're in the office with the boss."

Having to deal with a division chemical officer was a new experience for Maura. The infantry brigade she had been assigned to in Germany belonged to Corps, and the Corps chemical officer didn't care about or engage with anything they did, so all she had to worry about was making sure the brigade S-3 and Commander were happy with her. Turning to flip through the rolodex Maura discovered that in addition to the Division Chemical officers name and number, the tab also contained the assistant division chemo, Sergeant Major and other officers and NCO's positions and phone numbers. Picking up the receiver, she started dialing. After five rings, she was about to hang up, when she heard, "LTC Wise."

"Afternoon sir. Captain Collins from DISCOM. Master Sergeant Primo just told me you want me to come for an office call this afternoon."

"Yes." He replied brusquely, "I'm pretty busy today, but want to get this out of the way. Be here at 1700," and hung up before Maura could respond.

Hanging up the receiver Maura was tempted to ask her NCO if the Division ChemO was always this rude, but stopped short, realizing that would be unprofessional and put him in an awkward position. Maura looked across her desk at him, "Division ChemO wants me there at 1700. DISCOM XO told me the duty day starts with morning PT and they expect us to be at our desks no later than 0800. Given that officially the duty day is over at 1700, how about I follow you to Division Chem and then you can go home?"

"Sounds good ma'am, but I'll go in with you. You might have some questions for me and Sergeant Major and I have some stuff to go over, so no big deal."

Maura stood up. "Sounds good, thanks. I'm gonna go chat with the S-3. I want to sit through the USR briefing before I take over next month."

★ ★ ★

MAURA SPENT AN HOUR with the S-3 and returned to her desk with three thick black binders of information she had to go over before the Wednesday morning USR brief to the DISCOM commander. She put the binders aside and in preparation for her meeting with the division ChemO, opened the DISCOM Chem section Continuity Book. The sound of Master Sergeant Primo's voice startled Maura. "It's 1630 ma'am. You need to put the classified binders in the safe and do an end of day security check with me before we go to division chem."

Standing up, she closed the blue binder. "Thanks for keeping me on track." Maura picked up the three classified black binders and walked to the bank of safes. "Master Sergeant Primo, after PT tomorrow morning, look at your calendar and let me know if you have time to go to lunch together, my treat. We need to get to know each other and talk freely. This office isn't conducive to that, so I figured we could do a working lunch, if that works for you."

"We're good for lunch tomorrow ma'am. I usually don't get around to eating lunch, so it'll be a nice change of pace."

Maura looked up from the open safe drawer she had just put the binders in and spun the dial to lock it. "Darn, I was hoping you knew a good place to eat. This place is so large and spread out, I'm just not sure where to start and the O'club will get old quickly. Do you and your wife have some special places you go out for dinner?"

There was a short hesitation before Master Sergeant Primo answered. "I'm divorced ma'am. I usually meet some friends at the field house after work. We play some B'ball, then go to the Rod and Gun club to grab a few brews and something to eat."

Maura's face flushed. "Sorry, I should have asked if you were married, instead of assuming you are."

"Not a big deal ma'am." He replied and pointed to the SF 702 on the top of the safe. "If you'll initial and annotate the time you closed the safe, I'll do the double check and we can head down the hill to division."

Maura and Master Sergeant Primo walked into the Division Chemical office a few minutes before five. Stopping first to introduce her to the some of the officers and NCO's, they continued down the far end of the office, where Master Sergeant Primo stopped at the open door of one of the two private offices and knocked on the door frame. Looking up, Sergeant Major walked out from behind his desk to greet Maura. "Welcome ma'am," and pointed to the closed door adjacent to his. "Boss is still tied up with his 1630, but you're welcome to wait in my office until he comes out."

Maura didn't feel like making small talk so after shaking Sergeant Majors hand, she pointed to the nearby conference area. "Thanks Sergeant Major. I know you and Master Sergeant Primo have business to discuss and I don't want to extend your duty day any more than necessary. I'll sit there and wait for the colonel to finish." Before the Sergeant Major could object, she turned to Master Sergeant Primo. "See you at PT tomorrow morning." and walked away.

Sitting down at the long conference table, Maura pretended to read some of her notes, until the two NCO's walked into the Sergeant Majors office and closed the door. Closing her notebook, Maura recalled the very short conversation she'd had with the Division Chemical officer earlier in the day and realized it was his curt manner and hanging up on her, without even bothering to wait to see if she had anything to say, that had set her on edge. She had dealt effectively with difficult personalities and being treated badly when she'd arrived at the 1st Infantry Division Forward four years earlier; but she'd expected the Division Chemical officer to be more welcoming than the combat arms officers she worked with in Germany. She knew she was the first female chemical officer to be assigned to the 82nd and wondered if that was why he had been so terse. *Stop it. You can't feel besieged every time you go to a new unit. Maybe he's like that to everyone,* she mused silently. Exhaling deeply, she looked around and noticed some newspapers and magazines on a nearby rack. She found a recent Army Times and sat down to read it. Startled by the sound of a door opening and male laughter, she looked up as a male captain walked out of the Division Chemical officer's office. "Thanks for taking the time to talk to me sir," the captain said and walked away.

Standing up, Maura walked over, expecting to be told to come in. Instead, the Division Chemical officer turned his back to her as he dialed a number. At the same time, Sergeant Major and Master Sergeant Primo came out of Sergeant Major's office. Seeing her standing there, Sergeant Major peeked into the Division Chemical officer's office, turned to Maura and held up his hand. He stood with her until the phone conversation ended and knocked on the door frame. "Sir, Captain Collins is here for her office call."

"Got it Sergeant Major. I'll let her know when I'm ready for her."

"Airborne Sir! See you in the morning." Sergeant Major shrugged his shoulders and gave Maura an apologetic look as he motioned her and Master Sergeant Primo to follow him. He pulled out one of the chairs around the conference table and sat down.

Furious the Division Chemical officer appeared not to care that she had been waiting for him for more than half an hour, Maura managed to hide her feelings as she sat down and nonchalantly asked, "What's up Sergeant Major?"

"I figured we could get to know each other, while you're waiting for the boss ma'am."

I appreciate that Sergeant Major, but it's been a long day for everyone. You guys relax, have a drink, go home, whatever you usually do. I'll be fine."

Ignoring her suggestion, Sergeant Major replied. "We're good ma'am." Do you mind my asking how you feel about being the first female chemical officer to be assigned to the 82nd?"

Realizing Sergeant Major did not need to take the time to make her feel welcome, she relented and responded quietly, "I was actually…perhaps foolishly hoping I'd be treated like any other officer reporting to the 82nd. The DISCOM commander, XO, S-3, and Master Sergeant Primo, have been so welcoming, I was relieved that no one seemed to be making a big deal out of my coming here."

Before Sergeant Major could respond she heard the Division Chemical Officer bellow, "You can come in now Captain Collins."

Maura's attempt at a smile was actually more of grimace as she stood up and dryly announced, "Showtime gentlemen, thanks for looking out for me."

Walking into the office, the first thing she noticed was the glare the Division Chemical Officer greeted her with. Motioning her to sit in one of the two chairs in front of his desk, he turned his attention to the sheet of paper in front of him. As she sat down, she realized he had her Officer Record Brief on his desk. Without even one word of welcome he tersely remarked, "When branch sent me your ORB, I was quite frankly impressed that your first assignment as a second lieutenant had been at the *Big Red One* in Germany. But I was equally concerned to see that is the only assignment you have under your belt. You just finished the advanced course, but didn't have to compete to go to airborne school, because you were being assigned to the 82nd."

Maura's assignment officer had already told her the Division Chemical officer had called the assignment branch colonel to complain about Maura being female and too junior, to be assigned as a brigade chemical officer in the 82nd. Furious that the Division Chemical officer was treating her so badly, Maura chose to remain silent, but locked eyes with him, refusing to drop her gaze.

After a few uncomfortable seconds, the Division Chemical Officer sarcastically queried, "How do you feel about being assigned to the 82nd captain?"

"Honored sir." Maura replied tersely. "Apparently Branch feels I'm qualified and has the same confidence that I do; that I am up to the challenge. I did well in Germany, consistently max the PT test, have never fallen out of a run, and am looking forward to my assignment here."

"Time will tell..." he replied derisively, "bottom line, don't expect any favors or to be cut any slack because you're female. I expect you to mind your P's and Q's and not embarrass the Corps by not meeting the standard or getting pregnant while you're here. I meet with the brigade ChemO's once a quarter. You have a good NCO, he'll let you know what the battle rhythm is. Do you have any questions on what is expected of you?"

Maura couldn't believe what he'd just said to her and was too furious to say anything except, "No sir, do you have anything else for me?"

He glared at her for a second before curtly replying, "No!"

Standing up, Maura came to attention. "With your permission sir."

He waved his hand dismissively, picked up a manila folder on his desk marked *SECRET*, got up from his chair and went to unlock his safe, without saying another word.

★ ★ ★

MAURA WALKED INTO THE O'club and went straight to the bar, where Anne greeted her. "What have you been doing? It's your first day and you're already staying late at work?"

Maura sat down. "Sorry, Division ChemO said I had to be at his office at 1700. I didn't have any way to contact you to let you know I'd be late."

"Wow, you spent an hour with him? That's great! How'd it go?" Anne asked excitedly.

"Actually, it only lasted a bit over 5 minutes." Maura responded resignedly as she motioned to the bartender and said, "A Tanqueray and tonic please." Turning back to Anne, she added, "Don't want to talk about it right now, just want to relax and have a drink."

"Sorry," Anne replied and turned to the female captain seated next to her. "Natalie, this is my friend Maura I told you about. Maura, this is Natalie, my sponsor."

Maura smiled as she reached behind Anne to shake hands. "Nice to meet you Natalie."

Natalie responded, "I gather from your tone of voice, nothing much has changed in the 82nd. Is your sponsor a man or a woman?"

Maura took a sip of her gin and tonic the bartender had just put on the table and responded, "I wasn't assigned a sponsor; apparently there's a female captain in the med battalion who'll find out today that she's supposed to be my sponsor."

Anne interjected, "I don't know 'bout you guys, but I'm starvin'. Wanna get some dinner?"

Maura and Natalie nodded yes. Anne told the bartender, "We're headed into the dining room. Just put the drinks on my tab and I'll tell the waitress to add that to my bill."

Seated at their table, Anne looked at Maura. "While we're waiting for the waitress to come back with the menus, there's something I'd like to discuss. While Natalie was helping me get in processed today, she asked where I was planning to live. I mentioned we were both in the BOQ right now, but wanted to find a place off post to share. She discussed an option I thought might work for both of us."

"I bought a really nice three bedroom house on Flying Cloud Lane, in a new development." Natalie added. "My house is just a few miles outside the back gate, which is a breeze to get through, because most people live on the other side of Fayetteville. I love living there, but right now, I'm house poor. Originally I envisioned only having one roommate; but two can work, if you guys don't mind sharing a bathroom."

"That sounds like a possibility Natalie..." Maura pondered. "How big is the bathroom we'd be sharing and what would you want for rent?"

"The bathroom is pretty large. It has two sinks, lots of counter space. There's a large linen closet for towels and other items. I got lucky and locked in a 10% interest rate, so my house payment is $600 a month and utilities run around $100 a month. If each of you pay me $200 a month and we share the cost of food, that'd work for me."

Maura looked at Anne. "You good with this?" Anne shook her head yes and smiled hopefully. Maura turned back to Natalie. "Thanks for the offer, I think it could work, but I'd like to look at the house before I make a decision."

Natalie replied enthusiastically, "Absolutely. Look, why don't the two of you come over tomorrow night to check out the house and I'll make dinner."

The waitress returned with the menus and Anne opened hers immediately. "Sounds like a plan! Now let's order some food!"

6

FT. BRAGG, NC, TUESDAY, 10 JUNE 1980

THE NEXT MORNING MAURA walked into the DISCOM S-3 a few minutes before eight and Master Sergeant Primo arrived a few minutes later. "Mornin' ma'am. How'd PT with your fellow officers go?"

Maura looked up from her notebook. She had been making a few notes on things she needed to check on. "Good morning Master Sergeant Primo. The brigade commander sets a pretty mean pace, but I'm good. I'm glad you're here. I need to get those binders out of the safe and start reading them, but I don't have the combination."

"Sorry, come with me ma'am, I'll open it and give you the combo to that safe. I'll also show you where I keep the combinations to the other safes in the shop. As long as that piece of paper is marked TS and stays in the safe, you can always refer to it and only need to memorize one combination."

★ ★ ★

MAURA WAS READING THE USR continuity file when a female captain walked over to her desk and held out her hand in greeting. "Hi, I'm Beth Williams. Got a call from the XO yesterday telling me I've been assigned as your sponsor."

Maura shook the hand that had suddenly appeared on the page in front of her. "Hi, Maura Collins, nice to meet you. Sorry about the last minute notice."

Beth waved her hand dismissively. "Not a big deal. Same thing happened to me. Most of the guys assigned to the 82nd know each other from previous assignments and when they hear someone is inbound, they just volunteer to be a sponsor. Not many women in the division, so because the sponsorship system here is ad hoc, they didn't think about assigning you a sponsor."

Maura nodded understanding. "How long have you been assigned to the 82nd?"

Beth sat down in the chair next to Maura's desk. "Been here a little over a year and I was the first female officer to be assigned to the Med battalion. There were no women at the support battalions or here at the headquarters, but the guy I was replacing was still here, because he got the battalion S-3 job, so he was my sponsor. Holding out the glossy folder in her hand, she added, "I stopped by Army Community Service and got you a newcomers package. Inside is a post map and lots of good information about the local community, housing options, and lots of other information that will help you get settled. Being as it's almost lunch time, I thought we could go to the O'club for lunch so we can get to know each other. You can let me know what in-processing you've completed, and I can answer any questions you have about what we do in the DISCOM."

Excited at finding another female officer in the DISCOM, Maura responded excitedly "Thanks! I'll be ready in a minute, just want to leave a note for my NCOIC letting him know where I am and what I'm doing…oh and yeah, I need to sign out on the status board. Apparently forgetting to do that, borders on a court martial offense."

★ ★ ★

"I'LL HAVE A BLT and tea please," Beth told the waitress.

"I'll have a club sandwich.... fries and a Fresca." Maura said hesitantly. She wasn't particularly impressed with the Officers club lunch menu, but was really hungry. Maura turned back to Beth as the waitress walked away. "So, do you mind telling me a bit more about your experiences in the Army?"

I received a direct commission in the Women's Army Corps in 1974 and went to Ft. Sam for my medical service corps officer basic course. My first assignment was Garlstedt, Germany. I worked at an aid station on Clay Kaserne. I'd been there a bit over a year when one of the ambulance platoon leaders got relieved and I asked my boss if he'd recommend me for the job. He did and I got it. A year later, I became the company XO and a year later, as a brand new captain, I was offered command of the company, if I'd extend, and I spent the next two years in command."

Maura was impressed. "Wow, you are a real trailblazer! Did you find it difficult to work with the guys? Were you harassed a lot?"

"No," Beth replied. "Medical and med service types really don't care what your sex or color are, provided you can do the job and keep their patient stats good, which keeps the regular army types off their backs."

"Yeah," Maura mused, "I remember my brigade commander tearing into the brigade surgeon at monthly command reviews. He was out of shape, his uniform was always messed up, but he didn't seem to care, and that really pissed the CG off."

"Yeah, the medical types get really irritated with regular army types who care more about how they look in uniform and whether or not they can pass the PT test, than if they're really a good doctor or clinic administrator," Beth added.

Maura laughed, "The brigade surgeon at the first IDF I mentioned earlier, was single and we'd occasionally have dinner together at the O'club. He told me he already had a job lined up at Johns Hopkins when he got out but had to serve three years on active duty, as payback for the Berry Plan, which paid for his medical school training and kept him from being drafted and sent to Vietnam. I don't think he got a good OER, but he was a really good doc. The guy who replaced him was a great doctor too; but he came from a military family. His uniform, military bearing and physical fitness was as good, or better than the combat arms guys on the brigade staff. He ran with a group of us at lunchtime and always maxed the PT test. The CG loved him!" Realizing she'd been talking non-stop, Maura apologized. "Sorry, it's just interesting that in the military, if you don't fit the right profile; it doesn't matter what your qualifications are. Switching topics abruptly, Maura asked. If you don't mind, tell me how you ended up at the 82nd?

"After my advanced course and airborne school, I was assigned as the division med admin officer."

Maura looked at Beth questioningly, "Gosh, I didn't even know there was such a position. What do you do?"

"I'm responsible for tracking all sick call, injuries, and reports of illnesses and providing this information to the Division Commander."

"Wow," Maura exhaled. "Do you brief the division commander?"

"Sometimes, but mostly my boss briefs and I sit in the cheap seats in case the division commander asks a question he can't answer."

"What's the division commander like? Do you like him?"

Beth seemed nonplussed by the question and after a short hesitation replied, "He's an interesting leader. I'll let you make your own assessment of him when you meet him."

Maura was taken aback by this response, "The only reason I can think that I will EVER get to speak to or meet the division commander, is because I'm about to get court-martialed or something similar."

That response amused Beth and she laughed, "I guess no one told you he meets with all the female officers assigned to the division, once a quarter. You'll meet him in July when we have our next command performance."

"This is the first I've heard of it," Maura replied. "Do you know how many women are assigned to the 82nd?"

"I think with you, we'll be up to twelve."

Excited at the prospect of meeting other female officers in the 82nd, Maura excitedly asked, "Do you guys get together on your own, on a regular basis?"

Finishing the bite of BLT in her mouth, Beth took a swig of iced tea before answering, "Nope."

"Why not?" Maura asked in a shocked tone.

Surprised by this reaction, Beth just shrugged her shoulders. "I dunno, guess we're all so busy and in different units, we never really thought about it."

Maura was so surprised and disappointed that the women who saw each other every three months had never tried to get together socially or form a support network.

An uncomfortable silence set in that neither one of them knew how to change, so they finished their lunch in silence and went back to the DISCOM headquarters. Before leaving, Beth gave Maura a 3x5 card with her office and home numbers written on it and told Maura she could call if she needed anything.

★ ★ ★

MAURA STOPPED AT THE commissary annex on her way home and had just parked her car in the BOQ parking lot when she noticed Beth coming out of the BOQ with a really good looking older guy. Feeling badly about the abrupt silence that ended their lunch earlier that day, Maura yelled Beth's name as they walked toward her.

Beth curtly said hi as she passed Maura without stopping to introduce her partner Puzzled by Beth's abrupt greeting, and immediate departure, Maura walked to her BOQ room. She had just started taking her uniform off when there was a knock at the door.

"Who is it?" Maura yelled.

"Anne. You ready?"

"No," Maura replied, hurrying to the front door. "Come, in, I'll be ready in a sec."

Anne walked in and shut the door, as Maura continued changing out of her uniform. "What's with you being late all the time? You're only inprocessing. Is it that crazy at work already?"

Throwing her fatigue top on her bed and pulling off her pants, Maura replied breathlessly. "Sorta, the S-3 wants me to take over the USR as soon as possible and he expects me to be familiar with this month's report when they brief it later this week." Putting jeans on Maura continued, "There are several monthly reports due to the division chemical officer on the 15th and because the 15th is a Sunday, we actually have to have the reports to him on Friday. I need to make sure I understand and can defend the reports if needed, which means I have to read and understand all of the policies and SOP's before I sign and send them to division. I'm already in hot water with the division chemical officer and don't need to up a report with my signature that might have some errors on it."

"WHOA!" Anne said loudly. "How have you managed to get in this much trouble in two days?"

Pulling a polo shirt over her head and putting her feet in the loafers that were in front of her, Maura replied in an exasperated tone. "I'll tell you about it and some other stuff that has me totally out of sorts on the way to Natalie's." Maura grabbed her wallet and keys. "Let's go."

★ ★ ★

NATALIE OPENED THE DOOR. "Hi! C'mon on in" Maura and Anne followed her to the kitchen where Natalie pulled a cold beer out of the fridge for Anne and pointed to a wine glass and bottle of red wine on the counter. "Anne told me you don't drink beer or white wine, so help yourself and we'll start the house tour." After Natalie had shown them around the house, they went out back, where she had chicken and potatoes cooking on the grill.

"Nice deck and yard," Anne whistled.

Natalie put her bottle of beer on the nearby table and opened the grill to check the chicken and baked potatoes. "It's one of the best features of the house. We can relax and eat out here most nights. It's a great way to unwind after a long day at the office."

Pointing to the back of the yard Anne asked Natalie, "Are those tomato plants and corn?"

"Yup, I've got cucumbers, lettuce, peppers, and radishes growing there too. The salad I made for dinner tonight is all from the garden."

The smell and sight of the chicken breasts and large potatoes wrapped in foil was heavenly. Anne looked at Maura and whispered, "We'd be fools not to live here! Whaddya think?"

The bucolic picture of Anne getting up to help Natalie get the food from the grill to the table evoked memories of Amelia, Anne, and Maura meeting each other as brand new second lieutenants. Four years later, the three women were as much family as friends and if it had not been for that friendship, the last four years would have been much harder to endure. As Anne and Natalie sat down at the table, Maura announced, "Natalie, Anne and I have discussed your offer to move in and if that offer is still open, it's a deal."

Natalie excitedly clapped her hands. "Great! Can you guys move in this weekend?"

7

FORT BRAGG, NC, MONDAY, 23 JUNE 1980

MAURA WAS STILL SWEATING from the long run at PT that morning, when she walked into the DISCOM operations shop and heard the S-3 bellow, "Collins!"

"Sir?" Maura queried as she walked over to his desk.

The S-3 curtly replied, "Commander wants you in his office now!" immediately turning his attention back to the paperwork on his desk.

"Airborne Sir! WILCO." Maura strode over to her desk, hastily put her briefcase down, while grabbing a notebook and pen and reported to the brigade commander. Walking into the command suite, Maura saw the secretary had not come in yet, so she gingerly walked over to the commander's open door and poked her head inside. "Captain Collins reporting as directed Sir."

Without looking up from the paperwork he was reading, the brigade commander pointed to the chairs in front of his desk. "Sit down Maura, I'll be with you shortly."

Surprised by the terse reply and the scowl on the brigade commander's face, Maura sat down and for the first time since arriving at the 82nd, was a bit on edge. She immediately started wondering, *Did I do something wrong?* and was reviewing her actions of the previous week when she heard the brigade commander ask, "So Maura. Are you settled in yet?"

Looking up, Maura was relieved to see the brigade commander smiling. "Airborne Sir!"

"You've been here two weeks now, correct?" Maura nodded her head in affirmation. The scowl returned to the brigade commanders face as he picked up the binder he had been reading when she'd come into the office. "I got this Friday afternoon and have spent the entire weekend deliberating on who I need to assign to deal with this. Normally I wouldn't pick a company grade officer or someone so new to the division to handle something like this; but given the situation and the feedback I've gotten from both the XO and S-3 about your ability to fit in as part of the team, catch on quickly, and work with minimal supervision; quite frankly, your name was the first one to pop in my head, to be the Article 32 investigating officer." Picking up the binder, he stood up and extended it out to her. "I want you to know if you feel uncomfortable handling this, I'll accept that; but read this first and get back to me with your decision soonest."

Standing up, Maura took the binder, came to attention and crisply replied. "Check sir. Am I to assume that you want me to read this immediately and get back to you before COB today with my decision?"

"Yes Maura." The brigade commander responded as he reached for the phone.

Maura walked back to the operations shop, still trying to process what had just happened. MSG Primo greeted her as she approached her desk. "Mornin' ma'am. Saw the '3' limping as he came in this morning; was it a rough run this morning?"

Momentarily startled, Maura stammered, "uhh, yeah, XO was in charge and he set a brutal pace. We did five miles, instead of our usual three."

MSG Primo grinned. "Did anyone fall out?"

"You're joking right?" Maura replied incredulously. When MSG Primo started chuckling, Maura realized he had been teasing her. "Ok, got me on that one. You know these guys would die before they'd wimp out." Looking over at the major she asked, "How bad is he?"

"He looks like he's hurting pretty bad. He didn't take it too well when the XO gave him crap about limping and I saw him pop an 800 milligram of *Ranger Candy* shortly thereafter."

Maura shook her head, "Yeah, the combat arms types seem to live on Ibuprofen and coffee." Changing the subject she added, "Brigade commander just gave me a report he wants me to read now, so if anything hot comes up before I finish this and get back to him, I'll need you to handle it. You good with that?"

"No problem ma'am, got you covered. The HHC commander asked me to come over and help them with mask fitting, so they can get the required number of masks ordered to alleviate the shortfall you identified, but I'll give him a call and tell him something came up and I'll get there as soon as I can."

Maura smiled as she remembered alerting the XO to a readiness problem with protective masks on her first day here. "No, go over there, that's far more important. You call Division Chem and I'll let the '3' know we're both out of pocket; but if something comes up this morning, to call over to the NBC room and you'll take care of it." Considering the conversation over, Maura walked over to the S-3. "Mornin' Sir."

Looking up from the document he'd been reading the major acknowledged her. "Mornin' Maura. What's up?"

Holding out the binder the commander had given her, Maura asked, "Do you know what this is about sir?"

"Nope. Feel like enlightening me?"

"Brigade commander told me to read this and give him my decision soonest, so I'll be tied up reading this for most of the morning and Master Sergeant Primo is over at HHC all day helping them with mask fitting, so if something comes up this morning that can't wait, please call him at HHC and he'll deal with it."

The major nodded understanding. "If something comes up, I'll handle it until you let me know you've finished that requirement and are back on board."

Maura walked back to her desk, sat down, and gasped as she opened the binder.

POLICE REPORT

Case number 80-00345 Date: 20 June 1980
Reporting Officer 20 June 1980 CPT James Harvey

Event Details: Received 911 dispatch vic 2230 hours 20 June 1980 of gunshots fired at 2140 Cedar Creek Drive, Ambassador Motel. Upon arrival, motel manager directed us to room 213. One unconscious female was on the ground, another was sitting on the floor with 35 year old male with abdominal GSW. Medical personnel arrived shortly after and took victim to hospital. Two women were taken to police station and booked.
Summary: Upon arrival in room 213, female holding male victim reported that unconscious female had forced her way into the room and threatened to kill male and female. Male was able to neutralize shooter, but not before she discharged the weapon in his abdomen. After questioning, female shooting suspect admitted to shooting Dr. William Barksdale, her husband, intending to kill him and the other female, because they were having an affair.
Other female was identified as U.S. Army Captain Elizabeth Williams. Mrs. Barksdale was taken to county jail for processing and Captain Williams was remanded to Ft. Bragg personnel.

Shocked by the fact that Beth was part of the police report, Maura stopped reading and took a sip of water as she tried to regain her composure. After a few minutes, she resumed reading the rest of the documents included in the binder that contained a Provost Marshal report and a copy of the Uniformed Code of Military Justice section VII, Article 32.

★ ★ ★

MAURA CLOSED THE BINDER shut and took another swig of water as she tried to compose herself as she recalled seeing Beth in the parking lot of the BOQ with a good looking guy after work one day. *"Holy shit!"* she thought, as she realized the reason the commander had given her the binder was because he wanted her to be the Article 32 Investigating officer.

She'd learned some military justice basics, in her advanced course; but it never occurred to her that she might have to actually serve as an Article 32 investigating officer. She didn't want to investigate another female officer, let alone one she actually knew and was her sponsor into the 82nd; but on the other hand, she felt if she turned this down, it could affect her officer evaluation report (OER). Feeling the need to process this a bit more before informing the brigade commander of her decision, she got up and walked outside. *"Why me?"* she asked as she recalled several times in Germany when she'd looked heavenward, knowing she had to make a tough decision and was asking for guidance. Maura walked around the compound for quite some time before returning to her desk and pressing the intercom button on her phone that connected her directly to the commander's secretary. After a short explanation, Maura asked when the commander might be available to talk to her and was put on hold. After a few minutes she was told to come to his office.

The brigade commander smiled as Maura walked in his office and motioned for her to join him at the small round conference table. "So, do you have any questions about what you've read?" he asked.

Maura shook her head and ruefully replied, "I'm sure I do sir, but right now, I'm still trying process it all." Hesitating momentarily she blurted out, "You want me to be the Article 32 investigating officer don't you?" He nodded acknowledgement. "Gee Sir, why me?" she asked while simultaneously holding up her hand and continuing. "I know why, I just had to let you know I'm really uncomfortable with this and want to make sure you don't want to change your mind, before I tell you that I can't refuse your request, but do have some serious reservations and concerns I want to discuss with you, before you make a final decision."

The brigade commander roared in laughter, but stopped abruptly when he saw the look of consternation on Maura's face. "Sorry, I couldn't help it. The XO warned me that you are just about the most transparent, awkward, and totally honest officer he's ever met. Your response just validated that in a way I never expected. After a short pause, he continued, "I'm not accustomed to this kind of reaction from one of my staff and having women under my command is still a very new thing for me. To further complicate matters, you haven't been here long enough for me to gauge you as a person, let alone as an officer and leader; so I'll be as frank with you as you've been with me. I could assign this to the '3' or XO or even one of the battalion XO's, but I really feel that assigning you, as a fellow female officer is the fairest decision I can make both in the long term interests of the command as well as the officer in question. While you were going through the package I gave you, the JAG returned my phone call and answered a concern I had, that you probably didn't realize could have rendered my choice null and void." Seeing Maura tilt her head he smiled and continued, "I had to confirm that Captain Williams being your sponsor would not be construed as a conflict of interest and possibly complicate matters down the line, if the decision is to court-martial her for fraternization, adultery, and conduct unbecoming."

Maura stared at him before asking in an incredulous tone, "Why in the world would my being appointed be construed as a conflict of interest? Men can judge men, why wouldn't it be appropriate for a woman to judge a woman?"

The brigade commander laughed heartily again before replying. "Maura, I can see you are going to make the last fourteen months of my command very interesting. Someday I'd like to sit down and discuss why you decided to come in the army and what you think are the qualities of a good officer! This has nothing to do with your gender. It has to do with her being your sponsor and the fact that you have a personal, albeit it superficial, relationship that may affect your ability to be impartial."

Frustrated, Maura exclaimed, "I barely know her! We spent a lunch hour together, she gave me some paperwork and her contact information in case I had a question or needed something, but that was it. I haven't seen or talked to her since then. A look of consternation suddenly appeared on Maura's face.

"What is it?" The brigade commander asked cautiously.

Maura put her hand on her forehead and grimaced. "I actually did see her one more time..."

"Proceed," the brigade commander demanded sharply.

Exhaling loudly, Maura continued. "The evening after we had lunch, I came home and ran into her in the BOQ parking lot. She was with an older guy with long hair and she didn't see me until I said "hi" to her. I remember being surprised by her reaction, which indicated she wasn't happy to see me, because she mumbled something intelligible and turned away without saying anything else."

Getting up, the brigade commander replied apprehensively, "Hold on a minute" and dialed a number on his phone. He greeted the person on the other line in a familiar way and when he shared what Maura had just told him, after a brief silence, he responded, "Hold on, she's right here." He turned to address Maura, "I have the JAG on the line. Did you contact her and talk to her about this chance meeting in the parking lot?"

"No Sir."

"Have you had any other contact with her since then?"

"No Sir."

Talking into the handset, the commander repeated what Maura had told him and asked, "What d'ya think Joe?" Thanking the division JAG, the commander hung up and walked back to the table. "Sorry Maura, I didn't know about you seeing her in the parking lot, possibly with the man she had an affair with and the easiest thing to do was to call and confirm that this did or did not disqualify you from serving as the investigating officer. We're on a bit of a slippery slope here, but if your limited professional contact with Captain Williams becomes an issue with defense counsel, the JAG is comfortable it won't negate your findings." Sitting down next to her at the table he continued, I appreciate your candor and understand your concerns Maura; but after discussing this with the JAG, the few concerns I had initially, are mute. I'm even more convinced now, that this is the best decision, given the circumstances. I'll inform the XO and 3 that you are relieved of any responsibilities here, until the investigation and recommendations are concluded. Any questions?"

Maura blurted out, "Oh sir, if that includes me briefing the USR next month, the 3 is gonna shit a brick!" Gasping at the realization of what she'd just said, she stammered, "Sorry sir, that just popped out."

Laughing heartily, the brigade commander reassured her, "I'm well aware of how the 3 feels about having to do the USR. Don't worry, he can handle it and knows this wasn't your choice. Just do a good job on this; there'll be plenty of USR's for you to handle down the line. Do you know where the JAG is located?"

"No Sir."

Getting up, he motioned Maura to follow him as he walked out to his secretary. "Would you please give Captain Collins the phone number and directions to the division JAG office?" Turning to address Maura, he added, "Go there today. They're expecting you and the JAG has already assigned one of his lawyers to assist and advise you on procedural matters. The XO is up to speed on this and you can consult him on procedural issues or support matters only. You are to discuss this with no one except your JAG counsel, not even me. Conduct your investigation, write your recommendations and give them to me and only to me. Understood?"

Maura nodded understanding and the brigade commander walked back into his office.

★ ★ ★

MAURA WAVED TO ANNE as she entered the officer's club lounge. Anne pointed to the glass of red wine on the table. "I ordered for you."

Sitting down, Maura looked at the wine glass and quietly remarked, "Thanks, but after today, I think I need a gin and tonic."

"Holy crap Maura, what's up now?"

Resting her elbows on the table and cupping her chin in her hands, Maura mournfully replied, "You just aren't gonna believe it…DISCOM commander appointed me as an Article 32 investigating officer today." As the cocktail waitress passed their table, Maura waved at her. "Tanqueray and tonic" then pointing to Anne's half empty glass, "and another beer please."

Leaning toward Maura, Anne asked, "You haven't even been here a month, why would he pick you?"

"Because the officer being investigated is a female captain."

Anne took a swig of beer. "I'll drive you home tonight and we'll pick your car up in the morning. You're gonna need a lot of gin tonics tonight. Okay, give it up, tell me all the gory details."

"I can't talk to you or anyone except the lawyer they've assigned to help me, but thanks. One wine and one gin and tonic is more than enough. I can't have a hangover tomorrow morning." Changing the subject, she asked Anne, "Tell me about your weekend with Derek and how he's dealing with you deciding to move in with me and Natalie, instead of him."

8

FORT BRAGG, NC, WEDNESDAY, 9 JULY 1980

MAURA WALKED INTO THE DISCOM commander's office. "Airborne Sir!" Looking up from the blotter report he had been reviewing, he looked up, and motioned for her to sit at the round conference table near the window. Maura sat down and started arranging the paperwork she had brought with her in front of the chair next to hers. After a few minutes the DISCOM commander stood and joined her at the table. Indicating the sheaf of paperwork she had put out for him, he remarked, "I'll look at these later. Let's talk about the Article 32 proceedings and your recommendations first."

"Well sir, first and foremost, Captain Williams was very forthcoming and cooperative. Against the advice of her attorney, she provided a written statement about her affair with the physician. She met him shortly after arriving here. His elderly, widowed mother lives next door to the house she rented. Captain Williams was moving in and his mother fell getting groceries out of her car. She had a slight cut on her head and asked Captain Williams if she could take her to the ER, at the local hospital. She said she didn't want to go by ambulance, and if she could just get to the ER, they knew her and would take care of her. Captain Williams chose to stay with her until her son was off duty, because she was very disoriented by the time they got to the hospital. When Dr. Barksdale arrived, Captain Williams introduced herself and told him what happened. He thanked her and Captain Williams returned home. That evening there was a knock on her door and it was the doctor. He thanked her again for her kindness and told her his mom was fine, but weak. He had tried to convince his mother to stay at his house for a week or so, but she demanded to go home. He hated to impose on her, but was wondering if she'd have time to check on his mom in the evenings when she got home. When she agreed to that, he gave her his office and home phone numbers to call in the event he needed to come over to help his mother.

The next evening she stopped by to check on the senior Mrs. Barksdale. They visited for a while. Captain Williams wrote down her home number for her to call if there was a problem and told her that she would stop by every evening just to check on her. That second evening when Captain Williams arrived, she discovered Mrs. Barksdale had made dinner for the both of them. Captain Williams explained that she realized she was lonely and this was sort of like having her mom next door. She knew Mrs. Barksdale was lonely, so a routine of coming over several nights a week for dinner was established. About two weeks after their first dinner together, her son joined them. They talked and discovered some common interests. When he walked her back to her house after dinner, he mentioned that as an ER physician he has a really crazy schedule, but was wondering if she wasn't busy the following Tuesday evening, he'd like to take her out for dinner. She agreed and when he came to pick her up, she was surprised to discover his mother was not joining them. She told him she needed to go next door to apologize to his mom about not coming over for dinner as usual. He told her that wouldn't be necessary. He'd mentioned it to his mother earlier that morning. When he brought her home that evening, he asked if he could come in. He told her that he'd had a really good time and realized she was at least ten years younger than him and probably wasn't interested, but he was very attracted to her and was wondering if she would consider dating him, if she didn't already have a steady guy. She admitted to me that she was lonely and the notion that this good looking single doctor was interested in her, was quite exciting."

The DISCOM commander interrupted, "She said single?"

"Yes Sir. I questioned her about that as well and she said she hadn't asked him, but was naïve enough to assume that because he was asking to date her, with his mom living next door, he was single."

The DISCOM commander shook his head. "So the mother was okay with the affair they were having?"

Maura shook her head. "I asked her that question as well. She told me that he asked her not to mention they were dating to his mom; because since his dad's death a few years ago, she had gotten very possessive and he was concerned that if his mother found out they were dating, she'd get angry at Captain Williams and it gave him a lot of comfort to know that she checked on his mom every evening and had dinner with her."

"She believed that??" The brigade commander incredulously inquired.

"Airborne Sir!"

"Would you believe that if you were in her position?" he asked skeptically.

Maura hesitated before replying in a thoughtful tone of voice. "Under those circumstances, I think I might have sir."

Surprised by Maura's response, the brigade commander drummed his right index finger on the edge of the table before asking, "So, she never told the mother they were seeing each other and the mother never questioned him coming to her house regularly?"

"Airborne Sir! On the first question. On the second question, she told me that because he never knew if an emergency would delay him, they agreed he would call to confirm they were still on for dinner and she would meet him at the restaurant."

The commander asked derisively, "So, just when did they go from having dinner together, to..." and abruptly stopped midsentence, realizing what he was about to say was problematic.

Maura smiled. "Got it sir." Relieved that she'd taken him off the hook, he let her continue. "He told her he worked the 3-11 shift, but had an hour for dinner. They met for dinner at 7:30 on Friday nights; which meant Captain Williams didn't get home until after his mother was already asleep.

They'd been seeing each other for a bit over a month, when he told her that he had the next Saturday off and was wondering if she wanted to go to the Outer Banks for the weekend. From that time on, they'd meet for dinner at a local restaurant once a week and go to the beach one weekend a month."

Maura noticed the brigade commander had started tapping his right index finger on the edge of the table. She'd been told that whenever he did that, he was irritated or confused about something and is thinking through the issue at hand and was told to sit there and say nothing, until he asked the question he was trying to formulate. Maura patiently waited until he probingly inquired, "Okay, you said she met him because she lives next door to his mom, but when we were talking a few weeks ago, you mentioned she was in the BOQ parking lot, when you saw her with the doctor."

Maura blurted out, "Sir, I'm so sorry, there's so many moving parts to this story that I forgot to tell you that she moved back into the BOQ last month. Her landlord didn't renew her lease, because he's been reassigned to Bragg."

The brigade commander raised his eyebrows in disbelief and sarcastically asked, "So she decided to move back into the BOQ instead of suggesting she move in with her single boyfriend?"

"As soon as she knew about having to move out of the house, she DID exactly that!" Maura exclaimed, which caused the brigade commander to give her a questioning look. "I'm obviously not doing a good job of explaining the chronology sir. I think it might be better for you to read my report and recommendations before we continue this conversation."

Shaking his head, he replied tersely, "No, I have my reasons for wanting to have this conversation before I read your report and recommendations. "Continue," he ordered sharply.

Maura took a second to calm down before continuing. "When she found out she was going to have to move, she called him at work and asked if he had time to have dinner that evening, she had some exciting news to share with him. He told her he'd have to change some plans, but yes, they could have dinner together that evening. When she told him about having to move out, she asked him how he'd feel about her moving in with him. She told me she was devastated when he momentarily appeared angry and she asked him if she'd made him angry. He told her he wasn't angry, it was just complicated and he needed some time to think about it, could it wait until they got together later that week." Stopping for a second to see if the commander had any questions, Maura continued. "When they got together, Dr. Barksdale told Captain Williams that he really cared about her, but had a confession to make. That's when he told her that he was married."

The DISCOM commander interrupted, "So how long has she known he's married?"

"A bit over two months, sir."

"Okay Maura, is there anything else you want to discuss before giving me your recommendation?

Surprised by his abruptness, Maura hesitated before replying. "No sir, everything is in my written report; but there are a few other details that I'd like to mention as justification for my recommendation." After a few uncomfortable seconds of silence, Maura realized he was waiting for her to continue. "Sir, I talked to Captain Williams for almost four hours. She was very forthcoming and admitted that by the time she found out he was married, she'd fallen in love with him. He told her he was very unhappy in his marriage and if she'd be patient, he'd get a divorce and marry her."

Interrupting, the DISCOM commander asked, "Were you able to talk to the doctor and his wife?"

"Yes sir, that's what took so long. It took over a week for me to be able to talk to both the doctor and his wife."

"Did either of them corroborate Captain Williams' assertion that he was going to leave his wife and marry her?"

"Airborne Sir, both of them did. The wife said that he told her he wanted a divorce about a month ago and when she asked why, all he said was that he'd tried to make things work for much longer than he should have and he'd finally realized it wasn't going to work and he wanted out."

"So he didn't tell her about the affair and she didn't know he was having one?" The DISCOM commander asked incredulously.

"That's correct sir," Maura replied. "I specifically asked her when she'd found out about Captain Williams and she said about two weeks ago, because after telling her he wanted a divorce, he moved out. She wasn't sure where he was living, so one day the wife followed him from the hospital to his mother's house. She was parked outside trying to work up enough courage to beg him to give their marriage another try; when she saw him come out again. He'd changed out of his scrubs into civilian clothing. She followed him on base and waited in the BOQ parking lot. That's when she saw both of them come out, get in his car and go out to dinner. They returned to the BOQ after dinner and he left around 2200."

'Wait a minute," the DISCOM commander bellowed in frustration. "I thought they were at a motel downtown together when she shot him."

"They were sir," Maura replied firmly. "The evening I ran into them in the BOQ parking lot scared Captain Williams and she told him he couldn't meet her at the BOQ anymore. After further discussion, they agreed to only see each other on weekends, until he was able to get the divorce proceedings started and they'd get away on the weekends he was off, but on weekends he had to work, he'd rent a motel room for Friday and Saturday nights, so they had quality time together."

Maura could tell the DISCOM commander was getting frustrated and his terse command to '*get on with it!'* confirmed her assessment.

"Airborne Sir!" Maura continued, "Technically Captain Williams is guilty of all the charges against her and she told me that she realizes she should have stopped seeing him as soon as she found out he was married, but it just wasn't that simple. If you feel strongly that you need to make an example of her," Maura pointed to the document she'd laid in front of him. "You have all the ammunition need right there for a court martial. However, I am asking you to consider how emotionally charged this whole situation was and still is. Until recently, Captain Williams thought she was dating a single man and the fact that he does want to marry her, left his wife, and filed for divorce over a week ago, which is what sent his wife over the edge and ended up with her following them to the motel on Friday evening and trying to kill them and herself. Given the extenuating circumstances, I recommend in lieu of a court-martial, you consider giving Captain Williams the option of either a letter of reprimand or the opportunity to resign her commission."

Maura involuntarily winced when she saw the commander start tapping his finger on the table again and felt her entire body stiffen a few seconds later when he thoughtfully replied. "So, even though she's guilty of 3 court martial offenses, you think I should let her decide if she wants to resign her commission or continue her career, with a slap on the hand in the form of a letter of reprimand?"

Maura bellowed, "Airborne Sir!"

Standing up, the commander picked up the document and addressed Maura. "Thank you for your hard work and candor. I know this wasn't easy for you. I need to think about this before I make a decision." As the commander walked over to his desk, Maura realized the meeting was over and walked out of his office without another word.

★ ★ ★

"**ARE YOU OKAY CAPTAIN** Collins?" Maura stopped at the sound of the XO's voice behind her and turned around to see him coming out of his office with a look of concern on his face. "You're white as a ghost. Come in here for a minute"

Maura walked into the XO's office and he motioned her to sit in one of the two large overstuffed chairs as he walked to the small refrigerator behind his desk and came back with a bottle of coke. Sitting down in the other chair, he quietly ordered, "Drink this, breathe, and tell me what happened."

Maura took a drink of the coke, put it on the table between them and responded in a raspy voice, "I just gave my recommendation to the commander on my Article 32 findings. He tapped his fingers for a long time and told me he'd get back to me with his decision."

The XO chuckled. "Relax Maura, he does that when he has a hard decision to make. I don't know the details and I'm not asking for any. I've known him a long time and he only considers proposals he thinks have merit. Whether he accepts your recommendation or not, the fact that he told you he had to think about it, means you've forced him to question his initial inclination and he'll give it serious consideration." Realizing Maura was still unconvinced, he sternly ordered her. "Captain, stop biting your lip and relax. You did a good job."

"I know sir," Maura said quietly. "Thank you, I'm fine. I guess this was just a lot harder than I wanted to admit and when the boss didn't make a decision right then and there, I started to worry that I hadn't done a good enough job of supporting my recommendation." Standing up, she asked, "If it's okay with you sir, I'm going to check in with the 3 to see if he's had time to review the USR data I gave him last night and make any adjustments he wants, so we're ready for the brief to the boss on Friday morning."

"Whoa Maura! The boss told you to turn that over to the 3. Are you telling me that you worked the USR in addition to conducting this investigation?"

Realizing she'd made a mistake Maura hurriedly added, "Sir, there's a lot going on here. I've noticed the 3 hasn't been coming to PT, doesn't eat lunch, and is still here working no matter how late the rest of us leave. Three days after I heard you tell him he had to do the USR, I told him that it was going to take a week before I could talk to any other witnesses and I had a good handle on the paperwork, so if he wanted me to, I could start putting the USR together. In fairness to him sir, he thanked me, but told me that you had made it clear that I was to focus solely on the Article 32. I told him I'd let him know if I couldn't handle both tasks and really wanted to get in the swing of things. He very reluctantly agreed to let me help. So if you have to be angry at anybody, be angry at me sir."

The XO just shook his head and shooed her out with his hand. "Go to it captain."

★ ★ ★

MAURA WALKED INTO THE kitchen and joined Anne and Natalie at the kitchen table. Picking up the wine glass in front of her, Maura reached for the bottle of wine. "Hi, sorry I'm late."

"We figured you'd be late, so we waited until six to put the potatoes on the grill and waited to put our steaks on until you actually got here." Pointing to her salad, Anne continued, "We were starving, so we started without you. Your salad is in the fridge."

"Thanks," Maura responded as she took a sip of wine. "I'm not hungry right now, so don't cook my steak; but I'll try to eat the baked potato and salad."

Anne looked at Natalie explaining, "Whenever she's upset, she doesn't eat." Turning around, Anne admonished Maura, "If you keep this up, when you have to weigh in for the October PT test, you'll be under the required minimum weight for your height and they'll medically flag you."

Maura scowled at Anne and stood up. "I'll get my salad now and start eating. Will that get you off my back? I finished the Article 32 investigation and gave the commander my report and recommendation today; so the worst part of this is over." Maura walked over to the refrigerator and took out the salad, put some Good Seasons Italian dressing on it, sat down at the table, and took a large bite of salad and snarled, "Happy now?"

Realizing someone needed to break the tension, Anne forced a laugh, but admonished Maura. "When you get over your tantrum and start acting normally, I'll be happy. You're acting like a six year old who wants to stay outside and play, but has to come in for supper."

Maura realized Anne was right and let out a deep sigh. "Guilty as charged. I just need some time to unwind and chill."

Anne nodded understandingly and took a bite of her salad. Natalie asked quietly, "Did the commander take your recommendation?"

"No," Maura replied dejectedly. "He said he needed to think about it before he made a decision and the suspense is killing me!"

"Well he didn't reject it, so obviously he's considering accepting it, which is good, right?" Maura shrugged her shoulders and took another bite of salad.

"Can you tell us what you recommended?" Natalie quietly asked Maura.

Maura shook her head, "Sorry, I can't say anything, until I get his final ruling; but I can tell you I think I presented a strong enough case that he might agree with my request for leniency."

"Then let it rest. You did your best and worrying won't change anything." Standing up, Natalie announced, "I'm going to put the steaks on the grill. You two make nice."

Maura lifted her wine glass and asked with a lopsided grin, "We good?"

Waving her hand dismissively, Anne admitted, "I had a bit of a bad day too, so it's not all your fault."

"What happened?" Maura asked with concern.

"When we first got here, Derek told me he was subject to no notice deployments at any time and he wouldn't be allowed to contact me, or leave the compound, so I should go to the apartment, leave him a note to call me and if I didn't get a response that day, it meant he was deployed, and he'd call me when he returned. I called Derek's office today to confirm we were still a go for lunch today and when no one picked up, I drove to his compound. The sentry told me he wasn't there. When I pressed him for more information, he just repeated, "I can't say ma'am. It's really maddening."

Before Maura could respond, Natalie opened the screen door and yelled, "Hey you two, come on out here. I just turned over the steaks and they'll be done in a few minutes!"

9

FT. BENNING, GA, WEDNESDAY, 9 JULY, 1980

2ND LIEUTENANT LORI NELSON was tall with dirty blond hair and dark blue eyes. With her indomitable drive, competitive spirit, and desire to meet any challenges put in her path, she had survived four years at the United States Military Academy and was a member of the first class of women to graduate.

After graduation and commissioning at West Point, Lori reported to Fort Benning, Georgia, home of the Army Infantry, for Airborne school. Lori was thrilled to find her former West Point roommate, Roni, in her airborne class. Despite good intentions, they had only seen each other once since Roni left the Academy at the end of their yearling (sophomore) year. Roni, a spunky, dark haired woman from Long Island, New York, returned home after failing English and transferred to the State University at Albany where she excelled in the ROTC program. Roni became an Engineer officer the same month Lori and her classmates graduated from West Point.

After a grueling three weeks of unrelenting harassment, physical training, morning runs, class room instruction, and completing the required parachute jumps, Lori and Roni graduated and received their airborne wings earlier today.

Roni suggested they go to their favorite local 'greasy spoon' for a celebratory lunch. Looking down at the airborne wings that had been pinned on her uniform an hour ago at their airborne graduation, Roni told Lori, "Airborne school sucked, but was nowhere near as tough as Beast Barracks and Camp Buckner. I hated Beast due to my first squad leader who hated me. He kept telling me I was taking a slot away from a man. What an asshole! Camp Buckner on the other hand was kinda fun. I meet lots of our classmates and we even had some free time to relax and swim at Lake Popolopen. My problem with Buckner was with all the long and hard runs and tactical patrolling." Changing the subject she asked, "You excited about getting your wings?"

Lori nodded, "I was scared stiff waiting to jump out of the C130 but after the first jump, I loved the feeling of floating in the air like a bird and the last few weeks weren't as bad as I thought they'd be, but I'm glad it's over."

"The jumps were the easy part for me." Running an airborne shuffle is easier than sprinting up hills; but there were a few times, I wasn't sure I'd make the run. I wish I could run as easily as you Lori, but running's really tough for me. Thanks for encouraging me."

"That's what friends do," Lori replied dismissively. "Even though I run well, all the silly hazing we got from the cadre, reminded me of our days at school. I thought silly stuff like that was over."

Roni grimaced, "Yeah, I really didn't like that they singled us out. Do you think we'll ever get out of this fishbowl?"

Swallowing the last bit of her hamburger, Lori took a gulp of coke before responding. "Yeah, it gripes me too. It's as bad as that first day in July of 1976 when we arrived at West Point and were besieged by the press and resented by our peers. I just hope with time and our performance, people won't single us out, and we can just be seen as fellow military professionals. So, what did you do at SUNY for your Army training?"

"Some of the same stuff I already learned at West Point." Roni explained. "I was so far ahead of my ROTC peers when we went to summer camp, that I was selected to be a company commander."

"I'm surprised to see you wearing engineer insignia. You told Cate and me you were going to pick military intelligence or quartermaster. Why'd you go engineers?"

"Engineer officer was my third choice, but I've always loved math and thought it'd be a cool branch. The funny thing is, now I'm gonna be in the same Engineer basic course at Fort Leonard Wood, as some of my former West Point classmates. That'll be so weird."

"Ya, that'll be strange but fun. Six of the women in our class picked engineers and I know they'll be as psyched to see you again as I was and it'll provide all of you an instant support network."

"Well, I have a feeling we'll be under the gun at our officer basic courses. Too bad I'll be at Fort Leonard Wood, while you're at McClellan. It'd be nice to be roommates again."

"Maybe when we're both at Fort Bragg in a few months, we can share an apartment," Lori said hopefully.

"That'd be great!" Roni said gleefully. "I can't wait to graduate from my basic course, it seems like I've been in school forever."

"True!" Lori said, as she finished her drink. "I've spent the last four years studying and training to be an Army officer and I'll finally get a chance to prove myself. I'm really looking forward to being a platoon leader and leading soldiers!"

"Yup, I know the feeling," Roni said as she looked at her watch and got up from the table. "Well, it's been great hanging out with you these past three weeks Lori, but I've gotta get my gear washed and packed before I drive to Missouri tomorrow. I hate good-byes, but I'm looking forward to seeing you at Bragg in four months."

Lori stood up and gave Roni a big bear hug. "Take care Roni. You know my number if you want to talk. See you when you get to Bragg."

10

FORT McCLELLAN, AL, JULY 1980

10 JULY 1980 WAS the first of eight straight days of over 100 degree temperatures and the longest streak of consecutive 100 + degree days on record in Birmingham, Alabama. Lori drove from Fort Benning, Georgia with her air conditioning running full-blast. Arriving at Fort McClellan, Alabama, Lori parked her Honda Accord and walked into the in-processing building greeting the Army clerk with a broad grin, "Hi! I'm here to in-process for my officer basic course."

The military clerk respectfully acknowledged her, as he reached under the counter and handed her a stack of paperwork. "Okay, ma'am. Please fill these out." Adding as he pointing to a nearby table, "You can fill these out over there and when you're finished, give them to me along with ten copies of your orders, ID card, leave form, and driver's license."

Sitting down at the large table in the corner, Lori noticed a male 2nd lieutenant and a woman in civilian clothes filling out the same forms the clerk had just handed to her. The woman smiled and looked up and Lori asked, "Are you here for the MP Officer basic course?"

"No. I'm here for the MP advanced course. I got here a few weeks early so I'll have to snow-bird until my class starts."

"Sorry ma'am."

Extending her hand out in greeting, the woman grinned. "I'm surprised you think I look young enough to be a second lieutenant. Captain Doris Peterson. How 'bout you?"

"I'm Lieutenant Lori Nelson, pleased to meet you ma'am. I'm curious, what is snow-birding?"

"Not really sure why they call it snow-birding but because I reported in early, I'll be assigned some sort of odd job the company commander or school needs help with, but more importantly, I don't have to needlessly burn leave before my course starts."

"Thanks ma'am, interesting concept. I didn't realize we could do something like that," Lori replied as she as she sat down to fill out the required paperwork.

Having finished filling out the required forms, Doris stood up. "Nice meeting you Lori. Welcome to the Corps. We don't have a lot of women, so if you have any questions, I'm happy to answer them or help you find someone who can. I'm sure we'll see each other at the O'club or at school sometime this week. If you like, we can have a drink at Happy Hour on Friday."

"That'd be great ma'am. Thanks," Lori said she watched the captain walk away.

After providing the completed forms to the clerk, Lori was sent to post housing, where she signed for her bachelor officer's quarters, received two sets of keys and a post map with her new residence circled.

As Lori drove into the parking lot, she was not impressed with the drab, three story concrete building that would be her home for the next three months. Unlocking the front door to her BOQ, Lori was disappointed to find a very small apartment with a galley kitchen, no bigger than a large closet, a small living room with standard cheap quartermaster furniture, a very small bedroom with a single bed pushed up against the wall, and a small bathroom with a tub. After making several trips up the two flights of stairs, unloading her possessions from her car, Lori accidently bumped into Captain Doris Peterson in the hallway.

"Hi ma'am! Didn't expect to run into you this soon." Lori said huffing and puffing from lifting the heavy box she had in her arms. "Sorry about bumping into you with my box, just moving my stuff into my Q."

Doris held up her hand. "No problem. I'm surprised they assigned you to this BOQ. I was told that this building was reserved mainly for Captains and permanent party."

"That explains why the housing officer said it was my lucky day," Lori responded cheerfully. "How close are we to the school house?"

"We're right behind it. Just go out the back door, down the hill, and across the parking lot. Living in this BOQ is a great deal. They're brand new, you get maximum sleep time, the PX, commissary, and baseball field, are just around the corner. You can even walk home for lunch if you like; but I'd recommend going to lunch with your classmates and getting to know them better. The MP Corps is small and the friendships you make will last your entire career."

"Thanks for the advice ma'am. I've got a few more boxes to unload and unpack before I can shower and eat, so I better get going."

Before Lori could leave, Doris offered, "I'm starving and was just heading to the O'club to get some dinner. If you've only got a few more boxes and can take a quick shower, I'll help you get the boxes in and you can join me for dinner."

"Thanks ma'am, that sounds great! I'm tired and hungry too," Lori replied. "Let me get this box inside my BOQ and with you helping me, I will have one last trip. I can be ready in about 15 minutes, does that work?"

"Perfect," Doris replied. "Let me help you with that heavy box."

11

FORT McCLELLAN, AL, MONDAY, 21 JULY 1980

EXCITED ABOUT STARTING HER officer basic course, Lori walked into her classroom 20 minutes early and saw three other lieutenants seated a few rows down, talking to each other. Lori smiled as she sat in the row just in front of them and turned around. "Hi! I'm Lori. I'm originally from Duluth, Minnesota. Nice to meet you."

The blond haired female lieutenant cheerfully greeted Lori, "I'm Jenni from New Hope, Minnesota. We're practically neighbors, how cool is that?"

Lori smiled and replied, "Very cool!"

"I'm Mike Longhouse from Myrtle Beach, South Carolina," one of the male lieutenants drawled as he pointed to the remaining male lieutenant, who announced boastfully, "I'm Fred, from New York City, the best city in the world."

"So you say," Jenni retorted and added, "Minneapolis is just as exciting and cool as New York City and a lot less expensive."

The playful banter continued as a few more lieutenants entered the room scouting out a seat and struck up similar conversations. All conversation ceased abruptly when a captain walked to the front of the classroom and announced, "Welcome, I'm CPT Norris, your company commander while you're here for the MP Officer basic course. I want to go over the schedule for the next few months, before you fill out the forms and introduce yourselves. Open the 3-Ring notebooks you received at check-in, so we can review the administrative schedule and company policies."

Just then, the door opened and a long-haired man in civilian clothes opened the door and sat down in the last row.

"Who are you?" Captain Norris growled.

"Jeb Green. Here for my officer basic course."

Captain Norris frowned. "Well, first and foremost, when you address me or any other superior officer, you need to end your reply with "sir" and in addition to being late, you are out of uniform. Go change into your Class A uniform and then you can take return and take a seat."

"My uniform is in transit and should be here next week," Jeb replied nonchalantly, then adding, "Uh, Sir."

"Then I expect you go to the Post Exchange when it opens at 0900 hours this morning and buy yourself another uniform so you can attend class this week." Captain Norris responded sternly, "I don't know what college you graduated from, but you're in the Army now and I expect you to adhere to all of the Army customs and regulations!"

"Yes, Sir!" Jeb said his face turning red as he stood up and walked out of the classroom.

Captain Norris continued, "Back to the schedule, we have an in-ranks uniform inspection at 1300 hours today in the North parking lot. I see some improper brass placement on your uniforms. Get that squared away before the inspection today. For those of you who know how to place your brass, help out your classmates who are still struggling. Class starts every morning at 0830 hours unless we're in the field or taking a PT test." Looking around the classroom, he pointed, "Lieutenant Longhouse, what is scheduled for tomorrow morning?"

Looking at the schedule, Mike Longhouse replied, "Sir, it says we have a PT test at the schoolhouse, at 0600 hours. The uniform is OD (olive drab) T-shirt and shorts with running shoes."

"Correct. I expect everyone to be in formation before 0600. After accountability formation, we'll perform stretching exercises, followed by the PT test, which consists of 2 minutes of doing as many push-ups and sit-ups as you are capable of doing, followed by a timed 2 mile run." Looking to his left, the captain pointed again. "Lieutenant James, what time does class end each day?"

"Sir, according to the schedule, class ends each day at 1700 hours."

CPT Norris held up a piece of paper. "Okay, if there are no questions, everyone needs to sign the first form in your package indicating you understand and will comply with all of the rules and policies I have just described. Once you've signed this form, pass it to the front and take a break. Be back in your seats at 0945."

Lori walked over to Jenni as they walked out of the classroom, "He's not real fun is he?"

"Nope," Jenni replied. "Might be a long 3 months if we have to deal with him a lot."

Lori smirked adding, "Ya. Wanna check out the snack bar?"

"Yeah, I need another cup of coffee."

At the snack bar, Lori met three more MPOBC classmates, and Brad Boyle, a fellow West Point classmate who Lori had briefly met at school on branch selection day. After a few minutes of conversation, Brad announced, "Well, we'd better head on back; fifteen minutes isn't a long break and I don't want to get on Captain Norris' radar, on our first day."

Walking back to the classroom Lori asked, "Brad, where's home, and what's your follow-on assignment?"

"I'm from Tulsa, Oklahoma, and I'm headed to Fort Hood, Texas, which is really great, since I'm not too far from home. How 'bout you?"

"I'm headed to Fort Bragg, North Carolina. What regiment were you in? I never saw you at school."

"D-1. I saw you play basketball a few times, but that was it. You were really good."

"Thanks, I was in A-4, no wonder I never saw you. I rarely saw cadets from first or second regiment."

"Hope to see you at the officer's club to swap stories this weekend," Brad said as he waved good-by as they entered the classroom and walked to their respective seats.

★ ★ ★

AT EXACTLY 1300 HOURS, the class leader, 2nd Lieutenant Walt Jones, yelled, "Fall in!" for the uniform formation. The thirty-four MP officers got into formation and stood at attention. 2LT Jones yelled, "Report!"

In progression, the three MPs at the right end of each row, saluted 2LT Jones and shouted, "All present and accounted for."

2LT Jones returned each officers' salute and opened the ranks for the uniform inspection. With heels together, 2LT Jones executed an 'about face' as Captain Norris briskly walked up to him, he announced, "Sir, the class is present and ready for inspection."

Captain Norris returned his salute. "Take your post and write down deficiencies for me." Walking to the end of the formation, Captain Norris stopped at the end of the first row, asking the lieutenant, "Lieutenant Mabry. Did you get a haircut this week?"

"No, Sir."

"Well, you need one ASAP. Don't come back to class tomorrow without one."

Captain Norris addressed each lieutenant by name and noted at least one deficiency for each one. Lieutenant Jones followed closely behind Captain Norris taking copious notes in his small notebook. Twenty minutes later, Captain Norris stood in front of the platoon, ordering, "Parade rest! Each one of you need some work on your Class A uniform and your appearance. We will have another Class A in ranks inspection this Friday and I expect to see no deficiencies. Class will resume in 10 minutes. Fall out!"

As Lori and Jenni walked back into the building Lori, exclaimed, "Wow we were only out there 30 minutes and I'm sweating like a pig. It's super-hot here."

"Actually it's more humid than hot. What do you expect at one in the afternoon in Alabama? What'd you get written up for?" Jenni asked.

"My jacket wasn't pressed properly near the bust-line. How do I get the laundry to fix that? What about you?"

"Norris said I had strands of hair touching my shoulders? Do you see them?" Jenni asked.

"Yeah, I see two strands barely touching the top of your shoulders. That's pretty nit-picky if you ask me."

"He's trying to make an impression. At St. Cloud we didn't have cadre who were that strict. How 'bout you?" Jenni asked.

"Our inspections were much worse; sometimes lasting two hours in the hot sun. I hated the inspections under arms and the Saturday white glove room inspections. I always got demerits for something. Plebe year was the worst."

"Oh yeah, I forgot you're a West Pointer. That's so cool. I'd like to hear about it over a beer at the O-club sometime."

"Sounds good. Let's hit the latrine and get to class on time so Norris doesn't give us extra duty or some other nonsense," Lori said as she headed into the women's rest room.

★ ★ ★

LORI WAS HOT AND sweaty when she got home from class, so after taking a shower, and eating left over Hamburger Helper for dinner, she got a Tab from the fridge, sat down, and dialed Scott's number. Scott answered with, "Can I help you?"

"Hey Scott! I haven't talked to you in days and I wanted to see how you're doing at Benning."

"Doing great Lori. Can't believe I've been here four weeks already. Sorry I missed lunch with you and Roni last week, but wouldn't you know it, that's the time my Commander scheduled a counseling session with me."

"I was disappointed you couldn't make lunch but was glad you were able to attend the ceremony and see me get my airborne wings. So, what have you been up to lately?"

"I finally got all my field gear. I'm running an hour before class every morning because it's hotter than heck, so I get up early before the wet-bulb temp gets too high. Then I spend a few more hours at the gym after class lifting weights. I figure I've got to work out at least three hours every day to get ready for Ranger school."

"Yeah, it's hot and humid here too. School is going well and is a piece of cake since we had most of the stuff in our military science classes. I've made a few friends and I'm enjoying all the free time."

"Lucky you. I don't have much free time. Are you still driving down this Saturday?" he asked curtly.

Surprised by his crabby attitude, Lori replied hesitantly, "Yeah. Has something changed?"

"Nope. We can work out together at the gym on Saturday and Sunday morning. I'll need a few hours to pack my gear, but I can do that when you drive back to McClellan."

"Okay, any plans for Saturday night?" Lori asked.

"I thought we'd go to dinner and then catch a movie." Scott said offhandedly. "I heard *The Empire Strikes Back* is a great flick."

"Sounds good, I loved *Star Wars*. Can't wait to see you Scott. I know it's been less than a week since I've seen you, but I really miss you."

"Okay, well I've got to go Lori," Scott said brusquely. "I'm meeting the guys at the O'club, so I'll cut this short. See you Saturday. Bye!"

"Bye," Lori said quietly as she heard the distinctive click of the phone and realized Scott had not even waited for her to respond. *Was she paranoid or was something off with Scott? He seemed so distant almost like he didn't want to talk to her.* Shaking off her feeling of gloom, Lori finished her Tab, walked into her bedroom, got her laundry basket, and headed to the BOQ laundry room on the ground floor. Entering the small cramped room, she noticed a tall dark-haired guy with a pencil mustache sitting on a plastic chair reading a book. He looked up at her, said "Hi" and continued reading.

"Hi back at ya," Lori muttered under her breath as she quickly sorted the light and dark clothes into two piles and put her quarters into the two empty washing machines. Leaving her laundry basket on the table, Lori went back upstairs to wash her dishes and get ready for tomorrow's class.

When Lori returned to the laundry room to put her clothes in the dryer, the mustached guy who had cursorily greeted her earlier, looked up from folding a pair of black bikini underwear and said, "Sorry I was so absorbed in my book when you came in, I may have been rude. I'm Roger and I'm here for the MP career course. What about you?"

Not sure of his rank, Lori decided to play it safe, "Nice to meet you sir. I'm Lori. I just started the MP basic course."

"You don't have to call me sir when we're not in uniform." Roger said. So, how did you get billeted here? Lieutenants usually go to WAC circle."

"Yeah, not sure why the clerk assigned me here, but I'm really glad I'm not in the old WAC circle quarters. Some of my classmates told me the cockroaches there are as big as belt buckles."

Roger grimaced. "Yeah, I've seen them. Pretty disgusting. Where're you originally from?"

Lori smiled broadly as she told him, "I'm from Minnesota. What about you?"

"Nowhere really. I'm an Army brat, seven schools in twelve years." Roger replied thoughtfully, "I guess I'd say my grandparent's house in Lacey, Washington is the closest concept of a home for me. We'd go there between moves and almost every summer except when we lived in Germany and Japan. "I was in Minnesota once on a family vacation. We went to Cragun's resort. Ever hear of it?"

"Yes! It's in Brainerd and I love that place." Lori said excitedly. "I spent a week there camping with my family." Pausing, Lori added thoughtfully, "I've lived in one spot my entire life, until West Point. I can't imagine uprooting every year or two. It must have been really tough growing up that way."

"You get used to it. I'm the youngest of three. My two sisters had a harder time with moving than I did because I'd just join a sports team and meet other kids," Roger said as the washing machine buzzer sounded and he laconically picked up his laundry basket. "I'll let you finish your laundry. I'm in room 224, see ya 'round campus."

"Thanks sir, I mean Roger. Nice to meet you." Lori turned around to open the top of the washer smiling and thought, "*That was so cool meeting a good looking guy my first time in the laundry room.*"

12

FORT BENNING GA, FRIDAY, 25 JULY 1980

LORI ARRIVED AT THE Camilla apartments early on Saturday morning, excited at the prospect of spending the weekend with Scott. After getting no response to her first ring, a few minutes later, she impatiently rang the bell a second time.

Scott opened the door, gave Lori a quick hug and a "Hi Lori," before motioning her to come in the apartment.

A bit irritated it had taken him so long to answer the door and his brusque welcome, she asked, "Did I wake you?"

An exasperated look crossed Scott's face as he told her, "Nope. I, uh, was on the phone. Sorry to keep you waiting."

"That's okay. I know how it is. My parents call at the most inconvenient times." Looking around at the sparsely furnished old apartment, she added, "I realize you just moved in last week, but I'd love to see your apartment."

"Won't take long," Scott said dismissively as he grabbed Lori's small suitcase and pointed, "We're in the living room, you can see the small kitchen over there, and the bedroom and bathroom are down the hall."

"Is it me or is this place really dark?"

"It's pretty dark." Scott concurred as they walked down the short, narrow hallway and he added, "Okay, here's my bedroom." Scott set Lori's suitcase on the floor as they walked into the bedroom that was littered with clothing and field gear, along with an unmade bed. "Sorry the place is a mess," Scott's voice trailed off. "Just really busy with school, physical training, and other stuff. You know how it is."

"Yeah, I do." Lori said quietly, as she tried to hide her disgust and justify Scott's messy apartment in her mind.

"Would you like something to drink?"

Relived at the change of subject, Lori smiled gratefully. "Thanks, I could really use a Pepsi."

"Sorry, all I have is beer, Coke, and orange juice," Scott replied apologetically.

"I'll take a Coke; ice if you have some," Lori said pensively, as she followed Scott out into the hallway. She wondered why Scott hadn't bothered to get some Pepsi, knowing that was all she drank and she was coming to spend the weekend.

"Have a seat in the living room, I'll be right back," Scott said as he headed to the kitchen to get her a Coke.

Lori sat on the far corner of the sofa, which was the only other item of furniture in the room, besides a small brown bookcase that was overflowing with books, field manuals, and three-ring binders. Looking at Scott's duffle bags, steel pot, and other TA-50 gear spread out in the corner of the living room, she was taken aback by Scott's unkempt apartment and disregard for something as simple as her preference for Pepsi. This was an unpleasant and unexpected departure from the Scott she had dated at West Point. Scott had always been considerate, attentive to her wants, neat, and squared away.

Scott returned with two glasses of Coke, handing Lori the one with ice and sat at the other end of the couch and explained, "I bought an extra set of sheets, so I can sleep here on the couch and you can have my bed for the night."

Lori quickly told him, "That's okay. I can sleep on the couch for one night. I don't want to take your bed."

"It's the least I can do since you drove all the way here to see me."

Recalling Scott's unkempt bedroom, and wondering when the last time was that he'd changed the linen, Lori took exception. "No, Really, I insist. I'm smaller and shorter than you and will be perfectly comfortable here. It's been decided, I'm sleeping here, end of discussion. Now what's on for today?"

Scott shrugged his shoulders in acceptance as he thought out loud. "Well, could eat lunch at this great buffet I found…I need to go to the PX for a few things, and then the Commissary to get some food for next week. After that we can change and go work out at the post gym."

Wondering why he hadn't done his errands before she came to visit for the weekend Lori asked haltingly, "Okay, what about tonight?"

"I thought we'd get some take out for dinner and watch a VHS movie on my new TV before calling it a night."

Lori frowned, irritation creeping into her voice, "I thought we were going to see *The Empire Strikes Back*," she said plaintively. "What gives? We talked earlier this week and it's like you haven't even considered anything I told you I wanted to do."

"That's not true, I have thought about our weekend together," Scott said defensively, He then walked over to the television in the corner of the room, beaming with pride. "I bought it at the PX yesterday. It's a brand new Sony, state-of-the-art TV and I'd really like to watch a movie on it this weekend." Reaching into the black cabinet he'd bought to put it on, he pulled out a black, phallic looking device and excitedly exclaimed, "This is the video game joystick. It's my newest toy I bought for the game console that I've hooked up to the TV. You're gonna love it! I have a game called pong. It's really cool."

Torn between wanting to have a fun, relaxing weekend with Scott and being both surprised and irritated at his selfishness, Lori paused before suggesting, "Uh, sounds slightly interesting, maybe you can show me how the game and TV work tonight after we go out to dinner and a movie, like we talked about earlier this week. I was really looking forward to a relaxing dinner and movie with you."

Realizing, he wasn't going to get his way, Scott tried to cover his irritation. "Okay, grab your gym stuff and I'll grab my keys and bag." Scott announced resignedly, as he turned to walk down the hall, to his room.

Lori couldn't shake the nagging feeling that Scott didn't seem happy to see her. After eating at Olive Garden, they returned to Scott's apartment because Scott had wheedled Lori into watching *Raiders of the Lost Ark*, one of Lori's favorite movies, as a compromise. She tried to convince herself that she was overreacting and Scott really did care about her, he was just busy and stressed from school and trying to get in shape for Ranger School.

The movie had just ended when Scott's phone rang and he hurried into the small kitchen to answer it. Lori couldn't help but hear him say, "Hi! Uh, yeah, I'm a little busy right now. Can I call you back tomorrow?" There was a short pause before Scott said, "I'm sorry hon. I'll explain everything tomorrow. Thanks for understanding."

Lori was already on edge and couldn't shake the feeling that Scott was hiding something from her. "Who was that?" she asked as Scott came back into the living room.

"Uhhh, a good friend of mine," Scott stammered.

Recalling the term of endearment he used, Lori asked sarcastically, "How good of a friend? I wasn't aware you call all your friends *hon*."

"Well, it was my high school girlfriend." Scott admitted reluctantly.

"Why is she calling you now, on a Saturday night?" Lori asked derisively.

"Well, ah, well, I don't know how to tell you this Lori..." He stammered. "But I guess it's just best to be honest. I started dating her again, while I was home after graduation."

"What! Can you say that again?" Lori asked not able to comprehend what was going on just yet, as her face knotted up from all the stress she was experiencing.

"I started dating Janet again when I was home on leave."

Stunned, Lori paused before asking querulously. "When were you going to tell me? Is this serious?"

Scott shrugged his shoulders. "I'm not really sure how I feel. I like Janet but I really like you too. I was going to wait for a few weeks before making up my mind on who to continue seeing."

Lori felt her throat constricting. She blinked long and hard, trying not to let her tears out and yelled, "Are you kidding me? We've been going out together for the last three years! I thought our relationship was way past friendship and we were looking at a long term serious relationship." Feeling hurt and betrayed, Lori lamented, "That's why I picked Fort Bragg over Germany so I could be with you!"

"I thought so too, until I bumped into Janet at the gym. She'd just broken up with her boyfriend and needed someone to talk to." Scott recalled pensively, "I guess we just fell back into our old relationship."

"Isn't that lucky for Janet," Lori replied caustically. "I'm really upset Scott! How could you?!?" Lori screamed, unable to stop herself.

"Well, we weren't engaged or anything. I didn't *plan* on resuming my relationship with Janet," Scott whined.

"I really don't care what you planned Scott! I care about us! What's going on with us?"

"I don't know Lori. I'm confused. Janet just got her nursing degree and she's thinking about looking for a job near Fort Bragg. I really like both of you right now and thought perhaps we can all be friends. You'd really like her, if you took the time to get to know her."

Trying hard not to cry and let Scott see how much he had hurt her, Lori clenched her fists and shouted. "You're joking, right???" Lori asked incredulously. "I've been thinking of nothing but you and I making a life together and juggling my career and you dump this on me and suggest that we could be really good friends, if only I'd....."

Scott cut Lori off. "I don't want to hurt you Lori. I really care about you."

"Yeah, right." Lori snapped and stood up. "Well the good news is you can return the sheets you bought to use on the couch; because I'm driving back to Alabama now!"

"Slow down Lori. It's getting dark out there and I think you need time to get your emotions under control. Please wait until tomorrow so we can discuss this some more." Scott pleaded.

"What's there to discuss? You're not willing to give up Janet for me, so I know where I stand. I'm an Army Lieutenant, just like you. I've got to go wherever the Army sends me. Janet can follow you wherever you go and get a nursing job almost anywhere." Pausing, Lori plaintively declared, "I just never saw this coming." No longer able to suppress the hurt, tears poured from Lori's eyes, salting her upper lip.

"I don't want to upset you Lori. You're a great gal." Scott spluttered helplessly.

Hiccupping massive sobs, Lori stood up and walked down the hall, grabbed her suitcase and came back sputtering, "I thought we had something special Scott. All the time we were at school, sharing our hopes and dreams, consoling each other when things were tough, going to church together...I thought we were going to get married. I feel so betrayed Scott...How could you do this to me?"

"I didn't plan to run into Janet. It just happened."

"I love you Scott! I thought you loved me," Lori sniffled. "I thought we had a future."

"We do have a future Lori. I still want to be friends."

Shocked at his ridiculous suggestion, Lori asked, "You've broken my heart in pieces and you excuse that by telling me you want me to be your friend?"

"Don't leave Lori; sleep on it tonight, I know you'll be calmer in the morning and we can discuss this more rationally."

"Right!" Lori grabbed her small suitcase and walked to the front door. "I won't get any sleep tonight so I'll be more logical tomorrow...that makes a lot of sense. Good-bye Scott!" Lori yelled as she opened the door, slamming it behind her. Lori ran to the parking lot to her car. She hoped Scott would come running out, begging her not to leave and when that did not happen, Lori sat in her car for ten minutes trying to get her crying under control, before driving back to Fort McClellan. She cried off and on for the next hour or so and didn't remember her drive back to her BOQ. Opening the door to her BOQ, her eyes sore from crying, she walked into her bedroom, collapsed on her bed, and fell fast asleep with her clothes on. When she woke up the next morning, her first thought was that she'd had a bad dream until she noticed she was still in her clothes and her suitcase was in the living room. *Oh my God, what is going on? I spent the last three years with Scott and no one else and now he's involved with his high school girlfriend. What's wrong with me?* Lori thought as she turned over in her bed and slept another four hours.

★ ★ ★

LORI woke up the next morning thirsty and unsure how to combat the depression threatening to overwhelm her and drank two large glasses of water before sitting down to write her best friend.

Dear Reggie,

Sorry to dump on you, but I had the worst experience last night. Since you're my best friend, I wanted to vent my feelings to you and I know you'll understand, especially after your situation with the Dean last year. Okay, no easy way to say it, Scott two-timed me and I broke up with him at Benning last night. I discovered he's been dating his high school sweetheart since he went home for graduation leave; because she called him last night while I was visiting. When I asked him when he was going to tell me about it, he told me he'd planned to date both of us until he decided who he liked the best! Can you believe that??

I exploded and told him that I wasn't going to wait for him to decide, I was done with him. I waited in the apartment parking lot before driving back home last night, trying to get my crying under control, hoping he'd come after me, but he didn't. That's when I realized he'd already made up his mind. He just wasn't ready to deal with telling me. I'm so pissed!

Ok, thanks for putting up with my wild woman rant. Don't worry about me, I'll be fine, it's just gonna take a while. Know you stay busy, but drop me a line when you get a few and let me know how things are going now that you're a firstie and a squad leader at Beast. I miss you Reggie. Hang tough, you're on the home stretch!
Your friend, Lori

Feeling slightly better after writing a letter to Reggie, Lori changed into gym clothes and went for a long, hard run to clear her mind. Having finished her run, Lori was unlocking her BOQ door when she heard the phone ringing and rushed in to answer it.

★ ★ ★

"YOU DID WHAT WILLOW?" Lori screamed into the phone. Lori could not believe what her best friend from Duluth, just told her.

"Like we told you last Christmas, if our baby was a girl, we were naming her after you and just wanted you to know that Lori Ann Schuda was born last night at 10 pm."

"Wow, I just don't know what to say…" Lori paused, momentarily at a loss for words. "How are both of you doing?"

Lori could hear the pride in Willow's voice as she answered. "She's doing great. She's 7 pounds 8 ounces and is 21.5 inches long. We're stuck in the hospital for another day, but get out of here tomorrow. Can't wait. You don't get any sleep in here."

"I'm so happy both of you are healthy Willow! I remember you and Jeff told me at Christmas time you were going to name your baby after me if it was a girl; because I helped you guys get through some rough times and set up your first date together in high school; but I figured when it finally came time to name her, you'd have second thoughts."

Willow interrupted. "It's official, she is your namesake and we were hoping you'll agree to be her godmother and if possible, be here for her baptism."

"Wow, yes to godmother" Lori exhaled and added, "Send me the date soonest and I'll try to get a 3-day pass or take leave. This is so cool, you have no idea how much it means to me. I'm so happy for you Willow. You've got a wonderful marriage and now a beautiful baby. Life doesn't get any better than that."

"I know, we're so blessed. I can't wait to see you again Lori. The nurse says I've got to get off the phone. I'll get the date to you as soon as we get it set with our priest. Take care of yourself Lori and when you get a chance, let me know what's happening with you. Love ya, bye!" and then the line went dead. Lori was conflicted. She was overflowing with happiness and love for Willow but she was also sad about what had happened to her last week with Scott. Although she was tempted to tell Willow about her problems, Lori decided to wait for a few weeks before she sharing her sad news with her childhood friend.

13

FORT MCCLELLAN, AL, FRIDAY, 26 SEPTEMBER 1980

LORI ENTERED THE O'CLUB bar and immediately looked for her classmates. Jenni, Brad, Mike, and Fred yelled almost simultaneously, "You're late! We're over here!" Smiling Lori walked over and sat down. Brad pointed at the one empty beer mug and several pitchers of cold beer, "I got the first round, help yourself."

Lori gave Brad a thumbs-up as she took a long swig of the ice cold beer she had just poured into her mug. "Man, that tastes almost as good as the shower I took when we got back from our 2 week field exercise at Pelham Range, thanks!"

Jenni whined, "Yeah, I really didn't expect to spend so much time in the field in our course. I can't believe we're only focusing on our tactical mission. I joined the MP Corps to work the white-hat mission and work law enforcement ops. I didn't expect to spend so much time in the field and run tactical control points and main supply routes during our course."

"No kidding!" Mike chimed in. "I had no idea MPs acted as infantry in the field. I was shocked when General Lowe briefed us on our new mission focus. I thought we'd be maintaining law and order, not doing battlefield circulation control in the field for weeks on end. This infantry mission sucks. I picked MPs to catch the bad guys and help people, not act as grunts in the field for half my career."

"I'm glad we're out of the field," Fred said. "I was so sick of green eggs from a marmite container and C-rations, that I stopped eating a few meals."

"The C-rats weren't that bad. I actually like beans and weenies, and the crackers and peanut butter are okay. What's your issue?" Brad asked Fred.

Fred replied, "I kept getting Lima beans and that nasty pork meal. I practically lived on the John Wayne bars and crackers. I must have lost 10 pounds during the last 2 weeks!"

"You do look a little thin. I'm sure you'll regain the weight in a few weeks, especially if you keep pounding down the brewskis," Lori said.

"How about a few more pitchers of beer?" Brad asked.

"I can handle another one," Lori said looking at the empty mug in front of her. The rest of the group nodded their heads in agreement, as Mike stood up and went to the bar and ordered two pitchers of Coors.

"Yeah, this is so nice. Good food, good friends, good beer, what more could you ask for?" Jenni added.

"I could use more than a 3 day weekend to recover and wash my clothes. But, I guess an extra day off is better than only having 2 days off," Fred said.

Lori added, "Yes, it is. I plan on catching up on sleep and doing some PT. I hate the field, so much wasted time. I don't need to practice being miserable."

Mike chimed in, "That's for sure! I can deal with field duty if there's a purpose for it. I'm looking forward to my first assignment in West Germany."

Lori's face brightened with excitement as she said, "I loved Germany."

Surprised, Mike asked, "When were you in Germany? I thought you just graduated from West Point. Are you prior service?"

"No, I spent 6 weeks at CTLT two summers ago. I loved the country, and the soldiers were awesome too. Too bad I was a staff puke and not a platoon leader. I can't wait to get my platoon at Bragg."

"Six weeks isn't the same as three years," Mike said, dismissing Lori's comments. "I figure I'll be an MP platoon leader for a year or two and then work on company staff for the rest of my tour. Then I'll be back here for the advanced course."

"Sounds like you have it all figured out. What happens if your plan doesn't unfold the way you envisioned it?" Jenni asked.

"I'm not worried about it. I can have fun no matter where I'm stationed. I hear the Germans have the best beer, and their wine's not too shabby either. I also plan on traveling all over Europe on my days off."

Fred smiled and added, "Let's hope you don't go to a unit that spends half the year at Vilsek or Grafenwoehr pulling field duty. This two week exercise will look like a vacation if you're going to a tactical unit. Trust me, I'm prior service and my friends told me some real horror stories about their field time. C-rats for weeks on end, once a week you *might* get a cold shower, eating dust all day long, jeeps getting stuck in the mud, stressed out bosses during evaluations, no privacy in the tents, you get the picture. I'm glad I'm going to Fort Campbell, Kentucky. My girlfriend can fly down for long weekends and I can fly home to the city on leave. If you're stationed in West Germany, it's super expensive to fly home."

Mike replied, "Probably true, but I'll do okay. I don't mind the field as much as you do Fred. I actually eat the C-rats and will sweet-talk the cooks for some good grub. Life's too short to be upset or hungry. Pass the beer please!"

Lori looked past the bar and noticed Doris having drinks with Roger. They seemed to be thoroughly enjoying each other's company and Lori wondered, *what's Scott right doing now?*

"Lori, you with us?" Jenni whispered.

"Yeah, just daydreaming," Lori whispered back.

"You want to meet me at the gym tomorrow? I thought we could play tennis, go to lunch, and then maybe watch a movie. You game?"

"Sure, how about meeting tomorrow morning at 9 at the tennis courts right by the gym."

"Sounds great," Jenni stood up and announced, "Well guys, I've got to take off, I'm beat and need my beauty sleep. I've had lots of fun. Lori finished off her beer and added, "I'm gonna bug out as well. See you guys Monday."

★ ★ ★

A LITTLE TIPSY FROM the three beers at the O'club, Lori wasn't ready for bed so she pulled out some stationary and started writing a letter to her West Point roommate.

> No Cate I haven't died...Just busy as heck with field exercises, school, working out, and the usual stuff. You know same thing you're doing, except I no longer have a boyfriend. That's right...I broke up with Scott right after I got to McClellan. It sucks, but he basically went back to his high school sweetheart and my heart was broken for about 6 weeks. I felt like a zombie and was so lethargic. My new friend Jenni told me I was depressed. I've never felt like that before. I had no energy or interest in anything. Thank goodness OBC is super easy after our hard 4 years at school and I am coasting in my military police classes. I just couldn't focus for weeks. Now I am finally starting to feel better. Enough of my sorrows. How are you doing at MI school and how's it going with Jim?
>
> Your friend, Lori

14

FORT BRAGG, NC, WEDNESDAY, 22 OCTOBER 1980

AFTER SIGNING IN TO Fort Bragg, Lori met Maura and Anne at IHOP for lunch. Hearing Anne yell excitedly, "Over here!" Lori quickly walked over and gave both women a hug and slid into the other side of the booth, "So great to see you both! It's been a wild ride since we last saw each other in May."

"Yeah, we've had our adventures too," Maura said, "You go first."

"Well, the biggest news is I broke up with Scott not long after graduation."

"No way!" Anne exclaimed. "He seemed like such a nice guy and you seemed really into each other."

"I thought so too, but he got back with his high school sweetheart while he was on leave in Kansas City. Damn near broke my heart in two," Lori said morosely. "I'm still recovering from the shock. I just didn't see it coming."

"Wow, that's tough Lori. How're you holding up?" Maura asked.

Lori looked Maura in the eye, "I was really depressed for a few months but I'm slowly getting back to normal. I can't believe I let a guy affect me so much. I thought I was more independent than that."

"Don't be hard on yourself," Anne replied. "Guys have a way of getting into your life when you don't expect them to and if it doesn't work out, we usually get the worst of that deal." Seeing Maura give her the evil eye, Anne changed the subject abruptly. "You look great! I love your longer hair and the color is fantastic!"

"Ya, it's so nice to be able to have long hair again. As long as I put it up in uniform, I can do what I want with my hair."

Concern in her voice, Maura asked, "You look like you've lost weight. You sure you're over it and are okay?"

"Well to be honest, I've lost about 10 pounds, but I feel good. I kinda like my clothes hanging loose on me. The good news is that I've reduced my 2 mile run time by 20 seconds, so the weight loss has helped made me run faster, which given my assignment here is a good thing."

"It is here." Maura affirmed vigorously. "You gain instant credibility with the guys if you can make all the runs. It's stupid, but the Army values brawn over brains, especially at the junior officer level."

Anne nodded knowingly. "Yeah, at SWIK, we've got a few slow field grade officers, but they're mostly guys who got wounded in 'Nam, so when they aren't on profile or medical hold, and they show up for a unit run, we encourage them and cut them a bit of slack on the run pace."

"The major at Division Chem, is chubby but super intelligent and hardworking, so the division ChemO lets him slide on some of the runs, but that is definitely not the case with the DISCOM or maneuver brigades." Noticing the waitress had returned to take their orders, Maura said, "Enough about PT. Let's order."

As the waitress walked off, Anne asked, "How's Trish doing? Did she finish the quartermaster basic course yet?"

"She's doing great. She went to the motor officer basic course at Fort Knox after her leave in June and she still has a few more weeks to go at Fort Lee. She's been assigned to the 2nd Infantry Division. If I can get off early on Friday, I plan on driving up to see her before she leaves for Korea."

"That'll be tough but Trish can handle it," Anne said. "I was impressed with her ability to work well with soldiers and rapidly learn basic logistics processes when she was in Germany with me for CTLT."

"Ya, she's a no-nonsense kind of gal and is one of a few women who can run faster than me! I'm a little worried about the situation in Korea though. Trish got a letter from her sponsor saying she'd been assigned to the 2nd S&T battalion at Camp Casey, in Tongduchon. She told me he wrote that is was important for her to realize that they have a real world mission and that the situation there is pretty volatile and the 2nd ID is only a speed bump on the road for North Korean forces, if they ever come across the border."

Anne nodded understanding. "Yeah, I don't know a lot about it, but one of my NCOs was assigned to 2ID before coming here and when I asked him what it was like, he told me that once you got used to the reality that if the North Korean forces attack, 2ID has a *die in place* mission. You just do your job and when you get the occasional weekend pass, you try to see a little bit of the country. I'm relieved to hear you've heard from her. I wrote her twice and got no reply."

"True. She only wrote me once, but we talked a few times when we were both in the basic course."

Maura changed the subject, "I think the oriental culture would be a fascinating place to be stationed. The culture is so different than Germany or Europe. Perhaps I'll have a chance to see that part of the world in a future assignment."

"Are you going to be a lifer?" Lori asked mischievously.

"Ha! I don't know." Maura shrugged her shoulders. "Originally I thought I'd get out of the Army and move back to New York after my tour in Germany, but now I'm not sure when I'll get out. Guess it depends on what happens."

"I have my five year military obligation for my education and training, so I've got a few years to think about it." Pausing, Lori asked, "So what have you two been doing in the last five months since I last saw you?"

Anne answered, "I'm the logistics officer for the JFK Special Warfare Center, which everyone calls SWIK."

Lori interrupted, "What do the I and K stand for?"

Maura chuckled. "It's pronounced, *SWIK* but is actually spelled SWC"

Lori nodded understanding and Anne continued, "Derek had to go TDY a few days after I got here and he's been gone a lot. He's part of a new headquarters called JSOC that stands for Joint Special Operations Command. So when he's around, I spend the weekends with him."

Maura interrupted. "Speaking of which, Anne and I live off post in a house owned by another female captain at SWC."

"Cool," Lori replied.

"Her name's Natalie, she's an MI officer and was my sponsor." Anne added, "We'll have you over and you can get to know her. You're gonna like her." Anne glanced at Maura indicating it was her turn to talk.

"I was on leave and staying at my parents' place in the city when I came to your graduation, and returned to Ft. McClellan to finish the Health Physics course, before signing into Bragg in early June. I'm getting a better idea of what loggie toads like Anne and Trish do in my assignment at the DISCOM headquarters. I'm guessing you're assigned to the 82nd MP Company, which means you belong to the DISCOM too, so when you get a chance, stop by. We'll go get a coke or cup of coffee."

"Thanks Maura. I'm really excited to meet my commander and soldiers. I found out that because I'm regular army and a grad, that I'm assigned to the 82nd MP Company because a platoon leader slot is open, but it's up to the company commander to decide if he wants me."

"Of course you'll get a platoon. You're smart and in great a shape." I actually know the commander and I'll stop by his office on my way back to let him know what a good job you did in Germany when I was assigned to be your CTLT mentor. "So, are you going to live in the *Q*?" Maura asked.

"Not sure if you remember Trish and I talking about Roni, who was my first roommate in plebe year. She flunked out of West Point after her third semester. Since all she's ever wanted to be is an Army officer, she joined ROTC, at SUNY and she's now an Engineer. We're both tired of living in a fishbowl when you live in the BOQ and agreed to share an apartment off post."

"Sounds great Lori," Anne said. "You'll have a good friend to talk to and be able to save some of your quarter's allowance money by sharing costs."

"Yeah, it'll be a big help for me, but Roni comes from a wealthy family in Long Island. They think she's nuts for joining the Army, but give her anything she asks for, so she doesn't think about what things cost or worry about making ends meet."

"So when do we get to meet her?" Maura asked.

"Her company left a few days ago for a two week field exercise, but I'm sure we can go to dinner when she gets back."

"I see our waitress coming with our food." Maura said as she looked at her watch. "This has been great and we can confirm details later. Unfortunately, I've got a meeting at 1300, so I need to eat and scoot out of here."

★ ★ ★

THE NEXT MORNING LORI reported to her new MP company commander, Captain Archibald. In response to her loud knock on the door, he bellowed. "Report!"

Lori strode into the room confidently, walked up to Captain Archibald's desk, came to attention, and saluted crisply, "Sir, Lieutenant Nelson reports!"

Returning the salute, he said, "Stand at ease. Welcome to the 82nd MP Company Lieutenant Nelson. I'm happy to have you." Looking up from her Officer Record Brief, he continued, "Says here you graduated from the United States Military Academy in May, attended airborne school, and then the military police officer basic course, graduating as an honor graduate." Lori nodded and the captain continued, "I need a good motor officer. Are you up to the challenge LT?"

"Airborne Sir!" Lori responded smartly before adding, "But I thought I was going to be a platoon leader."

"We're short a platoon leader in Charlie platoon, so you'll be a platoon leader; but the motor pool is in dire need of effective leadership, so you'll be the motor officer as an additional duty."

After four years at West Point, where she learned to have a *Can Do* attitude and to never turn down an opportunity to serve, Lori simply replied, "Airborne Sir!" without the slightest understanding of what she was agreeing to.

Captain Archibald pointed to a nearby chair, "Bring that chair over here and I'll show you how we're organized and brief you on our Company mission."

As Lori moved the chair next to Captain Archibald's desk, she became acutely aware of his chiseled, extremely handsome face, raven black hair and extremely well proportioned and fit body. His deep, enticing baritone voice jolted her out of her reverie as he explained, "We are the *All American Military Police Company.* All of our personnel and equipment can be airdropped and we train extensively for night operations, which is the preferred time for airborne assaults. Our basic mission is to support the 82nd Airborne Division in military police operations and are required to be capable of deploying anywhere around the world within 18 hours. The company consists of a headquarters platoon, and four MP platoons. Three of my platoons provide direct support to the Division's three infantry Brigades, and the fourth platoon provides general support to the Division rear area. The company is required to conduct law enforcement activities in the Division area and support the provost marshal's office. Familiarize yourself with our organizational chart. Any questions?" Lori shook her head no and he continued.

"Now I'll explain our company readiness requirements. Because I'm required to have all my platoons ready for quick recall and rapid deployment, we maintain this high readiness posture using three six-week rotation cycles. During the training cycle, we sustain our war-fighting skills. The platoons continue to train during mission cycle, but train in a manner that allows them to meet the two hour recall and 18 hour deployment requirements. In this cycle, we have our day to day mission to assist, protect, and defend our fellow paratroopers by conducting law enforcement operations in the Division garrison. But during deployment and engagement, we are a combat multiplier. We provide combat military police support in the form of traffic circulation control, rear area security operations, enemy prisoner of war ops, and evacuation of non-combatants. We also provide combat support and combat service support for the Division to include actions such as controlling refugee movements, and conducting law and order operations. Do you have any questions on our mission or our organization?"

"No, Sir," Lori replied crisply.

"Good. As I mentioned earlier, you will be my Charlie platoon leader. I have a mandatory meeting every morning at 0830 in the company conference room for company commanders, XO's, platoon leaders, and key staff. In the event you have an excused absence such as leave or sick call, make sure your platoon sergeant fills in for you. We focus on training activities and personnel issues at our morning meeting. As a leader, I expect you to set the example in all you do. You've got a good platoon sergeant but he's overextended and is looking forward to your arrival. You ready to meet Sergeant Adams?" Archibald asked grinning.

"Airborne Sir!"

Captain Archibald stood up and escorted Lori down the hallway to the room she would share with her new platoon sergeant. As Captain Archibald entered the room, Sergeant First Class Adams stood at attention and bellowed. "Airborne Sir!"

"At ease, Sergeant Adams. Here's the new platoon leader I've been promising you."

Sergeant Adams eyes widened in surprise at seeing Lori as he shouted, "Airborne Sir!"

"Teach her everything you know," Captain Archibald commanded, before walking out the door.

Sergeant First Class Adams, a seasoned black soldier with twelve years' experience in the Army, looked directly into Lori's eyes and announced in a thick southern drawl, "Hello ma'am. I've been in the Army over a decade and never had no girl as my platoon leader. I'm not prejudiced, but make no mistake, I'm surprised and not used to having a gal be in charge."

"Thanks for your honesty Sergeant Adams. I've been a cadet at West Point for four years and have no doubt we will make a great team, but I need your help to learn as much as I can, as quickly as possible."

Adams continued, "I've had a few Pointers as leaders, some were good and some not. I try to give everyone a fair shake before I assess their worth. If you can run fast and make good decisions, you'll be alright."

"That won't be a problem, but I'll be asking you for feedback, based upon your experience on any tough decisions I may have to make."

"That sounds 'bout right ma'am, but we need to agree on who does what. I deal with all the soldier problems unless they're serious ones.

We have three good squad leaders and I let them lead their squads without getting into their business too much. I need you to go to all the company and battalion meetings, write up all the reports, and schedule all the training. I've been the acting platoon leader for three months since Lieutenant Chandler moved to the Provost Marshal's office so I know what your responsibilities are. Lieutenant Chandler was not into PT and he barely made the company runs. As a result, our platoon is weak on PT and range qualification. Our soldiers have the worst qualification scores in the company and I'd like to improve on that by scheduling more M16 rifle and .45 pistol range training and qualification times."

"I think those are good ideas Sergeant Adams. I actually like PT and am an excellent marksman. MP's should be in good physical shape and good shots. I'd like our platoon to be the best in the company and with both our efforts, have no doubt that we can accomplish that."

"You got that right ma'am. Well, here's your desk and after you finish your in-processing I'll introduce you to our squad leaders and show you the barracks."

Lori sat down at her slightly banged up, metal quartermaster desk for a few minutes. She was happy to see a large 18" by 20" calendar on top of the desk along with colored markers, two black skillcraft pens, three pencils, and a pad of paper, stapler, and paper clips on top of the desk. *So this is where I'll be spending most of my days.* She smelled cigarette smoke and grimaced as she watched her platoon sergeant smoking a Lucky Strike cigarette just six feet away.

Looking up after snuffing out his cigarette in the ashtray on his desk, Sergeant Adams said, "I'll take you to the S-1 shop ma'am." Lori stood up and followed her new sergeant down the hallway, happy to get out of the smoky room.

★ ★ ★

"HE'S DROP-DEAD GORGEOUS," Lori said into the telephone.

"Yeah, right. That'll be the day when a boss is a looker," Roni replied. "My company commander is a pock-marked pudgy captain who smokes all the time. I feel sorry for his wife. Is your commander married?"

"I don't think so. I didn't ask. Get this, I'm not only a platoon leader, I'm also the motor officer for the company."

"Sounds like extra work to me. Do you know anything about motor pools?" Roni asked.

"Nah, not yet. But I will. I'll be reading TMs, PM manuals, and all those maintenance SOPS at night and on the weekends to bone up on all the new material. I just hope the motor NCO knows his stuff and can train me," Lori replied.

"I'm glad I don't have *that* additional duty. I have physical security, mail, and NBC officer as my additional duties. As the junior lieutenant in the unit, I get stuck with all the crappy duties no one else wants."

"How was the field exercise?" Lori asked.

Roni replied dourly, "The commander didn't have a good training plan and we wasted or missed a lot of good training opportunities in the field. Our soldiers deserve better. We don't go back to the field 'til January, so hopefully by then, we can have a good and complete training plan to exercise."

"I have no idea about our training schedule. I sure hope I'll be able to take leave at Christmas," Lori said.

"I'm sure you can take some leave. I was told the Division has a block leave schedule over the holidays."

"Good. How about meeting me at the O-club tonight for dinner? I'd really like to catch up."

"Sounds good Lori. Meet you at six for drinks and dinner. I've got some real crap to share with you over beer!"

★ ★ ★

"THAT'S JUST WRONG," LORI said after Roni shared her field experiences and her company commander's actions at dinner.

"No shit! But what do I do? I know he's not happy to have a female lieutenant in his unit but he shouldn't share that with First Sergeant and key NCOs. At this point it's merely hearsay and second hand information, because my platoon sergeant told me what was said."

"Are you sure your platoon sergeant isn't making it up?" Lori asked.

"Why would he? He's very squared away, our platoon is a good one. He seems to like me and I think he's watching my back."

"Well what's your experience with your commander?" Lori asked probingly.

"Our first meeting was sorta formal and Captain Becker seemed tense. He smoked three cigarettes while he briefed me on the company mission. He cautioned me about making all the runs, but I run better than he does. Our relationship appears okay on the surface. We had no issues the two weeks we were in the field, in fact our platoon performed well. This is the first I've heard of him bad-mouthing me for no reason other than me being born female."

"What specifically did your platoon sergeant say?"

"He said, 'Ma'am, I don't want to worry you, but, the C.O. told us NCOs that he was none too happy having a girl in his unit, but we'd have to deal with it the best we could.' Captain Becker also told the NCOs I had to be closely monitored. That really pisses me off!"

"Yeah, that sucks Roni. Well, I think you have two options. You can ignore what you were told Becker said and work hard to show him you are a capable and good officer, or you can confront Captain Becker and ask him if he said that, but you risk getting yourself and your platoon sergeant in trouble."

"Not very good options if you ask me. Let me think about it a while Lori. Thanks for listening. I know this isn't as bad as what we went through at West Point, but it still is frustrating to have to prove myself all the time."

"Yep, I agree, but we're not gonna solve this anytime soon. So, how about some ice cream to make everything better?"

"Oh yeah!"

15

DULUTH, MINNESOTA, 26 DECEMBER 1980

"HEY LORI, CHECK THIS OUT!" Christa yelled whizzing by her older sister as she slalomed down one of the ski slopes at the Lutzen ski resort before racing up to a small man-made ski jump and sailing into the air. Landing gracefully, Christa stopped and turned around just in time to see Lori ski around the jump and leisurely stop alongside her sister.

"You're not turning into a chicken are you?"

"Nah, I'm out of practice and need to be smart and not break anything. I've gotta run with my platoon when I get back to the 82nd and I can't do my job if I come back in a cast." Lori looked admiringly at her little sister, "I'm impressed Chrissy. When did you become such of a great skier?"

Standing taller and grinning, Chrissy said, "Since you went to West Point, I've been skiing almost every week. I love the feeling of being outside and sailing through the air!"

"I know what ya mean. Even though my ski skills are rusty, I love being outside and physically active. One of the coolest things about being in the Army is they actually pay me to work out and be outside."

"I'm with you Lori! Let's head back to the lift and take a few more runs down the hill."

"Okay, but don't forget, I'm going over Willow's tonight to see the baby so we can only do a few more runs."

★ ★ ★

"MAN, YOU WEREN'T KIDDING, she sure is cute!" Lori said as she walked into Willow's house and saw Willow standing just inside the front door, holding the baby, who they'd named after her.

Jeff gave Lori a hug and said as he beamed with pride. "We think so. Here, let me take your coat."

Lori gave Willow a sideways hug and the three friends walked to living the living room.

Sitting down with the baby and motioning Lori to sit beside her, Willow asked excitedly, "So tell me all about your job in North Carolina."

Before Lori could respond, Jeff asked, "How about I go make all of us some hot chocolate while the two of you catch up?"

"Sure that'd be great," Lori replied and turned back to Willow. "Well, after airborne school and my basic officer training in Alabama, I'm now an MP platoon leader of 31 soldiers. We mainly support the 82nd Airborne Division in the field, but we have lots of training requirements and law enforcement missions. You wouldn't believe how much work there is to do. I have a good platoon sergeant who gave me his assessment of where we need improvement; so we're working on PT and marksmanship scores and we're making good progress." Pausing, Lori announced, "Enough about me, what's up with you and how are you and Jeff getting along with all the changes in your life?"

"As good as can be expected." Willow said contentedly. "Jeff is so helpful when he's home; but I'm the one getting up every few hours to breastfeed. We had no idea taking care of a newborn would be so all consuming. Don't get me wrong, I love being a mom, but I'm with Lori all day, every day. I feed her, bathe her, change her diapers, play with her, and get up when she cries. I barely have time to get anything done. Her nap times are the only time I have to do the laundry, clean the house, and make dinner. You have no idea how a baby changes your life."

"You're right. I don't. Maybe one day I will, but as for now, I don't even have a boyfriend."

"I wouldn't worry about that," Willow said. "You are the coolest woman I know. What guy wouldn't want to go out you?"

"There are plenty of civilian and military guys who aren't comfortable with women being in the Army. They think I'm weird or assume I'm a lesbian. Some of them resent me for taking a job away from a man and immediately dislike me. Due to circumstances beyond my control, I was born a woman, just like half the people in the world. Most men don't consider the fact that they could have been born a woman or bother to examine how they would feel, if they were in my position...." Lori stopped abruptly, as she realized the negative a picture she was painting for Willow. She reached for the cup of hot chocolate Jeff had left on the coffee table and took a sip before continuing on a more positive note. "Like you, I'm happy with my choices, but it's a lot more challenging and complicated than I'd anticipated."

Baby Lori started gurgling and Lori reached over to touch her gently as she asked Willow, "Are you going to be a full time mom or are you thinking about going to work?"

Willow sighed as she looked down at her new daughter, "I'm just enjoying the few months I have with Lori before I start a nursing job in the spring. My mom already told me she'll take care of Lori while I'm working. We're getting by on Jeff's salary but we agreed that if I work, we'll be able use that money to buy a house as soon as possible." Looking back at Lori, Willow observed, "My life here with Jeff and little Lori is so different than yours. We're lucky to have two sets of grandparents nearby, who want to see Lori all the time. It must be hard on you to not have family nearby."

Lori remarked wistfully, "Yeah, my life is totally different, but I sorta knew what I was getting into when I applied to West Point. Having said that, there have been several times when it was hard not to have family and friends nearby to help me through some rough patches like my breakup with Scott. I really thought we had a future together. I was devastated and for the first time in my life, really depressed." Seeing the look of concern and sympathy on Willows face, Lori added, "I'm fine. Now my focus is on my platoon, and my military friends have become my family in a way."

Not sure what else to say, Willow held out the baby and asked, "Would you like to hold and play with her for a while?"

"I'd love to! She's so cute and smiles all the time."

Willow laughed as she handed her namesake to Lori. "Trust me, she doesn't smile all the time. You should hear her holler when she's wet or hungry."

Jeff came back into the living room with a tray of sandwiches and sat down to join them. "Lori, we're so happy you're here. We hope you'll make time to visit us every time you come home."

"You can count on it," Lori said as she bounced the baby in her arms.

★ ★ ★

"REMEMBER TO CALL US every week. We need to know how it's going at Fort Bragg," Lori's mom said. Lori kissed her mom and dad good-bye and gave her brother Joe, who was finishing his senior year at college, and younger sister Christa a big hug before getting into her silver 1980 Honda Accord.

"I will. Thanks for everything and for letting me relax while I've been home on leave."

"Make sure you keep me informed of all the cool stuff you're doing in the Army. I still can't believe you're a police officer!" Christa said.

She's a *military* police officer Chrissy. She told you that before," Joe said shaking his head.

"Well, they're the same thing to me. I want to hear all about the bad guys," Christa replied.

"The way the Army is going, I will be spending most of *my* time on tactical field exercises, not doing law enforcement operations. Criminal Investigations Division (CID) has the Army special agents who bust the bad guys. I don't think I'll have any great stories to tell, but you never know. Well, I hate to leave, but I have a long drive back to North Carolina. Thanks for storing my boxes for me in the basement mom."

Lori's mom wistfully said, "We didn't mind storing your belongings and we hate to see you go Lori. Drive safe. We'll see you this summer won't we?"

"For sure mom. I'll be back sometime this summer. I've got to get going, but I miss you already!" Lori sadly said as she started the engine, and slowly backed out of the driveway. Waving goodbye to her family, Lori was excited about returning to Fort Bragg, but for the first time in a long time, felt sad leaving her family.

16

TANGIER ISLAND, 31 DECEMBER 1980

THE DOORBELL RINGING STARTLED Anne, as Derek yelled from the kitchen, "Can you get that?" Getting up from the chair where she'd been reading the latest Stephen King novel, *'Firestarter'* Anne laconically replied, "Got it." Then yelled. "The doors open. Just come in!"

The door opened and a rush of cold air preceded Maura and Eric, as they came into the expansive living room. Maura had a large shopping bag in her hands and Eric was carrying two suitcases. "I'll close the door," Anne announced as she walked behind Eric, before turning back to greet them. "You made great time. We weren't expecting you guys for another hour or so."

Maura put the shopping bag on the floor and laughed as she reached out to give Anne a hug. "Our flight arrived a bit early and we picked up the rental car at National. Surprisingly, we had no traffic, so speed racer here, acted like we were still on the autobahn in Germany and never let the speed dip below 80, once we got on 95 south. So we actually made the earlier ferry."

Anne looked over at Eric and smiled. "Welcome home. Hopefully you'll learn to drive 55 again, before you get too many speeding tickets."

Derek had come out of the kitchen and sardonically commented, "If you're anything like these two women, it'll take several tickets and hefty fines, before your lead foot gets retrained."

Eric walked over to greet Derek. "Yeah, that sounds about right. Nice to finally meet you."

"Likewise brother." Derek rejoined, as he slapped Eric on the shoulder and acknowledged by his greeting that while they had never met, he knew that like him, Eric was being assigned to the newly formed Joint Special Operations Command and was a fellow Green Beret. Eric's look of surprise and involuntary stiffening of his body, alerted Derek to the possibility that Eric hadn't told Maura that he was a special operator and was being assigned to the new command. Looking at Anne and Maura, who were talking and had not really paid attention to the two men greeting each other, Derek reached out to take the shopping bag from Maura and announced, "I'll put this in the kitchen, then show Eric around the house and we'll put your stuff in the bedroom. Why don't the two of you open a bottle of wine, get comfy, and we'll join you in a bit."

Without waiting for an answer, Derek motioned Eric to follow him. When they got to the guest suite on the other side of the house, Derek pointed to a fabric covered bench at the foot of the bed. "You can put the suitcase there and unpack later." As Eric nodded and put the suitcase down, Derek probed, "Sorry brother if I spoke out of turn. I thought Maura knew about your status and new assignment."

Eric waved his hand, "Not a problem brother. You just surprised me. I didn't know you were part of the community. You're assigned to the unit?"

"Yeah. I'm a team leader and we were told several weeks ago that you were inbound and would be the 3. Does Maura know?"

Eric shook his head in assent. "I told her while we were in New York at her parents."

Derek gave a large sigh of relief. "Whew, dodged a bullet there. How did she take it?"

"She told me she knew from my assignment in Berlin and the fact that I never discuss work with her, that I wasn't, to use her term, *your typical combat arms type* but she didn't care what I did, as long as I was assigned to Bragg for a few years and was happy with my assignment."

Derek laughed. "She doesn't have a clue, does she?"

Eric grinned wryly. "Nope, I'll explain what I can, when we get to Bragg. From what I know about her, she'll adjust."

"Yeah, Anne's adjusted well; but sometimes gets her nose out of joint when she doesn't hear from me for several weeks," Derek offered. "I think it's been tough on Anne not having anyone to talk to, because I told her she couldn't discuss my job or frequent absences with anyone and originally that included Maura. She accepted that, but wasn't happy, because I think those two tell each other everything…which is more than Anne tells me."

Surprised by Derek's candor, Eric responded reassuringly, "The good news is now they can talk to each other and be their own little support network." Pausing, Eric asked, "Do you know Maura and Amelia well?"

"I don't know Maura that well, but I know Anne considers her family and I don't know how well you know my Anne, but her childhood was a nightmare and she doesn't get close to, or trust people easily. I've heard about Amelia, but have never met her. I think she got out of the Army and lives somewhere in Alabama."

Eric nodded understanding. "Did Anne or Maura tell you how we met?"

"Only that you showed them around Berlin the first time they went to visit Amelia…" Derek responded thoughtfully, adding, "I seem to recall Anne saying something about you being some sort of super spook and telling me Maura went over the deep end when she met you."

Eric laughed, "That's my girl, she doesn't do anything halfheartedly. Speaking of Maura, I don't know about Anne, but if we spend much longer talking here and they come looking for us, I'm liable to get the third degree from Maura about what we're talking about, so why don't you give me the house tour you're supposed to and we can continue our discussion that way?"

"Yeah, you're right. This is the guest wing and you and Maura will have complete privacy." Walking to the other side of the bedroom, Derek slid open a small pocket door and turned on the bathroom light as Eric followed him in. "You've got all the necessities and on the other side of that door at the far end, is another bedroom. This suite has the full size beds and there's another suite like this further down the hall with two single beds in each bedroom.

Impressed with the obvious quality furnishings and size of the house, Eric remarked, "Pretty nice set up." Before he could say anything else, Anne walked in and announced, "I figured we'd join you guys on the tour."

Turning around, Eric and Derek smiled as Maura and Anne walked into the bathroom with a glass of wine in one hand and a beer in the other. Taking the beers that each woman held out for them, Derek said, "Oh yeah, I forgot, Maura's never been here either."

"This is amazing Derek! I can't wait to see it in the daylight. Anne showed me the kitchen, butler's pantry, and the living room. Being a city girl who grew up in a three bedroom co-op in Manhattan, I'm still amazed at the expansiveness of houses in the country."

"Most houses aren't like this one Maura," Eric responded. "The house I grew up in didn't have much more room than your parent's place."

Derek explained. "My mom was an only child and her parents left her lots of money. She and my dad love to sail and spend time on the beach, so she used part of that money to buy the land and build a vacation house for our family to get away and enjoy the outdoors. When my dad was assigned to the Pentagon, mom would bring us down every weekend on Friday afternoon as soon as we got out of school and dad would get here late on Friday evenings."

Anne knew that Derek often felt uncomfortable with people making a big deal about how privileged a life he'd led and interjected. "When Derek's dad was on active duty, they lived on base in military housing, so this house is the closest thing to a family home, he and his sister have ever known. This is Derek's parents' house most of the year, now that his dad is retired; but they travel a lot and leave for St. Augustine, Florida, right after Christmas and don't come back until April. His parents invited us to spend the holidays with them and Derek asked if we could stay until the third of January, if we agreed to do everything that was needed to close the house up. So we spent yesterday taking down Christmas decorations and before we head back to Bragg, we'll do the few other things that have to be done and drop off the keys with the management company that keeps an eye on the house and does what's needed for the four months the house stays empty."

"Well, thanks for inviting us here for New Year's Eve," Eric replied as he lifted his beer bottle in a toast. "Don't know about anyone else, but I'm starving and Maura mentioned something about eating dinner."

Relieved by Eric's change of topic, Derek announced cheerily, "Yeah, lets head to the kitchen. My mom taught Anne how to make her world famous crab and artichoke dip and after that, we've got a nice salad, garlic bread, baked potatoes, and porterhouse steaks for supper."

As the two couples entered the kitchen, Anne pointed to the large round glass table by the expansive bay window. "You guys sit there, I've got the dip in the warming tray and will have it over there in just a few minutes."

A few minutes later, Anne returned with the dip and crackers, followed by Derek, who'd brought a bowl of pistachios, small plates, and the open bottle of wine. Sitting down, Derek looked at Eric. "Beers are in the fridge, just help yourself when you need a refill."

Maura lifted her wine glass. "Here's to all of us getting to know each other better and having a relaxing New Year's Eve together."

"Hear, hear," everyone yelled as they lifted their glasses and took a drink. Eric was the first to dig into the dip and after the first bite exclaimed, "Oh man, that's fantastic Anne!" Grabbing the bowl of dip, he asked jokingly, "Okay, this is enough for me, what are you guys going eat?" Maura grabbed the bowl out of his hand as she put some dip on her plate and handed it to Anne. After taking a bite she exclaimed, "Wow Anne, this is great, I'm impressed. I don't ever remember you actually cooking anything and just assumed like me, you didn't know *how* to cook!"

"Thanks Maura," Anne replied dryly. My BOQ in Stuttgart wasn't exactly set up for cooking and eating out was so easy and inexpensive, that there really wasn't any reason to cook. We're so busy at work during the week at Bragg and I spend the weekends with Derek, so there really hasn't been any time or reason for me to cook at the house in Fayetteville. You forget my mom didn't die until I was 16 and I grew up in a house full of hungry men, so I started cooking with my mom, when I was around seven years old. As a matter of fact, I'm making quiche for breakfast and jambalaya for lunch tomorrow."

Holding up her hands in mock surrender, Maura conceded, "I'm appropriately chastised and looking forward to tomorrow."

In an effort to change the subject once more, Eric addressed Anne. "So Maura tells me you're assigned to *SWIK*. Rumor has it they're expanding and going through a lot of organizational change."

"Yeah, I'm the property book officer, so all I do is ensure we keep track of what we already have and assign new equipment as it comes in. It's a large operation and I spend most of the day updating the property book and conducting quarterly inventories and hand receipt updates. I think I have the highest security clearance of any property book officer in the Army, but aside from the classified briefings I had to take in order to get Indoc'ed, I don't know anything about what actually happens there."

"Yeah, but they couldn't do what they do, without you making sure they have what they need," Derek added in an encouraging tone. "So while you don't have an operational role, you're still a critical part of the team."

Anne flippantly retorted, "This coming from the guy who branch transferred from Quartermaster to Infantry, just after his basic course, so he could become a green beanie." Seeing the hurt look on Derek's face, she reached over to grab his hand. "I appreciate your support, just jerking your chain a bit, like you do to me all the time." In response to the mock scowl that Derek gave her, Anne added musingly, "What's that you tell me when the tables are reversed?" and then mockingly retorted, "Oh yeah, now I remember. It builds character and helps you keep a sense of humor about things!" Everyone burst into laughter as Derek ruefully grinned and responded, "You got me babe!"

After the laughter died down, Anne asked Eric, "Do you have your assignment yet?"

"Uhhh. Yeah..." Eric reluctantly replied, as he reached for a cracker and some dip and in an effort to not have to answer anything else, popped the food into his mouth, hoping the topic would change.

"Yeah, nice try Eric," Anne replied mockingly. "Derek does that same shit when he doesn't want to answer my question or wants the subject to change. So, is this sort of like your response to that question a few years ago in Berlin, when you told us if you told us what you did, you'd have to kill us?"

Not expecting such a flippant rejoinder, Eric inadvertently swallowed the cracker he'd just put in his mouth and started coughing, because part of it got stuck in his windpipe.

"Busted man," Derek said as he handed Eric his bottle of beer. "Just wash that down and suck it up. I deal with this all the time and you're gonna need all the practice you can, to worm out of this gracefully."

Maura looked over at Anne questioningly, while Eric drank some of his beer, to wash the cracker crumbs down his throat. Anne rolled her eyes. "Derek belongs to that new unit no one actually admits exists, disappears for days and weeks at a time, with no notice and when he finally comes back, expects me to act like nothing happened and this is just normal, everyday work stuff."

Maura looked over at Eric, "So, is that why you didn't answer my question last week about where you were being assigned? Last conversation I recall, is that you were going to find a low key, low vis job, so we could spend more time together?"

Anne reached for the wine bottle and advised Maura as she filled Maura's wine glass. "Don't fight it. It makes them happy and they love us, they just want to have their cake and eat it too. It'll take a while, but you'll get used to the sudden disappearances and reappearances, with no explanation offered and when you ask a question about work and he gives you a kiss on the cheek and asks how your day went, just let it be. You don't have a need to know and they can't answer your question."

Having swallowed the offending cracker, Eric looked at Maura and replied apologetically. "I really intended to do exactly that, but when the word went out that I wanted to come back to Bragg, an old boss called me and asked me to come to work for him and I couldn't say no."

Taking a sip of wine, Maura looked at Eric. "One question and I expect a simple, clear answer. Are you assigned to the same unit as Derek?"

Taking another sip of beer, Eric just shook his head yes. Looking at Anne, Maura apologized. "I was irritated you wouldn't answer my questions when I'd ask about Derek's whereabouts and job. Now I'm beginning to understand why you acted so weird!"

Derek answered before Anne could respond. "I told her she couldn't tell anyone when I suddenly disappeared without any notice to her, for OPSEC reasons. In fairness to Anne, she specifically asked if you could be the one exception and I told her I was sorry, but that was a no go." Derek got up and kissed Anne on the cheek. "I know that was hard for you and hate that I had you do that." He turned back to Maura. "Eric and I were going to tell both of you about this tomorrow and let you know that we're glad that at least now you can talk to each other and be a mini support group."

Looking back at Eric, Maura mused out loud, "I thought you were an Infantry officer with an intel additional specialty, but now that I think about it, you never confirmed or denied it, when I said that. You just smiled and said you were assigned to the Potsdam mission. If you're going to the same unit Derek is, that means you're a green beret." Eric started to respond, but Maura held up her hand for him to be silent. "No, I'm starting to get it." Looking over at Anne, Maura shook her head and smirked. "We sure know how to pick 'em don't we?"

Anne grinned, "We coulda done worse, I guess, but they've squirmed enough for one night and now we sorta know what they do and can at least talk to each other when we're frustrated or scared. Besides, it's New Year's Eve and we're supposed to be relaxing and having fun."

"You're right." Maura conceded. "So, how much longer before we eat? I'm starving."

★ ★ ★

"**THANKS GUYS, THAT WAS** a fantastic meal." Eric leaned back contentedly, having just finished the last piece of steak on his plate. "The steak just melted in my mouth."

Derek looked over at Maura and Anne. "You ladies finished?" Even though their meals were only half eaten, they both shook their heads yes. "Okay, why don't the two of you go into the living room and relax, while Eric helps me clean up and we'll go outside and start a fire in the pit."

Anne stood up. "C'mon Maura, they've got this and we can chat a bit." Looking over at Derek, she added, "Holler when you head out to the patio and I'll heat up the gluhwein."

★ ★ ★

DEREK AND ERIC WERE sitting around the fire pit at the edge of the patio, when Maura and Anne walked out of the kitchen, each carrying two large mugs of steaming hot gluhwein. Handing a cup to each of them, they both sat down in the wooden Adirondack chairs that Derek had covered with flannel blankets. Maura took a gulp of the gluhwein and sighed contentedly. "Wow Anne, this is fantastic; as good as the ones we drank that first Christmas in Berlin with Amelia. Where'd you find this?"

"Derek's mom made some for us on Christmas Eve and gave me the recipe. I wanted to surprise you guys."

"Mission accomplished," Maura replied contentedly as she looked over at Eric and Derek. The sight of the two men leaning toward each other, deep in conversation reminded Maura that it was Anne who suggested Maura and Eric join them for New Years, so the two guys could get to know each other in a more natural and relaxed setting. Stealing a furtive glance in Anne's direction, Maura was relieved to see that Anne's hands were cupped around her gluhwein as she sipped it mindlessly, her face totally relaxed and a slight smile on her face, as she looked out at the dark abyss that lay in front of them. It was a good sign. Anne rarely totally relaxed and this was a good sign that she trusted Derek enough to let down the guard she had built up, to keep her from being vulnerable or hurt by others.

The physical warmth of the fire along with the soothing effect of the alcohol was hypnotic. Maura peered into the dark abyss at the edge of the beach, mesmerized by the sound of the waves of the Chesapeake gently lapping the edge of the shore, when she felt the warmth of Eric's breath graze her cheek as he bent down to kiss her. "Hi there…remember me?" he whispered gently. Maura shook her head languidly up and down, as she instinctively turned her face to his and grazed his lips with hers.

"Of course," she whispered as she wrapped her arms around him and buried her face in his shoulder. Hearing the sound of Anne laughing gently nearby, Maura pushed herself away from Eric slowly and stood up. Taking Eric's hand, she turned to see Derek standing behind Anne, with his arms around her waist.

Sensing movement, Anne looked over at Maura and Eric remarking quietly, "If there's a heaven, surely it must be something like this." No one said anything as the two couples stood together on the beach in front of the still warm, but dying embers of the fire pit.

Derek broke the silence. "The local B&B does fireworks at midnight. We can go inside and wait to watch them, or just call it a night."

Anne turned toward Maura and Eric. "You're our guests. We'll do whatever you guys want."

Maura looked at Eric expectantly and in response to the smile he'd given her, said, "We can't thank you guys enough for inviting us here and for the wonderful evening; but if it's all the same to you, I think we're in favor of skipping the fireworks."

"That decides it." Derek took Anne by the hand and started walking toward the house. Once inside the kitchen, Derek locked the door and wished Maura and Eric a Happy New Year. Maura and Eric returned the greeting and the two couples headed to their respective bedrooms.

Once inside their bedroom, Derek took Anne into his arms and quietly asked, "Are you happy?" Anne nodded yes and folded herself into him. Her sweet smell was almost more than he could bear, as he buried his nose in her hair. After a few seconds he gently pushed her away, cupping her chin in his hand and lifting her face up to his. "Enough to spend the rest of your life with me?" he asked tentatively. He hadn't intended to bring the subject up tonight, but the emotion that had suddenly welled up inside him, seemed to have a mind of its own and the words came out of his mouth unbidden. He felt his pulse increase as Anne shook her head up and down without a second's hesitation and put her hands under his shirt and started lifting it over his head, while she hungrily sucked on his left nipple.

The two previous conversations they'd had on this subject, Anne had physically stiffened and pulled away. She'd told him she loved him, but wasn't ready to talk about marriage. When he'd pressed her for a decision the last time, she withdrew both physically and emotionally from him for several weeks. After much cajoling she agreed to move on, but asked him to give her some space and she would let him know when she was ready to talk about marriage.

By now she'd unbuckled his pants and was running her tongue down his torso. He could feel the heat rising inside his body. He reached down and lifted her off the floor and carried her over to the bed. Her breathing was shallow and raspy, as he took her clothing off. Their eyes were locked and never wavered, their hands and bodies knowing instinctively what to do.

Anne's mind wasn't able to keep up with her body. All she knew was that she loved and trusted Derek more than any human being she'd ever known except her dad. When he'd died, she bottled up all her emotions and pain. She wasn't sure what had opened up the flood of emotion that filled her heart and took her breath away, when he timidly asked her to spend the rest of her life with him. All of a sudden, all the fear she had of opening herself up to be hurt by loving someone again was destroyed by an overwhelming desire to be a part of him in every way and the fear that if she kept him at arm's length too long, she would lose him. She felt him enter her and her entire body shuddered. They had made love before, but it hadn't ever felt like this! She heard herself yell, *yes!* but it was like she was in someone else's body. She pulled Derek hard to her, urging him on. He grabbed her so tightly, she almost felt like she was going pass out, when this huge rush hit her and shortly after that, he relaxed and lay down on top of her, spent. He gently kissed her neck as he said breathlessly, "Damn, I don't know what happened tonight, but I definitely want more of this, so from now on, you can drink all the damn gluhwein you want!"

She couldn't help it and started giggling. Propping himself up, he inquired, "What's so funny?"

"You."

"I'm serious!" He said teasingly. "That was some seriously good shit and I want as much of it as I can get!" Then turning serious, he asked, "Did you mean it when you said you'd marry me?"

Anne lifted her head up off the pillow and kissed his lips. "Yup, you're stuck now." Her brow furrowed a bit and she tremulously whispered, "Do you promise never to not love me?"

Overwhelmed with emotion, Derek hugged her tightly in response, whispering, "I do."

★ ★ ★

MAURA AND ERIC WALKED into the kitchen to the sight of Derek and Anne laughing as Derek took a casserole out of the oven and Anne was cutting up fresh fruit. "Happy New Year!" Maura greeted them gaily.

Putting the casserole on a trivet on the kitchen table, Derek responded cheerfully. "Happy New Years to both of you. Pointing to the percolator behind him he noted, "Coffee cups are in the cupboard above the coffee pot. Sugar and cream are on the table. Breakfast will be ready as soon as Anne finishes cutting the fruit."

Maura walked over to Anne. "Can I help?"

Anne pointed to the cupboard behind her. "Thanks, no. Just help yourself to some coffee, sit down, and relax."

That's when Maura noticed the ring. Taking Anne's left hand, she asked, "What's this? I don't remember you having a diamond ring."

Anne smiled and nonchalantly replied, "Derek proposed last night and I accepted." Maura and Anne looked at each other and then simultaneously screamed and hugged each other.

Derek and Eric turned at the sound and looked at the two women hugging and jumping. Derek grinned. "I guess Anne just told Maura we're engaged."

"Congrats man."

"Thanks," Derek replied.

Anne and Maura calmed down and when they sat down at the table. Maura took Anne's hand and commented, "That looks like a very old ring." Looking at Derek, she asked, "Is that a family heirloom?"

Anne answered, "Yes, it was his grandma's engagement ring. When Derek told his mom he found the love of his life, she gave it to him. When he gave it to me and told me the story, I asked him how long he'd had it and he told me, he's had it for several years." Looking back at Derek, she reached over and gave him a kiss."

Eric raised his coffee cup. "To a long and happy life together." The four friends spent the next hour talking and eating breakfast. After they'd cleaned up the kitchen, Maura asked what the plan for the day was.

"Well, I thought you ladies could make something for lunch and we'll watch the game, while the two of you work on wedding plans."

"Can you believe these two?" Maura asked derisively. Anne laughed. "Its New Years and they are both pretty amazing…." Maura hesitated before breaking out in laughter. "Okay, go ahead you two, we'll entertain ourselves today, but you'll owe us big time."

Derek started walking toward the living room, motioning Eric to come with him. "C'mon brother, before they change their minds!"

17

FORT BRAGG, NC, FRIDAY, 4 JANUARY 1981

"IT WAS LOVE AT first sight," Roni matter-of-factly said while sitting in a booth at a mom and pop restaurant at Fort Bragg.

"Get outta here," Lori replied while they waited for their hamburgers to arrive.

"I'm not kidding. When I saw George walk into the room, I gasped, and my mouth dropped open. He had the most beautiful smile and warm brown eyes. I was apprehensive at going on a blind date but when I saw him, I knew it might be real."

"Nice. Who set up the date and where'd you go?" Lori asked.

"I was pissed I had to miss Christmas at home because my unit was on alert, but my sponsor suggested I go out with his wife and this 'nice captain from New York.' I don't remember the name of the restaurant, but we got there first and George got there around five minutes later. He was wearing this light blue sweater and brown leather jacket that showed off his broad shoulders. I was hooked at 'Hello.' "

"Okay, so he's a looker and from New York. What else made him so great?"

"He focused right in on me, gave me a huge warm smile, told me I looked wonderful, and he hung on my every word. He was amazed I was an engineer lieutenant. Told me he really liked strong women."

Happy for Roni, Lori asked a few more questions, "So what does George do? Will he be here a while?"

Roni replied, "George is an infantry captain who just arrived last month from his advanced course at Benning. He thinks he'll be here at least three years, possibly more. He's in the Division G-3, future operations cell, and he's excited to be in this airborne Division."

"I'm really happy for you Roni. You deserve a nice guy, especially with Captain Becker on your case."

Ignoring the Captain Becker comment, Roni replied, "Yeah, I'm looking forward to our next date, we've already had three in the last week, and each one was better than the last. Did I mention he's the best kisser?"

"No, but I'll take your word on that one. Sounds like you found a keeper."

"Oh, Yes I did! Here comes our meal," Roni said as the waitress brought their food. "So have you heard from Cate or Trish? Are they at their new assignments?"

"I hear from Cate every week, and Trish actually sent me a Christmas card with a long letter in it from Korea. Trish said the phone calls are so expensive she might have to start writing letters!"

"I don't know Trish, but Cate's the best. She tried so hard to help me my yearling year, but I still bombed my English class. So what's the latest with Cate?" Roni asked.

"She's madly in love with Captain Jim her teacher from West Point."

"Whatda ya mean? How'd she meet Captain Jim?"

"She had him for math class and they were dating while she was a cadet," Lori replied.

"Wait a minute… Cate, our star-woman, rule follower, was breaking the rules? I find that very hard to believe."

"Well believe it. Scott and I went on a weekend trip with them last year in the Poconos. They're crazy about each other and they both were willing to give up their careers to continue the relationship. Now they're both stationed in Hawaii and living off post in a place called Mililani. In our last phone call, right after Christmas, Cate told me they got engaged and they're getting married this July on the North Shore."

"How romantic! An illicit love affair, and now they're living together in paradise. Sounds dreamy."

"It was nerve-wracking living with Cate, hoping she wouldn't get caught with Captain Jim since he was faculty and they could have gotten caught fraternizing. I'm glad they're engaged and I'm thrilled she asked me to be her maid of honor. I told her I'd look at the training calendar and try my best to be there."

"That's so cool Lori!"

"Yeah, I just hope I can take leave and go this summer. I'd love to see Hawaii. It's a dream location."

"Shouldn't be a problem. The division has no field exercises in the summer because of all the moves and new soldiers coming in. Do you think Cate might invite me to the wedding?" Roni asked.

"I think she might. We have lots of history together from USMA, plus, I don't think too many people will attend the wedding due to the high cost of flying and staying on the island."

"Well, if she invites me, I'm going. I've never been to Hawaii and I wanna go! If we both go, we can share a hotel and maybe spend a few extra days there sightseeing and hanging out on the beach? I heard the beaches there are the best!"

"Sounds like a plan," Lori said. "I should have some leave accrued by then and I can't wait to see Cate again…it'll have been over a year since I last saw her."

"Do you think I can take a date?" Roni asked in earnest.

"You that serious about George already?"

"Yep. He's a definite and he makes me laugh. Guys are usually a pain, but when they have a sense of humor….that's what I need."

At that moment, the hamburgers arrived and Lori and Roni happily feasted on the juicy, scrumptious burgers and fries. While digging into their meals, Roni asked, "So what's Trish been up to in Korea?"

"Same ol' crap. Living on pins and needles with North Korea so close. I was surprised she wrote me such a long letter. She mentioned the mission, the company she is in, and her feelings. That's so unlike Trish. Normally I have to pry any emotions out of her. I think the stress and distance from America is making her homesick. She likes most of the guys in her unit but a few have made her a target because she's a female."

"So what's her job and how long's her tour?"

"She a quartermaster platoon leader at Camp Casey in a support battalion. She's in charge of Class VII materials. She's there on a one year unaccompanied tour and she'll be coming back here to Ft. Bragg in October. How cool is that!"

"That'll be nice. I really liked Trish the few times I met her at West Point," Roni said.

"I'm stoked. She and I had the best times on the basketball team and on CTLT. Maura and Anne were our sponsors and they were great. For fun we saw Berlin, Heidelberg, and Munich with them. After CTLT, Trish and I took the train and spent 10 days in Paris together on leave. We got to party hardy."

"That sounds too good to be true."

"It was. It's just another reminder of how different the Army is from West Point."

"How 'bout Trish? You think she likes the Army too?"

"Yeah, but she's in a tough situation. You know she's a lesbian don't you?"

"I didn't know for sure, but I suspected. She never had a boyfriend and she was very close to Julie at school," Roni replied.

"Yeah, she has to hide her sexuality or she'll lose her job. I'm still not sure about my feelings about homosexuality due to my strong Catholic upbringing, but I sure like Trish. I can't wait until she gets here!"

18

FORT BRAGG, NC, MONDAY, 7 JANUARY, 1981

MAURA WALKED INTO THE DISCOM ops shop and immediately heard the XO bellow, "Captain Collins!" It had been a long, tiring drive back to Bragg from Tangier Island last Thursday. Maura pasted a smile on her face as she groaned inwardly and couldn't help thinking, *You've been gone for two weeks and he's hyper, because the quarterly training brief and USR are being briefed on Friday morning.* Maura greeted the XO cheerfully in an attempt to calm him down. "Happy New Year sir!"

Maura relaxed a bit as she watched the tension go out of his voice and a grin appear on his face, but was taken aback when he tersely ordered, "Old Man said to report to him *AS SOON* as you get in this morning."

"WILCO sir. Let me drop my stuff on my desk, get my notebook and a cup of coffee." The XO just waved his hand at her as he turned his back to her and resumed his discussion with the S-3.

Maura grabbed her stuff and walked down the hall to the commander's office. It was too early for his secretary to be in, so Maura stuck her head inside his open door and knocked on the doorframe to let him know she was there. Looking up, he motioned for her to come in and take a seat. While she waited for him to finish his phone conversation, Maura took a sip of her coffee and tried to calm down. Luckily he was not on the phone long enough for Maura to get any more nervous about being summoned by the commander the second she had returned from several weeks of leave.

Hanging up the phone, the DISCOM commander immediately told Maura, "While you were on leave, I got a call from the ADCS (Assistant Division Commander for Support) telling me to get you to the commander's office. I explained you were on leave until the 3rd. You have an office call with ADCS and CG at 0900 today, so finish your coffee and get up there." Then as an afterthought added, "And report back to me when you return."

Maura stood at attention. "WILCO sir; but could I ask why he wants to see me?"

"I would have told you, if I could." He replied gruffly, "Now get your ass in gear. I'll let Mary know to fit you into my schedule today."

Maura left without another word. By the time she got back to her desk, she had finished the cup of coffee. Grabbing the camouflage map case she used as a purse, she immediately walked over to the sign out board. Driving to division headquarters at this time of the morning took twice as long as normal, because traffic was really bad until around 0900. Pulling into the parking lot, she swore under her breath, because the parking lot was almost full and finding a parking space would take time she did not have. By the time she parked her car, she half jogged to the entrance of the division headquarters, because it was already 0845. As she entered the building, it dawned on her that she didn't have a clue where the division commander's office was. Looking around, she saw the building directory on the wall to her right. Not knowing exactly how all the offices were numbered, she stopped a master sergeant who had just come into the building to get directions to the division commander's office. As she entered the command suite, she hesitated for a moment because there were several offices with secretaries and executive officers. Luckily the ADCS walked out of his office and seeing her, smiled and motioned for her to follow him. "Perfect timing Captain Collins. I'm headed to the CG's office now."

Maura had met the ADCS the first time she had briefed the USR, so they knew each other by sight, but that was it. Maura fell in behind him and stopped as he greeted a captain seated outside the CG's office. The captain stood up and smiled. "Go in Sir. CG is waiting for both of you."

Maura's mouth was dry as she followed the ADCS into the division commander's office. Looking up from the paperwork on his desk, he pointed to the long table by the window. "Sit down, I'll be right with you."

The ADCS sat to the left of the chair at the end of the table and indicated Maura should sit across from him. A few minutes later, the CG came over with a folder and sat down. "How are you doing Captain Collins?"

Maura had had long enough to get really nervous about this encounter and she hesitantly replied, "Uh, fine sir, I think…"

That response elicited laughter from the division commander. "Relax Captain Collins, if you were in trouble, you'd know it." Maura nodded her head up and down and tried to relax, but failed. Opening the binder, the division commander noted, "I see you spent several years in Germany, went to airborne school, the advanced course, and you've been assigned to the division since June. Correct?"

"That's pretty much it sir."

"The DISCOM commander and the ADCS tell me you're pretty good at what you do, in good shape, and seem to have your act together. What made you pick the 82nd as your assignment after the advanced course?"

Not sure how to answer that, Maura stammered, "Because branch told me I should sir?"

The division commander scratched his head and grinned. "Fair enough….I assume you realize your assignment here validates that you are on a fast track; so I'm curious as to why you don't have platoon leader time. Are you not interested in leading troops?"

By now, Maura felt like her head was going to explode. She still did not have a clue as to why she'd been summoned to the division commander's office and now he was asking why she had not had a platoon leader position. Her nervousness and irritation at still being in the dark about why she was here and what she perceived to be a stupid question, came through as she tersely replied, "Sir, I'm not sure how much you know about the Chemical Corps and leadership position availability, but as an example, the

82nd Airborne doesn't even have a chemical company that would allow me the *opportunity* to be a platoon leader. So, it's not that I'm not interested in a leadership position, but unless you know of an opportunity that I've missed, the answer is of course I'd love the chance to lead troops, but with the current Chemical Corps force structure and the combat exclusion policy regarding women; my opportunity to be a platoon leader is *zero*."

The CG looked over at the ADCS, who just smirked and said. "I told you she's direct and the most candid officer I've ever encountered." Turning to Maura the ADCS advised, "I'm not sure that's such a great thing for your career potential, but it certainly livens things up."

Before Maura could respond, the commanding general looked her directly in the eyes and asked, "*If* you had the opportunity to command, what would you say is the reason you should be chosen over any other chemical officer in this division?"

Caught totally off guard, Maura cautiously responded, "Well sir, quite frankly, I need a minute to frame my thoughts."

The division commander nodded yes and after a brief pause Maura continued, "Sir, I've only been here a bit over six months and I've been so busy doing my job in the DISCOM, that I really haven't had the time to interact with many of my fellow brigade ChemO's or the Division Chem staff officers. I only see them once a month for our update to the Division ChemO. I really can't say I'm more competent or deserving than any of them; but what I can tell you is that I've proven I have the mental and physical stamina to go toe to toe with *ANY* other company grade officer in this, or any other division you might choose to compare me to. Perhaps it would be better to ask the DISCOM commander, XO, 3, and perhaps the ADCS, to provide their assessment of my leadership potential."

"I've already done that Captain Collins; but I wanted to ask *YOU* that question, because as it happens, the 82nd recently received the force structure to stand up a chemical company. Unfortunately, it will take a while to get both the personnel and equipment authorizations in place; but I've been directed to stand up the company and get it operational immediately. My challenge is to find the right officer for a very difficult job. The qualities this new commander will need to be successful include not only physical and mental stamina, but a willingness and ability to be innovative in solving myriad equipment, facilities, and personnel shortfalls and get this company stood up, operational, and deployable, as quickly as possible. "How would you propose to do that?"

Maura didn't hesitate, "Would I have M12's with bladders, and vehicles to transport them sir?"

The ADCS interjected, "The Chemical school is sending us the M12's and bladders, but we'll have to take the vehicles out of hide."

"Thanks sir, then what I'd do first is get with you, the division G-4, and the G-1 to help me find resources to man, house, and train the company. Then I'd beg, scrounge, and borrow anything that will get us an initial operating capability. Given the constraints the CG mentioned, this won't be a textbook capability, but with the right people and a lot of hard work, we can get the job done."

"Well said Captain Collins. The only other question you need to answer is do you have the ability to get this unit operational in the next six months and do you want the job?"

Maura didn't hesitate. "Yes Sir!"

The CG stood up and said to the ADCS, "She's yours, set her loose on the staff and make it clear to them that she has our backing." Turning to Maura, the division commander held out his hand and as Maura reached out to shake it, he told her, "Congratulations Captain Collins. You are the first chemical company commander in the 82nd Airborne Division. Don't disappoint me," and walked back behind his desk.

The ADCS silently motioned Maura to follow him. When they got to his office, he had her sit down. "Okay Captain Collins, I'll need the rest of today to let the staff principals and the Division ChemO know that you are the CG's choice. Go back to the DISCOM and start working on your transition, I've already told the commander that if we select you, you'll be assigned to the division early next week. You'll sit in the Division Chem office until you figure out how to get a company headquarters, a first sergeant and XO, motor pool, billets, and soldiers. This is a fast moving train and failure is not an option. What are your questions?"

"Sir, I'm certain I'll have lots of questions along the way, but quite frankly, right now, I need to figure out what they are."

"Got it." He replied brusquely. "I have mixed feelings sharing this with you, but think you need to know that the CG asked the Division Chemical officer to provide him with ORB's of Chemical officers currently assigned to the division that have company command experience. When the division ChemO said none of the chemical officers assigned to the division had company command, the CG proposed having an Infantry officer as the commander. The Division ChemO told the CG that was not a good idea and proposed two officers, one on his staff and one of your fellow brigade ChemO's as potential candidates. The CG reluctantly agreed to this, but after interviewing the two officers, we agreed they didn't have what we were looking for. When the CG canvassed the brigade commanders for possible candidates, the DISCOM commander was adamant that we give you the chance to interview, before choosing an infantry officer. The reason I'm telling you this, is because when I told the Division Chemical officer you would be interviewing for the job…." the ADCS paused. "Let me just put it this way, the division chemical officer did not support your being interviewed, let alone being selected. This is going to make a tough job even harder; because you'll be working in his AO for a while; but you don't need to worry about his support." He said decisively. "I'll make sure you get full support from him *and* his staff. If you feel that is not the case, come directly to me. That's a problem you can't solve, but I can."

Maura pursed her lips. "I'm sorry to hear that sir, but not surprised. Won't bore you with the details, but much to my surprise, when I had my initial office call with the division ChemO, he made it abundantly clear to me, that he told branch the 82nd was not the place for a female chemical officer and I was on my own."

The ADCS frowned, "You do realize you could have reported this and if your allegations were proven true, he wouldn't be in the division now."

"Yes Sir, but that isn't the way I wanted to start off in the division and given that he's not in my rating chain, I just decided it was best to move on and prove him wrong."

"You realize, that now that I'm aware of this, I have a responsibility to report this?"

"Well actually sir, now that you mention it, I know that conceptually, but wasn't considering that reality, when I answered your question." Hesitating momentarily, Maura continued. "I know it's a bit irregular sir, but no one but you and I will ever know this conversation ever took place and I certainly won't mention it. Is there any way I can convince you to just let this stay between us? His disapproval of me won't affect my ability to do what needs to be done and bringing this up now, will just make my job harder."

"How so?" the ADCS asked.

"Sir, how comfortable do you think the rest of the division staff, not to mention the brigade, battalion, and perhaps fellow company commanders I'm going to have to ask to help me will be, once the word gets out that the Division ChemO is being investigated because of my allegations?"

"Quite frankly, I hadn't considered that aspect" he replied. Maura struggled to remain silent as the general thought out loud. "I'm really not comfortable with this, but given the circumstances, I'll grant your request."

"Not a problem sir. If I thought reporting this would make a positive difference, I would have done it, but it won't. Thank you."

Making it clear the conversation was over, the ADCS reached for the phone. "Okay Captain Collins, move out and draw fire! There's a helluva lot to get done."

Maura walked to the parking lot in a daze, struggling to wrap her head around what had just happened. As she drove out of the parking lot, she imagined the S-3's face when he found out that he'd have to start doing the USR immediately. Banishing that image, she silently admonished, *Take it one step at a time, one challenge at a time....*

19

FORT BRAGG, NC, THURSDAY, 5 FEBRUARY 1981

"SHIT!" MAURA YELLED, SLAMMING the phone down. The call she'd just received had informed her that the courts martial would start the following week. During last weeks' status brief she'd expressed concern about being able to stay on track with standing up the NBC company, if she were selected to serve on a courts martial jury. The CG had advised her to do her best to get struck off the panel by either the defense or prosecutor; but made it clear that removing her name from the courts martial duty order was not an option.

She'd reported to the court and went through the required *Voir Dire* and the usual *swearing to tell the truth, etc.* administered by the military judge; but despite her best effort, Maura was selected as a panel member. She figured she'd been kept on the panel, because she was the only woman in the group of enlisted soldiers and officers whose names had been selected from the current six month courts martial duty orders signed by the CG in October.

First Sergeant appeared in her doorway, "Problem ma'am?"

Maura tersely replied, "I'm on the panel for the rape case I told you about and it starts Tuesday." Seeing the look of concern on first sergeant's face, she added, "Yeah, I know. That's the day we set up the interviews to select platoon sergeants. You and the XO will have to conduct interviews and tell me who you recommend." Maura motioned first sergeant to sit in one of the two chairs in front of her desk as she dialed her XO's number on her phone. "Joe, need you to come in my office now." She had just pulled several files from her file drawer when the company XO walked in. Motioning him to sit next to first sergeant, she pointed to the stack of folders on her desk. "I have to report for duty on a general courts martial panel starting Tuesday. Here are the files of the candidates for our platoon sergeant positions. I'll look at the files later today and give each of you my preference in priority based upon my assessment of each candidate's qualifications. Make a copy for each of you, review them today and be prepared to give me your recommendations tomorrow morning after PT. We'll see how close we come to selecting the same top candidates and take it from there."

"So we're not going to conduct interviews?" The XO asked in a surprised tone of voice.

"I'm not, but the two of you will." Seeing the look of surprise on both of their faces, Maura validated her decision. "When I offered each of you your current positions, I told you we are a team and need complete trust in each other's capabilities and judgment. If I'm not around and decisions need to be made, I need to know you're prepared to make decisions, even under difficult circumstances."

First sergeant spoke up first. "We are ma'am, it's just that we didn't expect it to happen so soon and picking the platoon sergeants is one of the most important decisions we'll make."

"I agree, which is why we'll discuss our top five picks, based upon our ranking of all the files. I'll leave you with a scoring matrix and a few questions I'd like you to ask, in addition to any you want to ask. Tuesday evening, we'll get together to go over your score sheets, notes and recommendations, based upon the interviews you conducted. Any questions?" Both men confirmed they had no questions, took the pile of personnel records and left. Maura spent the rest of the morning devising a scoring matrix that had the leadership imperatives, values, and professional competency skills she deemed essential for the platoon sergeant positions along with weighting values and a scoring formula. Maura was signing out on the sign out board, when the XO returned from lunch. "Good timing Joe, I'm meeting with the MP company commander to work out the details of using their motor pool and mechanics for our vehicles. After that, I'm meeting with the HHC commander to look at the billets he's going to let us use until we get our own. I finished the scoring sheet and put it on first sergeants desk to make copies for each of us. Please make sure the master and copies of the scoring matrix, along with the personnel files are back on my desk before you guys leave tonight. I'll fill out as much of the scoring matrix as possible, based upon the information in each file. If the two of you will do the same this afternoon, we'll go over our preliminary results tomorrow morning, agree on who the top five candidates are and the rest is up to you two. Any questions before I head out to DISCOM?"

"No ma'am, see you in the morning."

Maura returned to her office after five that evening and had barely sat down to look at the files when her phone rang. "Captain Collins, 21st Chemical Company, Airborne!"

"You're the hottest Airborne commander I've ever met." Recognizing Eric's voice on the other end, Maura replied in a mock, stern tone, "You know, the spooks in the MI brigade monitor these phones colonel."

Eric ignored Maura's admonition and asked, "How was your day and am I coming your way or are you coming to my place tonight?"

"Well, remember that courts martial jury I was being considered for? I got a call from G-1 today and I'm on the jury. Trial starts Tuesday and could last the entire week. So, not a great day, especially given that I'd set up interviews that day with fifteen NBC NCO's to fill the six decon and three Recon platoon sergeants slots I have open."

"Can't you just reschedule them for the following week? Eric asked.

"No, some of them are coming on permissive TDY to interview and first sergeant and I need to go over the enlisted personnel files PERSCOM sent to make sure most, if not all of them are already airborne qualified, otherwise, we have to see if we can get priority placement for them to go to airborne school. Besides, I need to get everyone assigned to us, before our equipment arrives from the Chem School."

"Why wouldn't they automatically only send you soldiers who are already airborne qualified?"

"Because, unlike the combat arms, the chemical corps doesn't have a lot of airborne slots. Remember this is the only the second division level NBC company to be stood up."

Eric responded thoughtfully. "If you don't have enough chemical soldiers that are airborne qualified to fill your slots, have you considered having the G-1 send you files of airborne troopers here? You could do an OJT sort of thing to train them."

Frustrated by Eric's suggestion, Maura sarcastically asked, "Well Eric, let me ask you this, if you were standing up a new A team, and didn't have enough applicants that were trained in that MOS and had been to the "Q" course, would you consider assigning them as OJT, just because their airborne qualified?"

Eric replied testily, "C'mon Maura, I was just trying to help. Of course I wouldn't. Our mission requires unique capabilities, not normally found in the general enlisted ranks."

"My point exactly Eric. Your guys are good at what they do and unique, but so are our guys. Conducting a radiological survey, recon mission, or decon operation is not the same as learning to fire a weapon or drive a tank."

"Got it Maura," Eric replied resignedly. "I was just trying to help and don't want to argue with you. I haven't seen you all week and just want to spend some time with you and relax this weekend."

"Eric, I want to spend time with you as well, but this is a unique opportunity and if I screw this up, my career is over and just as importantly, I will hurt the chances other women will have to command. Please understand that you are important to me and I know I keep saying let's see how tomorrow night works, and it never does, but I can't control that." After a brief pause and no response from Eric, she continued. "Eric, cut it with the silent treatment. You're the one that decided to come to Bragg and I'm thrilled about that; but I NEVER in a million years expected to be asked, let alone chosen to command the first NBC company in the 82nd Airborne Division.

I figured I'd be the DISCOM chemical officer for two years and maybe get a position at Division Chem, which meant, no pressure and pretty normal duty requirements. Command at any level is demanding, but this situation is unique. You know better than I do, that the people and equipment pipeline does not respond well to unplanned additions, so I'm forced to beg, borrow, and steal anything I can until the system catches up with the requirements. Please be patient."

Eric conceded. "You're right Maura. This is an incredible opportunity and you're the most amazing woman I've ever met. I want you to know that I'll always support you professionally and personally."

Relieved at Eric's vow to support her, Maura felt the tension she had been feeling leave her body and said quietly, "You know we'd be together tonight and every night if that were possible, don't you?"

"I do. Look, I've got a meeting at SWIK in an hour, so how 'bout you call me when you get home tonight and we'll just catch up then?"

"Perfect. I'm going to try to get out of here by seven, but promise to call you no later than eight. Bye." Maura hung up the receiver and opened the first personnel file.

★ ★ ★

MAURA GOT HOME AND gave a half-hearted wave to Anne and Natalie who were in the kitchen. "Oh my gosh, is that Maura?" Anne asked in mock astonishment as she pulled the cork from a bottle of wine and looked at her watch. "It's only eight fifteen, does this mean you might start eating dinner with us again someday soon?" Adding as she started pouring wine into one of the two glasses sitting on the countertop, "Wanna join us?"

"Yeah, may as well..." Maura answered morosely, but stopped at the look of concern on both Anne and Natalie's faces. "Sorry, frustrating day. Thanks and yes, please pour me a large glass. I need to get out of this uniform and clean up. I'll join you in the den in a few."

The previous November, Natalie had used the rent money Maura and Anne provided to close in the large patio area, so they now had a den to relax and eat in year round. Maura returned, picked up the unclaimed glass of wine on the coffee table and sat down in the rocking chair. Natalie and Anne had been discussing the stress Maura had been experiencing since being selected for command and immediately stopped talking when she returned. Taking a sip of wine, she ruefully smiled at her friends. "I'm fine, just a lot going on. No need to worry about me."

Anne remarked facetiously, "Well we're actually making progress, you're actually home before we've gone to bed. That's a good sign."

Ignoring Anne's sarcasm, Maura looked over at Natalie. ""Did you guys save me any dinner?"

Relieved at the subject change, Natalie got up. "Yeah, I made some chili. I'll get it out of the fridge and heat it up. D'ya want some cornbread and cheese with it?"

"Thanks Natalie, no cornbread, but cheese would be great!" As Natalie walked out to the kitchen, Maura turned back to Anne. "Okay, out with it. Let's get the third degree over with and relax."

Anne shook her head. "I just keep waiting for you to realize you can't keep up this pace and start acting like a normal person again."

"I don't like it either, but I can survive on five hours of good sleep a night indefinitely." Maura took a sip of wine and continued. "It's totally insane, they want this unit stood up yesterday, but I'm having to beg other units for billet and motor pool space, fight with PERSCOM for personnel..." Maura stopped midsentence. "Enough, I know you're concerned and I get it, but I only get an hour or so every night to not think about all this and just want to relax. Can we do that?"

Anne shook her head and grimaced. "You got it. Just let me know when and if it gets to be too much, okay?"

Maura lifted her wine glass in acknowledgement. "You and Eric will be the first to know. I promise."

"Speaking of Adonis, have you heard from or seen him lately?"

Maura relaxed and laughed. "I talked to him earlier and called him before I left the office. We had a nice long conversation and he'll be over Friday evening for the weekend. Are Derek and Bill spending the weekend here?"

Anne nodded yes and Maura heard Natalie say, "It'll be a full house." Natalie walked over to Maura with a steaming hot bowl of chili and set it on the end table near the rocker, as she asked, "Wanna see if the guys want to go dancing Saturday night?"

"You know I don't like to dance..." Anne replied petulantly.

"Yeah, but everyone else, including Derek does!" Maura rejoined and Natalie added, "C'mon Anne, be a good sport."

Anne scowled at Maura and Natalie. "This isn't fair, but if everyone wants to do it, I guess I'll suffer through it."

Picking up the bowl of chili, Maura laughed and said to Natalie, "We need to ply her with some gin and tonics before we go out and she'll be much better company."

Anne walked over to the TV, turned it on, and grumpily barked as she returned to couch, "Eat your chili and let me watch MASH in peace." Ignoring Anne's tantrum, Natalie sat down in the love seat and Maura dug into the hot bowl of chili, realizing for the first time that day that she was starving.

20

FORT BRAGG, NC, MONDAY, 9 FEBRUARY 1981

MAURA WALKED INTO THE courtroom with a sense of dread. This case was in the local news and had recently gained national exposure. There had been several other female officers in the pool for selection to this panel; but she felt she had been singled out because she was the only one in command.

The bailiff directed her to the panel sitting area, which was on a raised platform to the left of the military judge. Two of the seven members of the panel were already seated. Maura moved to the open seat in the front row and sat down. Looking around, she saw the area where the military judge who had conducted the initial sessions would sit and then looked to her left at the accused, a staff sergeant, who was the NCOIC of the X-ray department at the hospital. Maura smiled briefly as several other panel members arrived and took their seats. Never having sat on a military jury or even seen a military trial, Maura wasn't sure if they were even allowed to talk to each other and gave a furtive glance sideways to determine if her fellow panel members seemed as nervous as she was.

The past weekend, she and Eric had talked about what would be expected of her and the strict rules about not discussing the case with anyone, either during or after the proceedings, or as civilians called it, *trial.* She'd also admitted to Eric that she wasn't comfortable passing sentence on someone. Maura unconsciously bit her lower lip as she recalled Eric giving her a stern lecture about her responsibilities as a commissioned officer. Reaching for the black Army issue leather purse, that she had stuffed under the wooden chair she was sitting on, Maura opened it and took out a piece of gum. Her mouth was dry and she hoped the rhythmic motion of chewing the gum would help calm her nerves. She was jolted out of her reverie as she heard, "All rise." She stood at attention, as the colonel who was the military judge sat down and motioned everyone else to sit. After lengthy instructions and swearing in of the panel, the judge turned his attention to the trial counsel and announced, "The accused will now be arraigned." The prosecutor commenced, "All parties to the trial have been furnished with a copy of the charges and the defense waived reading of the charges." The prosecutor continued with administering of oaths and referring to the court. The military judge motioned to both the accused and defense Counsel. "Staff Sergeant Murphy, please rise. How do you plead?"

"Not Guilty Sir."

"Based upon a pretrial agreement, should you be found guilty, the maximum punishment authorized in this case is six years confinement and a bad conduct discharge. Additionally a stipulation by the prosecution, and agreed to by the defense with your consent, is that there will not be a hung jury and the member panel is required to deliver a verdict with a unanimous decision. Do you understand the full implications of this decision and were you consulted about and agreed to this stipulation?"

"Yes Sir."

The judge turned to face the panel. "Members of the Court, it is appropriate that I give you some preliminary instructions. My duty as military judge is to ensure this trial is conducted in a fair, orderly, and impartial manner in accordance with the law. I preside over all trial sessions, rule upon objections, and instruct you on the law applicable to this case. You are required to follow my instructions on the law and may not consult any other source as to the law pertaining to this case unless it is admitted into evidence. This rule applies throughout the trial, including closed sessions and periods of recess and adjournment. Any questions you have of me should be asked in open court. Until you close to deliberate, you may not discuss this court-martial with anyone, not even amongst yourselves. You must wait until you are all together in your closed session deliberations so that all panel members have the benefit of your discussion. You must also not listen to or read any accounts of the case or visit the scene of any incident alleged in the specifications or mentioned during the trial. Do not consult any source of law or information, written or otherwise, as to any matters involved in this case and do not conduct your own investigation or research. During any recess or adjournment, you must also avoid contact with witnesses or potential witnesses in this case, counsel, and the accused. If anyone attempts to discuss the case or communicate with you during any recess or adjournment, you must immediately tell them to stop and report the occurrence to me at the next session. I may not repeat these matters to you before every recess or adjournment, but keep them in mind throughout the trial. While you are in your closed session deliberations, only the members will be present. You must remain together and you may not allow any unauthorized intrusion into your deliberations. Each of you has an equal voice and vote with the other members in discussing and deciding all issues submitted to you. However, in addition to the duties of the other members, the senior member will act as your presiding officer during your closed session deliberations, and will speak for the court in announcing the results. A general order of events can be expected at this court-martial: Questioning of court members, challenges and excusals, presentation of evidence, closing argument by counsel, instructions on the law, your deliberations, and announcement of the sentence. The appearance and demeanor of all parties to the trial should reflect the seriousness with which the trial is viewed. Careful attention to all that occurs during the trial is required of all parties. If it becomes too hot or cold in the courtroom, or if you need a break because of drowsiness or for comfort reasons, please tell me so that we can attend to your needs and avoid potential problems that might otherwise arise. Each of you may take notes if you desire and use them to refresh your memory during deliberations, but they may not be read or shown to other members. Are there any questions?"

"No Sir." They all replied in unison.

"Please take a moment to read the charges provided to you and ensure that your name is correctly reflected on the convening order. If it is not, please let me know." Everyone on the panel looked at the document in their hands and handed them to the bailiff, after which the military judge directed the Trial Counsel to announce the general nature of the charges.

The trial counsel stood and announced, "The general nature of the charge in this case is a violation of Article 120 of the Uniform Code of Military Justice. The charges were preferred by Private Wilson and were forwarded with recommendations as to disposition by the convening authority and investigated by Criminal Investigation Command."

"Continue with Specification of charges." The judge ordered.

"In that Staff Sergeant Murphy did repeatedly have supervisory control over PFC Wilson during the three month period in question at Womack Army hospital and with intent to commit rape upon said solider, constitutes conduct unbecoming and prejudicial to good order and discipline, and is of a nature to bring discredit upon the armed forces."

"Defense, call your first witness."

Maura listened intently to the sworn testimony given by both the accused and the victim, who were the only witnesses called to the stand. The defense attacked the victim's claims and veracity and the trial counsel repeatedly attacked the character, and professionalism of the accused. At the conclusion of testimony, the defense counsel requested the accused wife be allowed to address the court on the impact of a guilty verdict on her and her newborn child. Holding her baby in her arms, she pleaded with the panel to consider the inconsistencies in the victims account of what had transpired and the fact that if her husband were convicted, she and her baby would be homeless and without material support. With that admission, she burst into uncontrollable tears and had to be physically removed from the courtroom. Momentarily losing focus, Maura considered both the conflicting accounts of the parties involved and some of the far reaching consequences of the verdict, given the intense media interest in this case, as the judge announced the court would be adjourned for lunch, to be followed by panel deliberations.

As she left the courtroom with her fellow panel members, Maura considered her lunch options and called Eric at the office. Twenty minutes later, Eric walked into the foyer, where Maura was sitting in an overstuffed chair, waiting for him. Seeing him, Maura smiled and stood up as Eric announced playfully, "One slice of pizza and a Tab as requested ma'am."

Maura took the pizza and soda from his outstretched hand. "You're a lifesaver. Do you have time to stay and talk?" Eric nodded wordlessly and sat down in the chair next to hers. Suddenly realizing he didn't have any lunch, Maura extended the slice of pizza he'd just given her. "I'll share this if you're hungry."

Eric guiltily admitted, "A couple of us went to the greasy spoon just outside the gate after PT this morning. I had four cups of coffee, three eggs over light with grits, and two flapjacks with maple syrup at 9:30. I'm good for the rest of the day. You need to eat that, because if your deliberations go long, you may not get anything else to eat until late tonight." As Maura pulled back the slice of pizza and hungrily took a bite, Eric commented. "I was surprised when you told me the trial was over and you'd be going into deliberations after lunch."

Maura hesitated for a second, recalling the judge's admonition to not discuss the proceedings with anyone and responded cautiously. "There weren't a lot of witnesses called. Actually all the administrative stuff took longer than actual testimony."

Realizing he'd inadvertently made Maura uncomfortable, Eric smiled and pointed to her pizza and can of Tab, "Eat up, you don't have a lot of time and you'll definitely want to hit the ladies room before you go into deliberation." Standing up, he bent over to whisper in her ear. "Friday night, your place for the weekend?" Turning to look at him, she nodded yes. Watching him as he walked away, she blushed as thoughts of him naked in her bed involuntarily came to mind. Looking up at the clock on the nearby wall she took another bite of pizza, and determined how much time she had to finish lunch and go to the bathroom.

★ ★ ★

THE PRESIDENT OF THE panel, who was a lieutenant colonel, had just handed out the slips of paper they would use to record their vote. Pointing to a small box to his right he instructed, "Write guilty or not guilty on the sheet of paper, fold it over and put it in here. When everyone has voted, we'll tally the responses." What he said next shocked Maura to the core. "I'm confident we'll be out of here as soon as I record your votes, because it's obvious that while he's guilty of adultery, that girl is lying about him raping her and we should all come to a quick verdict." He then proceeded to write on the sheet of paper in front of him. Maura looked around at her fellow panel members who were busily writing as well and proceeded to record her vote. Maura was the last one to put her ballot in the box and she was greeted with a look of exasperation and irritation by the lieutenant colonel as he took the top off the box and vigorously shook the ballots for several seconds, before opening them. He had opened four ballots and announced "not guilty" as he put them in a pile on the side of the box. He opened the ballot in his hand and had already started to say "guil.." when he stopped suddenly. The initial look of surprise was replaced by a scowl as he bellowed incredulously, "How could *ANYONE* vote not guilty?" Neither expecting, nor getting a response from the panel members, who with the exception of Maura were all looking at each other furtively; the panel president shook his head and continued opening the remaining ballots. When he had announced and recorded the last ballot, he growled, "Obviously we have a moron in the room." Pausing for effect, he continued. "I know this is supposed to be by secret ballot, but given the constraints that we cannot have a hung jury and we need a unanimous vote to put this to bed, I'm going to ask whoever cast the one and only guilty vote, to explain why they cast that vote and we'll discuss your rationale and help you arrive at the correct decision."

Maura asked quietly, "Why don't you explain why you feel the one vote is incorrect sir?"

Glaring at her, he exploded. "I should'a known it was you captain! What the hell are you trying to prove?"

"Nothing sir, I just cast my vote like everyone else, but I'd be interested in hearing you tell the panel why you think the one dissenting vote was incorrect."

Putting both his hands of the end of the table, he bent over and scowled at Maura. "Do you actually believe her story that there was no consensual affair and he raped her?"

For just a second, Maura considered reproaching him for not answering her question, but decided to resist that impulse. "I believe there was a mutual attraction, there were most likely previous sexual encounters between the two. I admit to having doubts about the veracity of her accusation that he locked the door, pinned her to the x-ray table and forced her to have sex with him after she repeatedly told him to stop; but there is no doubt an affair did take place. Given the requirement for a unanimous vote, along with the constraints that we cannot find him guilty of one charge and not guilty of another charge and if we find him not guilty, no punishment will be given, I cannot enter a not guilty verdict."

One of the three enlisted panel members spoke up. "Ma'am, I acknowledge your unease with finding him not guilty, given the constraints put upon the terms of sentencing as agreed to by the defense and prosecuting attorneys prior to this proceeding; but this is a career soldier with a family, who made a bad decision and I would be happy to give him a general discharge; but if we find him guilty of all the charges, he gets a bad conduct discharge and has a federal conviction, that will keep him from being able to find any decent job on the outside and definitely not a job in a hospital x-ray department."

Another panel member jumped in on the conversation. "And he has a wife who has forgiven him and a brand new baby to support. No disrespect meant ma'am, but it would be unfair to make his family suffer for his one time lapse in good judgment."

Maura pursed her lips. "I didn't come to this decision without significant anguish and sorrow that his family will suffer so grievously for his bad choice and I came very close to letting that be the deciding factor in my decision; but this case has gotten a lot of news coverage and while I am not overly concerned about the perceptions of the civilian population regarding this case, I am concerned about the message a not guilty verdict will send to both the male and female soldiers who are also following this case." Seeing that she now had their full attention, Maura continued. "I feel strongly that a not guilty verdict will embolden other male soldiers to believe that they can justify rape in cases that will surely follow this one; but more importantly, I am very concerned about the message it will send to female soldiers now and in the future, about how they will be treated when they accuse another soldier of rape. I am very concerned that if we deliver a not guilty verdict, there will be many women who will be afraid to come forward with valid rape charges. There are larger issues at stake in the verdict we are about to deliver, than one family suffering."

"You have got to be shitting me!" The panel president exclaimed.

Maura could feel the anger rush through her body and considered blowing him out of the water for just a second; but was able to contain her fury, because she'd seen from the non-verbal cues some of the panel members evidenced, that she might have caused them to reconsider changing their original verdict and she was afraid if she lost her temper, she'd lose their support. Unable to trust her voice not to quiver or crack, Maura just sat back in her chair, making it evident that she had nothing else to say.

Exasperated, the panel president roughly grabbed additional slips of paper to be disseminated amongst the panel members. "Okay captain, you've had your say and we'll take another vote. But I want your word that if all of us except you find him not guilty, you will change your vote to comply with the majority vote."

Maura turned to look at him. "No sir. I don't have to and I won't." Maura had to contain herself as she saw his face turn red with fury. "Captain, your obstinate behavior is unprofessional and illogical! I feel as strongly as you do, that a not guilty verdict is the only reasonable verdict; so I guess we're just going to have to put up with your nonsense until you realize that your only option is to change your vote."

Struggling to control the anger and frustration that was boiling over inside her, Maura responded by looking around the room at her fellow panel members, before finally resting on the panel president. "Then I guess you plan on dying here sir, because there is no way, no how, that you will ever get me to change my vote. Had you engaged me in a professional and conciliatory manner, there may have been a chance of my changing my vote, but quite frankly, your attempt to shame and bully me, has only deepened my resolve to stay the course, not because I'm stubborn, but because I truly am looking at the possible long term implications of this verdict and cannot in good conscience, ever agree to a not guilty verdict." Maura looked down at the paper slip on the table and started writing. Folding the ballot, she got up and put it in the box and returned to her seat announcing, "Your turn gentlemen." After what seemed an eternity all the new ballots were in the box and the panel president proceeded to open and record the votes. As he read not guilty, on the first two ballots, Maura felt the muscles in her jaw involuntarily stiffen. When he recorded guilty, on the third ballot, she assumed that was hers, but when the next two ballots were guilty, she felt such relief and gratitude, that she immediately silently thanked God for his help and struggled not to cry. Maura forced herself to abstain from the measured and quite lengthy discussion among the dissenting panel members. This was followed by the master sergeant who had appealed to her for clemency after the first vote, addressing the panel president resignedly. "Sir, I think we've talked this one to death. We need to vote again and see what happens."

Maura struggled to keep her poker face as guilty verdicts were read and in the end, there was still one dissenting vote, but this time it was a lone not guilty vote. Maura was clenching her jaw so hard, it was killing her; but it was the only way she could keep from repeating the challenge the panel president had given her after the first vote. After a few seconds, one of her fellow captains haltingly addressed the panel president. "Sir, could I respectfully suggest we give you a few minutes to think about this and conduct another vote when you're ready?"

The panel president rubbed his eyes and silently nodded assent as he stood and walked to the window to look out and deliberate what his vote would be on the upcoming round. It took quite some time, but he finally turned back to the group and handed out new ballots.

★ ★ ★

THE PANEL FILED IN followed shortly by the return of the military judge, as the bailiff announced, "The court is called to order."

After the trial counsel confirmed that all parties to include court members were present, the military judge addressed the panel. "Have you reached a verdict?"

The panel president stood and stiffly replied, "Yes Sir."

"Is the verdict reflected on the Sentencing Worksheet?"

"Yes Sir."

"Please fold the Sentencing Worksheet and give it to the Bailiff so that I can examine it." The bailiff took the worksheet and handed it to the judge who after reviewing it announced, "I have examined the Sentencing Worksheet and it appears to be in proper form. Bailiff, you may return it to the President." The bailiff walked over to return the form to the panel president, as the military judge continued. "Defense Counsel and Accused, please rise." Once they had done so, the judge looked at the panel president. "Please announce the sentence of the court."

"We find the defendant guilty of all offenses preferred by the government."

All heads turned as the defendants wife shrieked and collapsed. As soon as the bailiff, removed the hysterical mother and child from the courtroom, the judge solemnly announced, "Accused and Counsel, please be seated. Members of the Court, before I excuse you, let me advise you of one matter. If you are asked about your service on this court-martial, I remind you of the oath you took. Essentially, the oath prevents you from discussing your deliberations with anyone, to include stating any member's opinion or vote, unless ordered to do so by a court. You may of course, discuss your personal observations of what happened in the courtroom and how the process of a court-martial functions, but not what was discussed during your deliberations. Thank you for your attendance and service. You are excused. This court is adjourned."

The waiting reporters accosted Maura and her fellow members as they walked out of the courthouse. The panel president surprised Maura by stepping out in front of them and spreading his arms out in a protective manner. "Ladies and gentlemen of the press. Military courts do not work like civilian courts and we are prohibited from talking to you or anyone else about the proceedings. I respectfully request you allow the panel members to proceed unimpeded and reserve your questions for the trial or defense counsels."

Maura had barely unlocked her car door, when the panel president accosted her verbally. “How does it feel to destroy the future of a soldier, because you insisted on imposing your will on others?” Maura sat down and closed the car door without responding to the accusation. As the furious lieutenant colonel walked away, Maura sat there for quite some time, coming to terms with her anger at the private for getting away with her lies, recalling the tearful exit of the sergeant’s wife and the reality that she could have chosen to avoid inflicting that trauma had she not felt so strongly about the long term implications for others if she had sided with the original not guilty, majority vote. She needed to get her head straight before returning home this evening and dealing with the questions her friends would pepper her with, until all of this died down and was forgotten. She considered stopping to see Eric on her way home, but knew if she did, she might tell him everything, which would violate the judge’s instructions. By the time she turned the key in the ignition and drove away with a very heavy heart, the reporters and members of the court had long since departed. She knew she would spend several sleepless nights, but would grow more confident over time, that she had made a decision that was as just as the circumstances had allowed.

21

FORT BRAGG, MAY 1981

SERGEANT ADAMS WALKED INTO the office and seeing Lori with her head in her hands asked, "What's up ma'am?"

Lori looked up shaking her head in disbelief. "How in the world do soldiers think they have money in the bank just because they have checks in their checkbook?"

"What are you talkin' about Ma'am?"

"I was told by the commander that Private Zimmer had his new truck repossessed because he sent in another check that bounced."

"That dumb-shit, ah, I mean, that dummy. I'll schedule a counseling session with Zimmer and set up a platoon training session to teach all of our troops about balancing a checkbook. I hope he's learned his lesson....but you never know."

"That's not the worst of it," Lori said. "A social worker just called me about Specialist Mackey. The social worker inspected Mackeys' on post quarters and Mackey failed his inspection. He might have his two young children removed from the house because it's been deemed unsafe and there are allegations of child abuse."

With obvious concern in his voice, Sergeant Adams responded, "I'll talk with Mackey today. I knew he was having marital problems but I had no idea his kids were in danger. What specifically did the social worker say?"

"She said as soon as she walked into their quarters, there was a strong stench of urine and feces. Both children were unsupervised and filthy and the two year old had a super dirty diaper."

"Was the mom there?"

"Yes, but Mrs. Mackey was sleeping in another room when the four year old boy let the social worker in the house around two in the afternoon. The four year old also told the social worker he was hungry because he hadn't had anything to eat all day."

"Crap. I'll let you know Mackey's version after I talk with him."

"Sounds good. I've got to go to the motor pool for another inspection right now. I'll see ya in a few hours."

★ ★ ★

TOM PICKED LORI UP at her apartment that evening. "Hey Lori! You ready to go?" he asked impatiently. Tom was a Special Forces captain, tall and muscular, with striking brown eyes. It was only their second date, but Lori was already attracted to him.

"Ya, let me grab my purse."

"Great. I've been wanting to see this movie for weeks."

Lori grabbed her purse off the kitchen table and asked, "So what's Excalibur about? I have no idea."

"The Camelot story. You know, King Arthur's Knights of the Round Table. Part action, part fantasy. I think it'll be a good flick. You can pick the next movie we go to."

"Who said we're going to another movie?" Lori teased.

Revealing dazzling white teeth as he grinned, Tom replied, "I've got this great feeling about us. I figure we'll go to quite a few more movies while we're stationed here."

Grabbing Tom's hand, Lori said, "I like your intuition and I can definitely get into an escape movie after my crummy day at work."

Tom opened the pickup truck's passenger door for Lori and quietly asked, "You wanna talk about it?"

"Not much to say. One of my soldiers might be abusing his kids and the company motor pool still looks like crap. I think I'll have to find a new motor sergeant."

"Wouldn't be the first time a motor sergeant had to be replaced, but the child abuse is a different story. What's up with that?"

"This afternoon, my platoon sergeant spoke with Specialist Mackey after the pediatric doctor reported numerous bruises on the backs and thighs of both of the specialist's kids. Mackey denied everything. Said his two and four year olds were wrestling and gave each other the bruises. He said the social worker just came at a bad time…they never have pet poop in the house, and normally his wife takes great care of the kids and only naps when they nap. The social worker said the house reeked of urine and feces and there was evidence of repeated instances of dog and cat feces and other stains on the carpet…. Why does he have kids and pets if he can't take care of them? That just pisses me off!"

Not saying anything for a few seconds Tom said, "I have a real sweet spot for kids. That soldier and his wife are scum. Kids don't wrestle and give each other bruises when they're that young. Was the wife sick?"

"No, Mackey said she just dozed off in the bedroom that one afternoon… I don't buy it at all."

Tom added, "Yeah, that really sucks. I'd probably support the social worker's recommendations on this one."

Lori sighed, "Yeah, well, enough about work; you still running the half-marathon next month?"

"Planning on it. I enjoy running and it really helps me unwind after a long day. I also get to run long some mornings for PT, that's one advantage of being in Special Forces. You and I should run together once in a while."

"I'm not a distance runner, but I can run five miles without too much of a problem. I love running but I have to run with my platoon during the week. If you promise to keep it under five miles and not to run too fast, I'd enjoy running with you on some weekends."

"I'd make sure you set the pace. How about this weekend?"

"Sorry Tom. I'm flying up to West Point to see my best girlfriend and some of my basketball teammate's graduate. I'll take a rain check though."

"You got it. What's your friend's name?"

"Her name's Reggie. We've been through lots of fun and tough times together. Reggie and I have this unique connection. I can't really explain it. We're more like twins than friends."

"Yeah, I've got a friend like that. Dave and I can complete each other's sentences most of the time…sort of eerie."

"Yes, Reggie and I have the same ideas and we like the same things. It's great having someone to confide in." Seeing the post theater, Lori added, "I'm so glad you asked me to come with you tonight."

"I wouldn't have come by myself. You make everything so much more fun Lori."

"Thanks for the compliment. I love hanging out with you too. You're smart, funny, and willing to try new things. Plus you understand all the Army stuff I do at work."

"Got that part covered. I must say though, I've never dated an Army officer before…so this is new ground for me….but I kinda like it."

"Do you get teased by your friends?" Lori asked.

Tom replied, "A little, but I could give a rats ass. I've never done conventional things. Dating you is so much better than the usual girlfriend issues I've dealt with. You're not into shopping and putting on your face like my last girlfriend. I sometimes had to wait an hour before we went out so she could put on her makeup. Frustrated the crap out of me. What a waste of time."

Lori added, "I am odd when you think about it. I love comfort over beauty. I'm not into shopping or wearing jewelry like many of my girlfriends. I just love being outside and being physically active. If you're into that type of woman, we'll be a good match."

Tom smiled as he pulled into the theater parking lot, "You sound perfect to me. Plus, you're easy on the eyes and don't talk my ear off like lots of gals."

★ ★ ★

ON 27 MAY 1981, Lori was in Michie Stadium at West Point wearing her Class A, green uniform for Reggie Howard's graduation. Security was been tight given that this was only President Ronald Reagan's second public appearance since John Hinckley Jr shot him on 30 March. Lori, and all the graduation attendees, had to walk through metal detector machines before entering the stadium. Lori sat with Reggie's mother, father, grandmother, and Kim, Reggie's younger sister.

"You look so nice in your uniform Lori," Reggie's mom said. "Thank you for flying here to commission Reggie. She's so excited to see you."

"I'm excited to see her too. Last year was a tough year for me without having Reggie to talk to every day. You know we played basketball and softball together for three years."

Mrs. Howard smiled, "Yes. Reggie talked about you from the git-go. She's been looking up to you since her plebe year. She also told me she wanted to be an MP, just like you."

"I'm flattered she picked MPs and I'm so happy I get to commission her today. I've promoted a few of my soldiers, but I've never commissioned an officer into the Army. This is an exciting day for everyone."

"It most certainly is!" Mr. Howard said beaming with pride. "I'm so proud of my girl. You know how hard it was for her to graduate. You were there for her and helped her through this place. We will always remember that Lori."

"Thank you sir. I'm proud of Reggie too."

Reggie's grandmother spoke, "Can't believe they got the President of the United States to be the speaker today. Seems like he was just in the hospital after that nut tried to kill him."

Mr. Howard said, "Mom, Reggie said President Reagan's Chief of Staff has a son graduating with the Class of 1981 today and the rumor is the Chief asked his boss to be the commencement speaker. Interesting how things work; it's all about friendship and connections."

"I'm so glad you learned what we taught you Henry, and haven't forget how politics works," Reggie's grandma replied.

"Oh I know. I learned from one of the best," Mr. Howard replied to his mother.

At that moment, *Pomp and Circumstance* began playing and the graduating cadets marched into the stadium wearing their full dress over white uniforms. Lori and the Howard family craned their necks looking for Reggie.

"It shouldn't be that hard to see her. How many black women cadets are graduating?" asked Mrs. Howard.

"Well, I know of only two other black gals in the class of 1981. But you're right, not very many," Lori replied. "I'm so happy for Reggie."

"Mom, dad, there she is! Look to the left side of the chairs," Kim said. "Make sure you get a picture."

"I'm taking a whole roll of photos. This is a once in a lifetime achievement!" Mr. Howard said as he snapped four photos of Reggie before Reggie sat down in her folding chair. A few minutes later, President and Nancy Reagan walked onto the stage.

"Look Henry! There they are," Mrs. Howard whispered to her husband as the crowd started clapping.

"Yes, yes, I see them..."

Lori was catching key phrases of President Reagan's speech..."You are the guardians of freedom...you become the keepers of the peace...I accept without question the words of George Washington, 'To be prepared for war is one of the most effectual means of preserving the peace.'...Obviously you did not choose this profession with the thought of making a fortune. Samuel Johnson 200 years ago said, 'An officer is much more respected than any other man who has so little money.' ...I have asked Secretary of Defense Weinberger to form a defense manpower task force to review the entire military manpower question and to make proposals which will increase the effectiveness of the active and reserve all-volunteer forces..... studying ways in which we can make enlistment more attractive for the kind of young people we need in our military forces...you can transmit the historic heritage which is in the very air of West Point. The first Purple Heart medal was awarded here..."

After President Reagan's remarks were over, the superintendent presented a cadet sabre as a token of appreciation, Mrs. Howard exclaimed, "I am so inspired! The speech was wonderful and patriotic and I'm so happy to be sharing it with my baby on her most special day." Lori and the

Howards along with thousands of family and friends watched the cadets go up and receive their diplomas on the stage. The ceremony culminated with the cadets throwing their white cadet caps into the air after the class president announced, "Class Dismissed."

As the Howard family and Lori made their way onto the chaotic football field, throngs of children ran into the seating area, collecting the caps as the graduates started hugging each other and looking for their loved ones. Mr. Howard spotted Reggie first, "There's my girl!" and they all walked over to Reggie who was beaming from ear to ear.

"Hi guys! Was that great or what?"

Mrs. Howard responded first, "Oh Reggie! We're so proud of you. We knew you could do it!" and then she hugged and kissed her oldest daughter.

Mr. Howard added, "Honey, you will be a fantastic Army officer. I am so proud of you too."

"Aw sugar, you are so beautiful. We love you," exclaimed Reggie's grandmother with tears in her eyes as she hugged and kissed Reggie.

"Thanks everyone," Reggie said smiling. "Thanks for flying out for my graduation and commissioning me Lori. This means so much to me!"

Lori said, "Regg, it's my honor to commission you into the Army. It was so great seeing you and all your class graduate."

★ ★ ★

LATER THAT AFTERNOON, REGGIE changed into her Army class A green uniform, and went to Trophy Point with her family for the brief commissioning ceremony. Lori and Reggie faced each other with their right hands held up and Reggie said:

> "I, Reggie Howard, having been appointed as officer of the Army of the United States, as indicated above in the grade of Second Lieutenant, do solemnly swear that I will support and defend the Constitution of the United States against all enemies, foreign and domestic, that I will bear true faith and allegiance to the same; that I take this obligation freely, without any mental reservations

or purpose of evasion; and that I will well and faithfully discharge the duties of the office upon which I am about to enter; so help me God."

22

OAHU, HAWAII, JUNE 1981

SEEING LORI AND RONI as they exited the airplane, Cate and Jim waved excitedly as they walked over to greet them. Placing leis around their necks followed by a welcome kiss on each cheek, Cate exclaimed, "I'm thrilled you both made it for the biggest day of my life."

Jim hugged Lori. "I think it's so cool you both got to take leave and come for a week. I know how stressful the 82nd can be." Turning to address Roni, he said, "You must be Veronica. Nice to meet you."

"Call me Roni. Only my mom and grandma call me Veronica. Boy it's really humid here! I hope you have air conditioning."

"We do have two A/C units in our rental off post. One's in the kitchen and the other one's in our bedroom. We have fans in the guest rooms for our parents when they arrive tomorrow."

Lori remarked, "Cate, thanks for the great smelling leis! They're beautiful! How thoughtful. What kind of flowers are they?"

"Plumeria. They're my favorite. It's an island custom to greet visitors with leis when they arrive. I hope you like your lei too Roni."

"Quite nice. I've never been leied before," Roni said grinning.

Smiling at the joke he had heard before, Jim asked, "So are you guys hungry or thirsty?"

Lori answered, "I'm not. They gave us plenty to eat and drink on the plane. I can't wait to see the island. I've been waiting to come to Hawaii for the past six months."

Cate said, "I'm so glad you came four days early so we can show you the island before we take off on our honeymoon. We decided to fly on the puddle-jumper to Maui. We both have ten days of leave for our wedding and honeymoon. I'm over-the-moon happy everything is going so smoothly and I'm not stressed out like so many brides-to-be."

"I take it getting married on the beach is more casual than a New York wedding?" Roni asked.

"That's for sure! The money we saved by having a small wedding and reception is paying for the airline tickets we bought for our parents to attend our wedding and a down payment on a nice two bedroom house we found in Mililani. We move in next month," Jeff said.

Cate added, "Most important is I've always dreamed of getting married at sunset on the beach and we'll be surrounded by our favorite people! I found this gorgeous white dress in Honolulu last month and Jeff's wearing his Army whites. I just hope the weather cooperates."

"I'm sure it will," Lori said optimistically as they followed Jim to the baggage claim area and waited for Lori and Roni's suitcases.

"I'm happy your here Lori. I've met some nice lieutenants and friends here that you'll meet at the wedding, but we've shared so many special memories after living together for four years that you were my only choice for maid of honor. Roni, you kept my sanity during plebe year. I just loved your defiant attitude with some of the creeps."

Roni smiled and replied, "Well I haven't changed. Sucks that I got kicked out for failing English, but I know how to handle all the engineer soldiers and officers I work with every day. Some are super smart, but most are dorky and have no people skills. I just work my magic on them and I usually get what I want. The real Army is so much better than being a cadet in training."

"There's our suitcases Roni," Lori said pointing to the arriving luggage. "How far is the drive to Mililani Cate?"

"Not far. Takes 15-20 minutes. It's much cooler in the middle of the island where we live. I know you're just going to love this island. We have a few days of sightseeing planned. I thought we could go to the Arizona Memorial now, if you're up to it, followed by dinner at this cool marina restaurant close by," Cate replied.

"Sounds great to me! I need to walk and stretch out my legs from the long flights. Wow! Look at the palm trees and flowers," Lori said when they went outside while following Jim to his parked car.

"Yes, the flowers are truly incredible. I pinch myself every day I wake up knowing I'm in such a beautiful place," said Cate. "Even the morning runs aren't too bad and you know I don't like PT."

Roni chimed in, "I remember Lori taking us to the gym to practice the indoor obstacle course quite a few times so we'd pass. Boy was that a tough test. I had a hacking cough for three days afterwards."

"I knew when the cadets took the IOC because my classroom sounded like an infirmary for a week. Even worse was when the plebes came to class after their boxing classes. Half of them looked glassy-eyed and the other half looked dead," Jim said.

"True. Some of the guys would move to the back of the room but a few would nod off at their desks and you'd hear the thud when they're heads hit the desk. I felt bad for some of them," Lori said.

Roni added, "I don't remember that. I remember our 80 hours of hand-to-hand combat and self-defense with dragon woman. She had that high-pitched monotone voice that was so annoying. Then she made us practice so many falls that we all ended up with bruises all over our bodies. I'm surprised we didn't die of blood clots."

Cate joined in, "Self-defense was one of my worst classes, that, and swimming. I was a rock and almost drowned one day. That was so scary."

"Cate honey, the good news is now you can swim and you're putting your swim lessons to good use here in Hawaii." Glancing in the rearview mirror Jim added, "We try to go to a different beach every weekend when we're not in the field. Occasionally we'll drive to Hanauma Bay with our coffee thermos and lawn chairs to watch the sunrise. Here we are," he said as they turned into the Arizona Memorial parking lot.

Surprised, Roni said, "This is so close to the airport."

Getting out of the car, Cate mentioned, "Most attractions are only a short drive away. Pearl Harbor is just a few miles away from the airport and the USS Arizona Memorial visitor's center is new. It opened on Memorial Day last year...The USS Arizona Memorial is the number one attraction here in Oahu, not including the beaches. It shouldn't be too busy this time of the day, but I have to warn you, it's very sobering."

Upon arriving at the newly opened visitor center, Lori began reading the short synopsis of the Arizona Memorial while Cate, Jim, and Roni, wandered through the visitor's center, looking at the exhibit photos and reading the historical accounts of the fateful day.

> On December 7, 1941, a calm Sunday morning, the color detail was on deck of the battleship in anticipation of raising the American flag. The *Arizona* came under violent attack by Japanese aircraft, and at 8:06 am the starboard side of the ship received a fatal hit by an 800-kilogram bomb. The explosion ignited furious fires in the forward part of the ship. The explosion and fires instantly killed or trapped 1,177 sailors and marines. Many of the 334 survivors displayed remarkable courage in assisting their shipmates to safety.

"Hey guys, the next boat leaves in 10 minutes, so let's meet on the dock in 5," Cate said to the group as she walked to the rest room and put on some fresh lipstick before joining Roni at the drinking fountain and all four friends walked outside for their tour to begin.

★ ★ ★

CATE AND JIM WERE getting married by an Army chaplain on the North Shore of Oahu at the Turtle Bay Hilton hotel beach with their parents, Lori as the maid of honor, Jim's brother as the best man, and a small group of close friends and family attending.

"What a glorious sunny day we have for our wedding," Cate said when Lori and Roni arrived in her dressing room as she was getting dressed for her beach wedding.

"You couldn't have asked for a better afternoon. Oh my God, Cate! You look gorgeous!" Lori sputtered.

"Not too bad for a haole," smiled Roni, proud of the new slang she had picked up since landing on the island. "Actually you look beautiful Cate, you know that."

"Thanks for your compliments. I've been looking forward to this day for over two years. I'm so happy the day is finally here! Let's get going. I don't want to be late for the biggest day of my life."

Cate's beautiful smile stretched across her entire face as she joined Jim on the beach, followed by Lori. Cate wore a long beaded white dress and a white haku lei on her head, in lieu of a veil. After the short ceremony, the photographer took several photos of the small wedding party, while the small group of guests snapped pictures with their Polaroid instant cameras before walking back to the hotel for the reception.

Entering the hotel, Roni came up to Lori and confided, "That was wonderful, I loved the intimacy of the small group of immediate family and friends. Best of all was the ocean backdrop. Just beautiful."

"Yup. I know what you mean. The ocean backdrop can't be beat. Cate and Jim look so happy."

Roni replied morosely, "Yeah, but this whole scene only makes me miss George more. I was so disappointed when he told me he couldn't ask for leave, because his unit had a field exercise."

Lori commiserated. "Yeah, I felt the same way when Tom told me he was being deployed, but at least we're together and we'll have fun in spite of the Army's terrible scheduling." Lori pointed toward Cate and Jim as they approached the champagne fountain followed closely by their family and other guests. "You ready for some champagne, great food and a bit of dancing?"

Roni smiled her big grin, "I'm always ready to party! Bring it on Miss Sunshine."

23

FORT BRAGG, NC, OCTOBER 1981

"WHAT THE HELL!" RONI yelled walking into their apartment that evening, seeing Lori with her foot propped up on the coffee table and a pair of crutches against the couch. "What happened?"

"While I was running at PT this morning, I looked up and I stepped right on a large rock and rolled my ankle *really* bad. Sergeant Adams made me go on sick call even though I thought I could ice it and take some aspirin. The doctor said it's a bad sprain and I need to ice it and stay off of it for a week."

"That sucks the big one," Roni replied.

"Yeah, I'm on bed rest for the next three days and then I'll go back to the hospital for a checkup. First time I've ever had crutches."

"I had 'em twice and they're no fun. If you walk a lot, you'll get really sore underarms from all the rubbing. Let me change and make us some dinner."

Lori said, "That'd be great Roni. I'm starting to get hungry and I didn't know what to do about dinner."

As Roni turned toward her bedroom to change out of her uniform, the doorbell rang. "I wonder who that is," Roni said as she went to the front door. She opened the door and saw Tom holding a beautiful bouquet of yellow roses, "I heard we have an invalid on our hands," he said.

"Yes, we do. Come on in Tom. Lori'll be glad to see you. Have you eaten yet?"

"No. So if you're asking me to dinner, I'd be happy to have what you're having," then looking at Lori, Tom said, "Hi Honey!" giving Lori a quick kiss on the cheek and then holding up the flowers.

"Hey Tom! How'd you know I was laid-up?" Then noticing the flowers, "Ahh! What pretty roses!"

"I called your office to see if you could take off for lunch, and Sergeant Adams told me about your accident this morning. Figured the least I could do was cheer you up. How bad is it?" Tom asked, looking at her bandaged ankle and foot elevated on a pillow on the coffee table.

"Pretty ugly right now, with lots of swelling and some purple from the blood pooling around the ankle. I've been icing it off and on all day like the doctor said. I took two more aspirin an hour ago. Now I'm feeling okay."

"Yeah, I hate getting hurt or sick. Makes you remember how vulnerable you are. Can I get you anything?"

"I could really use a glass of water. I'm pretty thirsty right now," Lori said.

"You got it," and Tom went into the kitchen, returning with a large glass of water with two ice cubes in the glass. "You need to stay hydrated and keep taking the pain meds. You'll heal faster when your body's not in pain."

"I guess; I just don't like taking medicine."

"For your own good and the good of your troopers, you need to get well soon. Last year I had a bad sprain after a jump, and it took me six weeks before I could run on it. I did exactly what the doctor ordered and now I'm back in shape. It's better to heal correctly than to keep reinjuring yourself. I've seen buddies who think they're ready for action when they're not. I don't want that happening to you."

"Okay, I get it. I'll take my recovery slow and steady, but I won't like it."

"Nobody does…you just have to suck it up."

Roni came back into the living room with a small plate of cheese, salami, and crackers and said, “I can have some Hamburger Helper and a salad ready in about 20 minutes, is that okay with you Lori?”

“Sounds great! I just started getting hungry a few minutes ago. Tom?”

“I haven’t had Hamburger Helper in ages. Sounds good to me! You have a beer?”

“Yeah. George just brought me a case of Coors yesterday and I put some in the frig. Help yourself,” Roni replied and then she walked back into the kitchen.

“I really like your roommate,” said Tom as he walked into the kitchen to get himself a beer.

★ ★ ★

TWO WEEKS LATER LORI was seated in Captain Archibald’s office for her annual Officer Evaluation Report counseling session. “So how’s the ankle doing?” Lori’s commander asked.

“Pretty good, sir. The doctor said I need to wait another three weeks before I start running on it, but I can walk fine and my combat boot is a great support for the ankle.”

“Glad to hear it. Most paratroopers have twisted or sprained their ankles, just part of the job here in the 82nd.” Pulling out a piece of paper Captain Archibald continued, “Now I want to discuss your performance over the past year Lori. I will say I was reluctant and apprehensive about having a female platoon leader in my company last year when you arrived, but it’s turned out to be a positive thing. It’s really helped that you run well and you’re a good role model for our young female MPs. But what I admire the most about you is how you turned our substandard motor pool into a fully functioning machine. The last inspection we exceeded the requirements. That has never happened before in this unit. I know you’ve spent many extra hours in the motor pool and after you fired the motor sergeant and replaced him with Sergeant Turrow, great progress was made.”

“Yes, sir. It was hard to fire the motor sergeant, but after I smelled alcohol on his breath, it was an easy decision. Thank you for your support.”

“Yes, well that leads me to your platoon. When you got here last October, Charlie platoon had the worst PT and range scores in the company.

Now you have the best scores. I attribute that to your leadership and focus. What do you think?"

"Sir, Sergeant Adams is my right hand man. Without him, we would not have been successful. He deserves most of the credit."

"True enough. He's a good soldier with lots of potential and I'll take care of him. Today's session is about you. Not only do I consider you the best lieutenant in the company, your decision-making, ideas, and ability to bring out the best in your soldiers is superb. I wish I could clone you."

Lori started blushing and Captain Archibald continued, "We received the best scores at our annual field exercise last month and most of the reason for that was because of your sound leadership. Your training focus and hands-on approach to leading your platoon is first-rate. I know you'd like to continue being a platoon leader, but I have two new lieutenants arriving next month. That coupled with my executive officer (XO) PCSing next month means I have a slot free. I'd like you to be my XO Lori. Would you like the job?"

"Yes, Sir! I mean, I really like leading my platoon and working with Sergeant Adams, but I think I'd do well at planning company training and making sure the admin and supply issues are taken care of. But won't Lieutenant Dundy be upset about my new job? He's the most senior lieutenant."

"You let me worry about Dundy. He needs more platoon leader time and he needs to improve his organizational skills. I know you're a good writer, and you have the attention to detail that is sometimes lacking around here. I think you'll be a major asset to me and the unit. Let's plan on you moving over to the XO slot in about four weeks, that'll give you time to finish writing your annual platoon training schedule, completing your range training, and writing your NCOERs. I know Sergeant Adams will miss you, but he'll get to train another new lieutenant. He's good at that."

"He's excellent Sir. He's taught me more about soldiers in one year than I learned in four years at West Point. He is a fantastic leader and trainer."

"Yes, I know that. Between you and me, I expect to see him on the next promotion list. You may be working with him again in the near future. Any questions?"

"No, Sir. Thank you for your guidance and coaching throughout the past year," Lori replied.

"That's my job. Now take a look at your OER, sign it, and have Specialist Graf make a copy for you. Don't worry about missing PT. You've already proven yourself physically. I need you to coach the weak runners at PT in the mornings. That's all I have."

Lori stood up, saluted her commander, and happily walked out of the room.

★ ★ ★

"HE SAID WHAT?" RONI asked when Lori told her about her counseling session with Captain Archibald.

"He said I was going to be his XO starting next month," Lori replied.

"You're going to be the XO as a 2nd Lieutenant? That's really weird. All the Company XOs I know are 1st Lieutenants… Well, if anyone can do it, you can. Way to go Lori!" Roni stood up and gave Lori a great big hug.

Slightly embarrassed at the affection, Lori quietly said, "Thanks Roni. I'm almost a 1st Lieutenant, but I *was* shocked when he offered me the job."

"No shit. I'd be totally shocked too." Abruptly changing the subject, Roni added, "So, remember my company commander?"

"How could I not remember him…he's a turd, and treated you like crap."

"You got that right! Well, I was so happy when he had his change of command last week. I couldn't take his attitude anymore. At least the new CO is giving me a fair shot."

"That's cool. What's he like?" Lori asked.

"Too soon to tell, but he called all the officers and NCOs into a meeting right after the change of command and gave us his leadership philosophy. Then he asked each of us to write three things the company was doing well and three things that needed to be improved. I'm hopeful he will read our ideas and try to make changes to improve the morale of the unit," Roni said.

"Sounds like he's a breath of fresh air compared to the old commander."

"I hope so; say, have you heard the rumor that Scott got married to that gal he was dating?"

"Yeah, Maura told me about it the other day. She saw their announcement in the paper."

Slightly relieved, Roni continued, "I thought you might be upset they got married. I know you really liked him."

"I thought I loved Scott, but I'm so much happier with Tom. Tom's the real deal. He's not as cute as Scott, but he has real character and treats me with respect. I couldn't be happier. I wish Scott and Janet well." Lori continued, "Besides, Scott and his new wife dated in high school and were dating for over a year before they got married. I knew Scott was more excited about her than me when I overheard him call her *hon* on the telephone."

"That must have crushed you. If George two-timed me I'd pull his hair out and cut off his balls."

"I can almost see you doing that Roni… I was shocked and completely unaware Scott had another girlfriend. I think that's why I was depressed for a few months. I just didn't see it coming. Well, enough about that….Reggie called me from her MP training at McClellan last night when you were out with George. She's sailing through the last few weeks of the course. She'll be here in two weeks."

"That'll be perfect. I'm moving into a new apartment with George next week and my room will be cleaned up when she gets here. It'll be great both of you can share the apartment together."

"Have you told your parents about moving in with George?" Lori asked.

"Naw, they don't care who I live with as long as I'm happy. Besides, they know how crazy I am about him and they met him last month over Labor Day weekend. Why? Would your parent's freak out if you and Tom were living together?"

"Yeah, my parents are very conservative and religious. They want me to be married or at least engaged before I start living with a guy and because I was raised that way. I feel that way too."

"I get that. I have this feeling George and I will be getting married sooner than later. I'm just crazy about him and if he doesn't ask me in the next month, I'm gonna ask him to marry me!"

Lori grinned. "George doesn't stand a chance Roni. You've always been very focused when you decide to go after something you really want."

24

FORT BRAGG, NC, SATURDAY, 21 NOVEMBER, 1981

MAURA WAS STARTLED AWAKE by both the phone ringing and Eric drowsily mumbling, "Hullo?"

It took Maura a second to remember she was at Eric's for the weekend. Turning to look at him, Maura saw his face go from sleepy disorientation, to intense concentration, as he immediately sat up and swung his feet onto the cold wood floor. "Do you have the police report?" she heard him ask tersely. Getting up, she put on the robe she used when she spent a weekend with him and went to the bathroom. When she returned, Eric was hurriedly getting dressed.

"Should I go home and you'll call me when you get back in town?" Maura asked quietly, as she sat down on the edge of the bed.

Eric pulled his shirt over his head and kissed her as he sat down on the bed with her. "No, that was the commander. He got a call from our duty officer, who told him the cops reported they found one of our guys dead in his house. Details are sketchy, but I'm gonna meet the commander at the soldiers house and figure out what's goin' on. You go back to sleep. Not sure when I'll get back, but can't imagine this taking more than a few hours." He got up, grabbed his wallet from the top of the dresser and walked out.

Maura sat on the bed contemplating whether or not to lay back down. Accepting that Eric was subject to no notice deployment and couldn't talk to her about it or let her know when he would return, she was relieved that he wasn't being deployed; but was unnerved by his revelation that one of his soldiers was dead and the police were involved. Maura realized she was too wired to go back to sleep, so she took a shower and got dressed. Walking out to the living room, she saw the new Steven King novel, *Cujo* that she had started reading a few weeks ago. She generally loved anything written by Stephen King, but this particular book was particularly graphic and unsettling and given what Eric had just told her, she wasn't sure if she should read it right now. Silently admonishing herself that this was fiction and she'd brought the book over this weekend because she was dying to see how it ended, she walked into the kitchen to fix coffee and planned to spend the day sitting in Eric's recliner reading.

★ ★ ★

MAURA AWOKE TO THE smell of Eric's breath and the caress of his lips on hers. She opened her eyes and lifted her arms out to stretch, as he drew away and announced. "True loves kiss, awakens the sleeping princess." Picking up the open book lying on her lap, he looked at the title and admonished her. "Reading this shit will rot your brains."

Sitting up, Maura reached for the copy of *Foreign Affairs* lying on a nearby end table. "I can only read so much of this stuff," and laid the periodical back down as she brought the recliner back to sitting position and stood up. Taking the book from Eric's hand, she put her bookmark on the open page, closed the book and laid it back on the table. "What time is it?"

"Just after eight."

"Have you eaten breakfast?"

"No, why?"

"Why don't you go take a shower? I'll fix fresh coffee, eggs, sausage and toast, and we can sit down and talk about what happened."

Taking Maura by her waist, he drew her next to him. She grinned, as she felt his erection and he asked, "How about taking a shower together and eating breakfast afterwards?" Maura responded by taking his hand and walked towards the master bedroom.

★ ★ ★

NEVER HAVING MADE IT to the shower, Eric kissed Maura as he rolled off of her, onto his back and simultaneously rolled her into his chest, whispering, "I love you."

Maura looked up surprised by his unexpected declaration of love. "What happened?" she asked in a concerned tone.

"One of our detachment commanders is dead. The cops took the commander and me into the house. He was lying on his back in bed, with bullet holes in his forehead and chest."

"Do they know what happened? Was anyone else shot?"

"No one else was shot and the cops told us that his wife told them she woke up to the sound of gunfire and an intruder turning around and running out the bedroom door."

Maura rolled off Eric's chest and sat up. "Is she okay?" Maura asked anxiously.

"That's the part that has us and the police questioning her claims," Eric said tersely as he sat up and got out of bed. Maura got up as well, as he continued, "She wasn't shot and can't explain why the intruder didn't shoot, let alone kill her. The shots that killed our guy were fired at point blank range. All the intruder had to do was shoot her in the forehead and there'd be no witness to his act."

"Did you know him well?"

"Yeah. He was drafted in '73, decided to apply for OCS and the degree completion program in '77. After OCS, he went to the 'Q' course and his first assignment, which is when I met him. He was scheduled to change command next month." Shaking his head in disbelief, he added, "He'd come out on both the major's list and the CGSC list earlier this year. When I took him out for lunch as a way of showing how proud I was of him, he confided to me that he'd told branch he needed to get out of SF and wanted to apply for Defense Language school for Russian and a Foreign Area Officer additional specialty." Turning to look at her, Maura saw the pain of loss, in his eyes. She wanted to reach out and hug him, but knew him well enough, to know that if she did that, he would probably stop talking, so she just sat there quietly, until he continued. "When I asked him why, he told me the requirement to leave our families in the dark about anything we do, had taken a serious toll on his marriage and he suspected his wife was cheating on him. He figured a year at the staff college, followed by a year at DLI in Monterey, would allow them to get back on track and being a brand new field grade Russian FAO, would probably get him an assignment somewhere in D.C. where he couldn't talk about what he did, but his wife wouldn't worry every morning that he might not come home that night and wouldn't know where he was, or if he would even make it back home alive."

Putting his arms on Maura's shoulders, Eric's eyes locked on hers as he asked, "If I were to ask you to marry me, could you handle my never being able to talk to you about what I do and never knowing if I'll come home that evening or ever, until I walk in the door, acting like nothing unusual happened and just pick up, where we'd left off?"

Surprised by Eric's earlier verbal admission of love and the unexpected change in narrative, Maura wasn't quite sure how to respond and decided to use humor to give her a chance to figure out what was really going on and how to respond. "Is that your idea of a proper marriage proposal?" She asked playfully.

Not expecting that reply, Eric paused before saying uncertainly, "What would you say, if it was?"

Laughing, Maura shook her head in admonition. "You don't get off that easily. You either are, or are not asking me to marry you. No guts, no glory, soldier!"

Eric replied with a thundering laugh. "You don't ever give an inch do you?" followed by a look of acceptance and peace, before quietly announcing, "If you can handle the secrecy and uncertainty of the specialty that I've chosen, I am."

Maura gave him a piercing glance and replied musingly. "I was beginning to wonder if you would ever ask." Seeing the look of hurt and surprise on his face, she held up her hand. "This is only the second time you've actually said those words out loud to me. I never doubted you love me, but there were parts of you that never let me, or anyone else in, which caused me to wonder if you could commit to marriage. I'm not really comfortable with your reluctance to open up to me emotionally, or let your guard down; but I know what I'm getting into, love you beyond distraction, and yes, I can and do."

Relieved, Eric asked in a teasing tone, "Guess I can't back out now, can I?" as he took her in his arms and rolled her back into bed.

25

NEW YORK CITY, 25 DECEMBER, 1981

BECAUSE OF THE DEMANDS of being in command, Maura and Eric had decided to wait until Christmas Eve to fly home to her parents for the holidays. She had told her parents they wouldn't land at LaGuardia until after 10 in the evening. Her mom told her it didn't matter how late they arrived, just call when they landed and they would pick them up. Maura and Eric chose to take a cab to her parents. Maura used the house key her mom insisted on her keeping, and when they walked into the apartment, they found both her parents asleep in their chairs, with the TV blaring loudly. Maura put her finger to her mouth, tiptoed to the TV to turn it off and motioned Eric to follow her. When they'd entered her bedroom, Maura closed the door and whispered, "If we're quiet we can go to the bathroom, unpack and go straight to sleep without waking them up."

"Shouldn't we wake them up so they can sleep comfortably in their bed?" Eric asked.

"We can." Maura replied. "But then we'll have to put up with mom fussing at us and insisting she fix us something to eat, so we can catch up.

We'll be forced to tell her that we're engaged, and it'll be at *LEAST* seven in the morning, before we get to bed. I'm exhausted and just want to sleep. I'd rather write a note, tape it to the TV screen, letting them know we're asleep in my room and see them in the morning." Eric grinned knowingly and taking that as agreement, Maura went over to the small desk in the corner, took out a sheet of paper and tape from one of the side drawers, wrote the note and quietly tiptoed out to living room. Returning, she quietly closed the door and ten minutes later, they were sound asleep.

★ ★ ★

MAURA AND ERIC OPENED the bedroom door and seeing no one, quickly made a beeline to the bathroom. On their way back to her bedroom to change from their robes into clothing, they encountered her father, who put his finger to his mouth and indicated they should follow him into Maura's bedroom. Closing the door, he quietly admonished them. "While I'm glad I didn't have to wake up and drive to LaGuardia last night, you are both in big trouble with mom."

Maura reached out to hug and kiss her dad. "We can handle it dad. I love mom, but after a very long and tiring day, the thought of several hours of answering never ending questions and eating food we didn't want, was more than either of us could handle. "

"I get it Maura, but with both you and your brother out of the house and you only coming home once a year, she goes overboard; because she loves and misses you."

"I get it dad. I love her too, I'll apologize to her and let her fuss at me for a bit."

"I've had to endure listening to her rant and rave about you not calling us, or waking us up, so we could get changed and in bed." He couldn't help laughing as he added, "I didn't even get a cheery Merry Christmas, let alone a good morning kiss from her…" but added philosophically, "I did get coffee and she's in the kitchen cooking breakfast. She told me to knock loudly on your door and tell you to get your lazy butt up and come to breakfast."

Maura opened the bedroom door and turned to Eric, "Let's go take our punishment and beg forgiveness."

★ ★ ★

MAURA WALKED UP TO her mother, who had her back to them and was bent over as she prepared to take the biscuits out of the oven. "Merry Christmas mom!" Maura announced gaily, grabbing her mother's waist and giving a hearty hug.

Turning around to face Maura, her mom had an angry glare on her face for just a second, before she started crying and hugged Maura exclaiming, "I'm very angry with you young lady." Pushing Maura back so she could look at her, she scolded, "So, what do you have to say for yourself?"

"I love you mom, but you and dad were sleeping so peacefully and we were so exhausted; I thought it best, to just let you sleep, until you woke up and found the note I thoughtfully wrote to both of you, telling you I love you, we were home safe, sweet dreams and see you in the morning."

"Uh huh, smarty pants…did you rehearse that before getting up this morning?" Mrs. Collins asked in a mock stern tone of voice.

"Nope ma," Maura responded playfully. "Eric came up with the words." Turning to look at Eric, Maura bent over double in uncontrollable laughter at the sight of the look on his face at her false admission. Turning back to her mom, she gasped in between laughs. "Sorry ma, yeah, you know me, I'm just a natural smart aleck, but I do love you and I apologize if I hurt your feelings. Can we make up and enjoy our week together? I have so many things to tell you and dad." Without waiting for an answer, Maura pointed to the covered skillets. "I'll get serving platters for the eggs, sausage, and biscuits." Turning to her dad and Eric, she instructed, "Could you guys put the coffee pot on the table, so we can all sit down, and eat this wonderful meal mom has made?"

★ ★ ★

HAVING JUST FINISHED GIVING thanks for the safe return of Maura and Eric and his wonderful wife who had prepared this amazing feast, Mr. Collins picked up the platter of eggs and handed them to Eric. "You're our guest, you go first Eric." Maura grabbed the coffee pot and started pouring coffee into hers, Eric's, then her mom and dad's cups.

After swallowing his first bite of food, Eric addressed Mrs. Collins. "Wow, this is great, thanks and Merry Christmas!"

Nodding approvingly Mrs. Collins looked over at Maura, who had just taken a sip of coffee, but hadn't touched a bite of her food yet. "What are you waiting for? Your food'll get cold." she admonished.

Maura immediately picked up a sausage in her hand and took a bite. "Great ma!"

Mrs. Collins responded with a look of reproach and Maura put her sausage link back on the plate, picked up her fork and took a bite of egg, followed by a bite of her still warm biscuit, and repeated with a mouthful of food, "Mmm Yummy," as she reached for her knife and started cutting the remaining sausage link into bite size pieces. Before Mrs. Collins could say anything else, Eric, who had never seen this side of Maura or her mom before, had been trying not to burst out laughing and coughed loudly as the coffee he'd just swallowed, went down the wrong side of his throat. Grabbing frantically for his napkin, he put his hand up indicating he was okay, but Maura grinned at the look of pure amusement in his eyes and took the attention off of him by addressing her mother in a sincere and loving tone. "Mom, it really is good to be home and thanks for the wonderful breakfast. When we're finished eating, Eric and I have some news we want to share with you."

Mrs. Collins gasped, "Maura Collins, you will tell me right now!"

Feeling a combination of frustration and amusement, Maura first looked at her dad for help and seeing no support there, she turned her gaze to Eric, who nodded 'yes' to her questioning look. Maura held up her left hand, while twisting the huge diamond on her engagement ring that she had turned into her palm, to the front of her ring finger."

Grabbing Maura's hand, Mrs. Collins shrieked. "Oh my God!" Then looked heavenward, clasping her hands in prayer. "Thank you Lord!" and got up to hug Maura as Mr. Collins held out his hand to Eric, "Congratulations son, you have no idea what you've gotten yourself into, but I guarantee you, life will never be dull."

Eric returned the shake, and barely got out, "Thanks sir, It's okay, I know what I'm getting into," before Mrs. Collins came over and gleefully hugged him.

26

FORT BRAGG, NC, JANUARY 1982

"THIS FIELD EXERCISE SUCKS ma'am," Lori's female admin sergeant said, shivering in the cold as they walked to the mess tent for lunch.

"Yes, it does, but as soldiers we need to operate in all kinds of weather conditions," Lori replied.

"That's not what I'm upset about ma'am," Sergeant Strayer said.

"Oh, so what sucks?"

"I'm torqued off because I'm expected to make and get the coffee and I'm not the junior enlisted working in the ops tent."

Lori asked, "Do you think you're being singled out to make the coffee because you're a woman?"

"I'd say yes. I don't think it's fair. SPC Miller can make the coffee; he's junior to me and I don't even drink coffee!"

"Sounds like you have a legitimate gripe. Let me talk with Master Sergeant Rungle and see if I can't smooth this out. Is everything else going okay Sergeant Strayer?"

"Yes, ma'am, not too bad. I miss my two year old, but my husband can handle him for a week."

"That's good to hear. Let me know if anything else needs my attention and I'll be sure to talk to MSG Rungle today about your issue."

"Thanks ma'am. I appreciate it."

★ ★ ★

LORI APROACHED HER OPS Sergeant at the conclusion of the afternoon battle meeting. "Master Sergeant Rungle, could I speak with you a moment?"

"Sure ma'am, what's up?"

"Sergeant Strayer seems to think she has to make the coffee because she's a woman. Is there a reason why she's making the coffee for the ops cell rather than SPC Miller?"

Perplexed, Rungle responded, "Why no. I thought she wouldn't mind making the coffee every morning. I didn't think about it too much."

"Well, since she doesn't drink coffee and SPC Miller drinks coffee and is junior in rank, I think you may want to reconsider who makes the coffee."

"Sure thing ma'am. I appreciate the G2. Again, I didn't think it was a big deal but I didn't know Strayer doesn't drink coffee. I'll change the coffee making duty tomorrow morning. And while I have your ear, I think someone might want to go out and check the TCPs. I get a feeling something is not right out there. I'm having trouble getting a few teams on the radio."

"I will go check on them and see what the issue is," Lori replied.

"Thanks ma'am. I'll handle it for a few hours while you're out. You might take SPC Miller with you."

"Good idea. If he's ready to go, have him meet me at the ¼ ton jeep in 5 minutes," Lori said. She turned around, left the tactical operations tent and pulled her maps out and put them on top of the jeep. As she scouted the topography, distances, and location of the MP tactical control points, SPC Miller arrived. "Good afternoon ma'am."

Lori looked up from her map, "Hi SPC Miller. You ready to be the navigator? I have my SF 46 military license and I need some field driving practice."

"Sure ma'am, I'm happy to get out of the tent for a while."

Lori drove to the location of the first TCP and noticed two MPs were sitting in their ¼ ton observing the bridge. Stopping the vehicle she said, "Let's go see what's up," while getting out of the vehicle.

The MP soldiers saw 1LT Nelson approaching their vehicle and they put on their helmets and stepped out of their vehicle. The senior MP saluted Lori and said, "Hello ma'am."

Lori returned the salute. "How's it going out here guys?"

"Fine ma'am. Nothing to report at this time."

"I heard you missed reporting your last Sitrep. Is there a reason for that?" Lori asked.

"Yes, ma'am, our radio's not working. The platoon sergeant is trying to get another one for us, but I don't know how long that will take," the senior MP said.

"How long has your radio been down?"

"About 3 hours now. I expected SSG Brown to be here with a replacement any time," he said.

"It doesn't make sense to have a TCP without comms. What will you do if you see action near the bridge?" Lori asked.

"Ma'am, we'd high-tail it out of here and go to company headquarters and report the incident."

"Okay, thanks for the info. I'll track down your missing radio. Stay alert and stay warm." Lori said before returning to her vehicle.

Lori started driving in the direction of the Command Post and while on a long straight-away she decided to go a little faster. As she glanced to the left, she did not see the large ruts in the dirt road. SPC Miller grabbed the windshield and yelled, "Oh Shit!" as the jeep went airborne and flew a few feet in the air. Upon landing, SPC Miller's helmet flew off onto the road. Surprised, Lori slowed down and stopped the vehicle. "Whoa ma'am! That was fun," SPC Miller said smiling and getting out of the jeep to retrieve his helmet.

"Well it wasn't intentional," Lori said while looking in her rearview mirror; noticing another ¼ ton approaching her vehicle. "We've got company. I hope it's the platoon sergeant with the radio."

As the vehicle approached, Lori recognized the passenger as the battalion commander. *Oh shit*, she thought. She got out of her vehicle for her expected ass-chewing. She saluted LTC Martin after he stepped out of the door. "Good afternoon Sir," Lori said.

"Lieutenant Nelson, what are you doing?"

"Sir. I'm practicing driving. I'm embarrassed I did not see the rut in time to avoid it," Lori replied getting red in the face.

Trying to contain his smile, LTC Martin said, "Yes, well, you need some more practice. So, where are you going?"

"Sir, I'm trying to track down a radio for TCP Mike. They're without comms."

"I just heard that and they should be receiving a replacement radio within the hour. So, how's the exercise going?"

"So far, so good, Sir. It's a great training opportunity for our soldiers and we're improving our command and control at the headquarters."

"Well, good," turning and looking at SPC Miller, LTC Martin added, "You learning anything out here?"

"Yes Sir. I learn something new every day."

"Good. Stay alert, stay alive," LTC Martin said as he sat back down into his seat and his driver drove down the dirt road.

★ ★ ★

THREE DAYS LATER, LORI was in her apartment talking with her roommate. "That field exercise was so cold I thought I'd never thaw out."

"What? My friend from Minnesota was too cold?" Reggie teased.

"Just 'cuz I'm from Duluth doesn't mean I like the cold. I mean, I like skiing, snowmobiling, and ice skating for a day, but to stay out in the snow and cold for over a week in a tent isn't my idea of a fun time."

"Yeah. I don't like the cold either. How was your Christmas leave?"

"It was perfect. I slept in every day, my mom waited on me like a princess, I saw all my high school friends, although there's fewer every year that aren't married, and I went to the high school gym every other day and played pick-up basketball."

"Did you go skiing?"

"Ya, I did, but only one time. My ankle was sore after about 2 hours. I guess it hasn't healed completely from my bad sprain."

"That sucks."

"Yes it does! I thought the ski boot would provide stability and I only went down the easy hills but I guess you move your ankle more than you know when you ski. So how was your Christmas?"

Reggie replied, "It was good. I hadn't been home since graduation leave and my parents, grandma, Kim, and all the in-laws were so happy to see me. I felt like a celebrity; it was weird."

"What'd they ask you?"

"You know, the relatives ask the same type of questions we had when we were cadets, what do ya do in the Army? Do you like wearing a uniform? Why'd you pick military police? Are there cute guys to go out with? They also asked me what I thought about the new Supreme Court Justice, Sandra Day O'Connor, since she's the first one President Reagan appointed."

"What did you say about her?"

"I was honest and told them I've been so busy with my new job, I haven't stayed up with current events. Then they gave me an earful."

Smiling Lori said, "Oh ya, sounds just like my relatives. I am happy there finally is a female in the Supreme Court. About time if you ask me!"

"True…progress is slow but it's a coming."

"Guess what! Trish actually sent me a letter from Korea saying she's finally arriving at Fort Lewis next month. Maybe we can get together for spring break and we'll have the old gang back in place."

"That would be cool Lori. Where should we go?"

"I'd like to meet in Florida but Las Vegas would be closer for Trish and Julie."

"Good idea. Let's try to make it happen."

★ ★ ★

ON FEBRUARY 6, 1982 Lori, Reggie, Maura, and Anne were in a New York City church for Roni and George's wedding. Cate and Jim had flown in for the week from Hawaii to attend the ceremony.

Thirty minutes before the ceremony Roni was alone with Lori in her dressing room and confessed, "I'm not sure I should be doing this."

"Are you nuts! You asked George to marry you! I know you love each other. What's the problem?" Lori asked.

"This is for life and a huge commitment," Roni whined. "Plus, I've got all those people out there, its kinda nerve-wracking."

Lori smiled and said, "You'll love being married to George once the ceremony is over. Your dark curls look spectacular against your white satin lace dress. Relax Roni, you're gorgeous and everyone out there are either relatives or very close friends who love you just as you are and only want you to be happy. You can do this."

"Yeah." Roni replied tentatively, then exclaimed, "But shit, this is so crazy. I've never felt my stomach jump around like this before and I'm not comfortable being in the limelight."

"This is a once-in-a-lifetime event and it's understandable you're a little nervous. I know I'd be if I were in your shoes."

"Thanks Lori," Roni said quietly. "You're right. No reason to be nervous, George is the only man for me and we're going to be deliriously happy."

Smiling Lori took Roni's hand. "That's what maids-of-honor are for. Come on, it's show-time."

27

TANGIER ISLAND, VA, SATURDAY, 3 JULY 1982

AMELIA AND CHARLES WALKED into the kitchen and finding it empty, Amelia looked out the sliding glass doors leading to the deck. Amelia slid the glass door open announcing, "There they are." Walking out to the deck, Amelia cheerfully greeted, Anne, Derek, Maura and Eric, as Charles followed behind. "Good morning!"

Anne responded to Amelia's greeting, "Mornin' sleepy heads." motioning her and Charles to join them at the table, as the remainder of the group stood up to greet them. Anne hugged Amelia and nodded at Charles. "Amelia, you know everyone at the table except for Derek."

"Nice to meet you Amelia," Derek responded. "I've heard a lot of nice things about you and glad you and Charles could join us for the holidays this year." At the mention of Charles' name, Derek gave a curt nod of recognition to Charles and immediately turned his attention back to Amelia. "Maura and Anne were very disappointed that you couldn't make it last year."

In the hope that neither Charles, nor anyone else had taken note of Derek not walking over to shake hands with Charles, as was his usual custom, Anne hurriedly added. "Charles, I'm sure you remember Maura from the wedding and this is Eric, her fiancée." Taking a cue from Derek, Maura and Eric, cheerfully greeted Charles and Amelia, but Eric did not move forward to shake Charles' hand as Anne pointed to the two empty chairs at the table.. "C'mon, join us. We've got lots of coffee and when you're ready to eat, I'll take you back to the kitchen. I have a large bowl of fruit salad, and pastries for you."

Amelia was keenly aware of the less than exuberant welcome Charles had received from the group as she and Charles sat down. Maura handed the coffee pot to Amelia, who poured a cup for Charles, then herself. There was complete silence as Amelia and Charles poured sugar and cream into their coffee and took a sip. "I needed that," Charles said as he exhaled loudly.

"Thanks for leaving the key in the mailbox last night. We didn't get here until well after midnight and didn't want to wake you guys, just to let us in." Amelia said as she looked up from her coffee cup.

"Yes, and thanks for the great directions," Charles added. "After working all day and the two hour delay in our flight from Atlanta, I was relieved to find the rental car desk at the airport still open. They gave us a map, but told us we had to hurry if we wanted to catch the last ferry over to the island."

"Yeah, we went to bed, thinking you'd missed the last ferry and would call us in morning," Derek responded.

"Well, the DA wasn't keen on my taking any time off this summer because our caseload is so high; but Amelia made it very clear that missing spending the holidays with you guys two years in row, was not acceptable, so I got as much time off, as I could, but just could not convince my boss to let us spend a whole week here

Anne asked, "Would you guys like some breakfast now or would you rather wait?"

Charles didn't hesitate. "Breakfast sounds great. We didn't eat supper last night and we're both starvin'."

Amelia took her coffee cup and stood up. "I'll root around in the fridge and fix breakfast for the two of us. Would anyone else like anything?"

"No. We ate around an hour ago," Anne said. "But I'll come in with you, to help. We can catch up a bit, while the guys get to know each other." Anne looked over at Maura, "Wanna join us?" Maura nodded and as the three women headed to the kitchen, they heard Charles ask, "So guys, Amelia warned me that you might not be able to tell me exactly what you do in the military aside from killing people; but I'd be interested in hearing whatever you can tell me

"Oh my Lord!" Amelia gasped once the three of them were in the kitchen and the patio door was closed. "I told Charles to make an effort to get to know the guys and ask them questions about themselves and what they do, instead of talking about himself....she paused. "I know how ya'll feel about him, but he really is trying," she added plaintively.

"I hear ya Amelia, we warned the guys about Charles and told them to be nice." Amelia nodded resignedly before asking, "Could I make eggs, bacon and biscuits? Fruit salad and pastries are fine for me, but Charles eats the same thing for breakfast every mornin'."

"Reaching under the counter for a frying pan, Anne pointed to the refrigerator, "The bacon, eggs, butter and jelly are in the fridge. Maura, can you get the biscuits out of the freezer?"

The three men looked up and stopped talking as the women returned to the deck with a fresh pot of coffee and the food. Anne put the tray at the end of the table where Amelia and Charles were sitting and set out the coffee pot, butter, jelly, and a large plate of steaming hot biscuits in the middle. Amelia handed Charles a plate with three eggs over easy and bacon, put her plate in front of her and reached for the coffee pot to refill her coffee cup, as she sat down.

Charles immediately reached for a biscuit, slathering it with butter; then breaking open one of the egg yolks, he lifted his egg filled fork to his mouth, followed by a large bite of the biscuit in his other hand. Mumbling contentedly, he proceeded to devour the food on his plate. Amelia lifted the plate of biscuits, proffering them to Derek and Eric. Anne took the plate from Amelia. "I'll pass this to the guys after you take yours Amelia." Amelia took a biscuit and started to eat her breakfast. Derek and Eric gleefully reached for the biscuits and there was blissful silence as they drank coffee and enjoyed the fresh biscuits. Charles had swallowed the last bite of biscuit and bacon and after he finished of the coffee in his cup, he announced, "Thanks ladies, that was fantastic." Looking at Amelia, he leaned over, took her hand, and turned to the four friends, who were racking their brains for a way to start a new conversation. "I apologize for my lack of manners, but I was absolutely starved and once I got that first delicious bite, I just couldn't stop. Looking at all three women, he added, "Thank you, I really appreciate it."

Trying to put everyone at ease, Derek waved his hand dismissively. "We've been there man." Pointing to Eric, Derek added, "There've been a few missions where we didn't eat or sleep for twenty or more hours and when we got some food and coffee, anyone who'd have gotten in the way of us filling our bellies at that moment, would have been risking life and limb."

Both Amelia and Anne shot Derek a look of thanks for making light of the situation and Eric addressed Charles. "So, now that you know a bit about what we do, tell us what you do and why you started working in the D.A.'s office instead of going to a large law firm."

Charles leaned back, languidly explaining, "Tuscaloosa doesn't have big fancy firms like Atlanta, Boston, or other large cities and my dad is a federal judge, who started his career in the D.A.'s office and has mentored me all my life. I'm the youngest DA in the history of the office and this was the path he put me on. I just never considered any other options."

"I get that." Derek responded. "My dad mentored me as well, and while I didn't follow his plan exactly, I never considered doing anything except being a military officer. So you're a prosecutor and you want to be a federal judge?"

"No," Charles replied cautiously. "My dad has lots of connections and he told me to make a name for myself in the D.A.'s office and get involved in local politics."

"So how does one do that and what's the end game?" Eric asked.

Charles hesitated, "I wouldn't normally discuss that, but y'all are Amelia's friends and have no interest in Alabama politics, so I guess I can speak frankly, but have to ask that everything discussed here be kept in strictest confidence."

"Okay." Derek and Eric said simultaneously, as the three women made eye contact and wondered where this conversation was headed.

"A year after I was assigned as a prosecutor, the lead assistant D.A. was diagnosed with brain cancer and was dead seven months later. The D.A. came to me shortly after the diagnosis and said he and my dad agreed that in addition to my current case load, he was going to suggest to the assistant D.A. that he turn some of his day to day supervisory tasks over to me, so he could concentrate on getting better. That set me up to fill his position when he passed. The original plan was to have me take over as D.A. when the current D.A. got elected to Congress; but he became been the subject of a criminal investigation and went to prison two years ago. I took over and was elected in my own right, last year. I've done well enough, that my dad has already started the process of getting me nominated as the Republican candidate for governor next year.

After a short period of stunned silence, Derek mused, "Okay, so you're the D.A., you'll run for governor next year and you really think you have a good shot at being elected even though you're still in your 30s?"

Charles didn't hesitate. "No doubt about it. After a successful term as governor, I'll be positioned to put my hat in the ring to run for the United States Senate."

Amelia abruptly stood up and started clearing dishes. "Enough Charles, we're here to relax. We leave on Monday morning and I want a break from all this political intrigue." Softening her tone, Amelia looked at Maura and Anne. "Didn't you say something about a boat ride today?"

"Yes." Derek answered. "We'll drive to the marina at noon. Anne has sandwiches and drinks ready to go in the cooler."

Having put everything on the tray, Amelia picked it up and started walking back to the house. "Wonderful. Charles, please open the door for me. I'll help Maura and Anne clean up the kitchen. You can take a shower and I'll take mine after you."

Charles nodded and got up. Derek and Eric said a shower sounded good to them as well. The three women were cleaning up the kitchen when Anne blurted out, "Okay Amelia, what's goin' on?"

Amelia retorted defensively, "Nothin's '*goin' on.*"

Anne backed off. "We talk several times a month and you never mentioned Charles taking over as D.A. let alone running for governor. Are you okay with it and if yes, when were you going to tell us?"

"I didn't plan to tell any of you, any of this!" Amelia blurted out. "I just wanted to have some fun, spend some quality time with the two of you and have Charles spend time with the guys."

Confused, Maura asked, "Then why did you abruptly stop Charles and banish him to the bathroom?"

"Charles can talk about himself forever!" Anne exclaimed. "I figured everyone had listened to Charles long enough and it was time to go have some fun. Simple as that!"

"Whoa, Amelia, calm down," Maura advised, as she put her arm around Amelia. "Your life is so different from ours and staying connected takes effort. We're interested in what you guys are doing and you're the one that asked us to give Charles a chance to prove he's changed. The only way to do that, is to chat with him and let him be himself."

"Yeah," Anne rejoined as she put her arm around Amelia on the other side. "Charles will never like me, so if he monopolizes the conversation or activities, we can handle that. Now promise us you'll relax and enjoy our time together."

"Sure." Amelia demurred. I guess I'm just nervous because I want all of you to like him and for us to be comfortable together, when circumstances allow us to be together.... Charles and I have some news we want to share with all of you. Is the plan still to grill something for dinner and eat here tonight?" When Anne nodded yes, Amelia relaxed and announced, "Fine. I'm gonna take a shower and change. See you in a bit," and walked out of the kitchen.

★ ★ ★

THAT EVENING AFTER DINNER everyone moved over to the row of Adirondack chairs with their drinks to watch the beautiful sunset. Before sitting down, Charles motioned Amelia to join him and lifted his wine glass. "We want to thank you for a fantastic afternoon on the bay. I didn't realize we were going to catch our dinner and I can't wait to develop the pictures of me actually catching a fish."

Derek raised his glass "You're very welcome and I'm glad you enjoyed the fresh catch, because we'll be doing this again tomorrow night."

Charles nodded and put his arms around Amelia as he addressed Anne. "Anne, I know things have not gone well between you and I for many years now; so I want to publicly apologize to you, for any hurt I have caused you. I'm ready to bury the hatchet and hope you are too."

Everyone just looked at Charles in stunned silence as Amelia quickly added. "Anne, I know you have it in you and I know you know how much it took for Charles to do this."

This elicited a smirk from Charles, who walked over to Anne and held out his hand. "I really mean it. Truce?" All Anne could do was nod 'yes' and extend her hand to Charles, who pulled her out of her chair and brought her over to where Amelia was standing.

Amelia took Anne's hand and looked up at Charles expectantly. Charles quietly asked,

"Anne, would you do us the honor of agreeing to be godmother to our first child?"

Anne's jaw dropped as she asked uncertainly, "You mean, when you get pregnant?"

Amelia laughed. "No silly, I'm already two months pregnant and your godchild will be here in seven months. I'm hoping all of you will be able to take leave and attend the baptism."

Still unable to talk, Anne just nodded 'yes' again. Charles turned to Derek. "We know you are only engaged, but with the certainty that you will be married sometime in the future. We are hoping you will agree to be the godfather. I know you don't know us and you're not Catholic, so may not understand just how important being a godparent is. You don't have to answer us right now, just discuss it with Anne, she knows how this works and will let us know when you've made you decision."

Maura was the first one to regain her composure as she stood and proposed a toast. "Congratulations Charles and Amelia. We are so happy for both of you and once all of us get over the shock of this wonderful, but unexpected announcement, I know we will all find a way to be at the baptism and Anne and I will just have to figure out a way to make at least one of the baby showers, we're sure your friends and family will throw for you."

Everyone raised their glasses and gave a resounding, "Hear, hear!"

28

LAS VEGAS, NEVADA, JULY 1982

THE HIGHLY ANTICIPATED REUNION in Las Vegas was finally happening. Trish and Julie, who had flown in from Seattle and El Paso respectively, ran into each other at the airport and shared a taxi to the Rivera hotel, where Lori and Reggie were anxiously waiting to greet them.

The first thing Trish and Julie heard upon entering the cavernous lobby was Lori yelling their names, followed by Lori and Reggie coming up to greet them. "Great to see you guys! Can you believe it's been 2 years since we've all been together?"

Trish hugged Lori first and asked incredulously, "Has it been that long? Wow!"

"Great to see you Reggie!" Julie exclaimed, returning Reggie's welcome hug.

After all hugs were exchanged, Reggie shook her head in wonderment. "My old basketball pals. It's so great to be together again."

"We're gonna have a great week in the city that never sleeps," Julie said excitedly.

"You betcha," Lori said. How 'bout you and Trish get registered and meet us in our room? We're in room 524 and I've got some rum and coke for old times' sake."

Trish smiled, "Cool. We'll be there as soon as we get registered and throw our bags in our room."

Trish and Julie knocked on the hotel room door just as Reggie finished her first rum and coke. As they entered the room, Reggie said, "Perfect timing, I'll fix your drinks and we'll all sit down and relax."

"Swell. I could use one. It's been a hell of a week," Trish said. "My ass-hole boss really goes out of his way to make my life as miserable as possible. He treats me like I'm the scum of the Earth."

"What's his problem?" Lori asked sympathetically.

"I reported in 3 months ago and he practically snarled at me when I met him. Told me the first woman in his company lasted only two months and he treats me like the scum of the earth. He doesn't think I should be in the army. He gave me the worst platoon in the company, told me my additional duties were supply officer, security officer, mail officer, and arms room officer. The problem is, I'm so busy with my platoon and all my additional duties, that I don't have time to do anything else. If I hadn't had a platoon in Korea and already been a security officer, I'm not sure I could have handled all his abuse."

"That really sucks Trish," Reggie said handing Trish and Julie their drinks. "I'm glad you were able to get leave this week. Lori told me you were worried about him approving your leave request, but I didn't know it was this bad."

"I never wanted to punch a guy so much in my life!" Trish exclaimed. "I've worked every day except Easter Sunday since I got to the unit. If he'd disapproved my leave, I just might have killed him." Trish took a large gulp of her rum and coke before adding, "Every other platoon leader got two weeks leave this summer, so he had to approve my leave request or risk an IG complaint. He's not stupid, he's actually quite cunning and knows exactly how much crap he can dish out without getting in trouble. To think I have another 9 months of hell until he changes command." Trish reflected glumly.

"Do you have any support in the unit?" asked Reggie.

"Sorta, a female lieutenant reported in three weeks ago and I've taken her under my wing; because he hates her too. My platoon sergeant can't believe all the crap I'm tasked with and he helps me a lot. He's been in the Army 10 years and told me Captain Jack is the worst commander he's ever seen. He's working hard to help me square away the platoon, since it's his platoon too."

"Wow, I thought my company commander was bad," Julie said. "Mine looks good in comparison. Is there any chance of moving to a different position?"

"Eventually, but not anytime soon," Trish said. "I have eight female soldiers in my platoon who've never had a female boss before. I'm their role-model and they depend on me to shield them from the commander, so it's not all bad. What about you Reggie? What's your job like?"

"Not too bad. I'm working in battalion ops until an MP platoon opens in the 65th MP Company next month. My boss is a major who doesn't talk much but seems okay. He's swamped with constantly putting out fires and last minute changes to the training schedule. The battalion commander is a dick, but luckily, we rarely see him. He doesn't even lead the monthly battalion runs because he has a P3 profile. The guys like me 'cuz I'm a good runner, but Lori might be getting screwed too."

"It's too early to tell," Lori reflected. The new CO is coming to us from battalion staff next month. Rumor is, he's very self-centered and a real flamer. If that's true, it'll be a tough transition from Captain Archibald, who is squared away and leads by example."

Trish responded thoughtfully, "Seems to me that finding good leaders in the Army, is a mixed bag. My CO in Korea was a good role model and treated me fairly. Then I got to Fort Lewis and get a guy who makes the upperclass hazes at the academy look nice."

"We did have some jerks at school," Julie acknowledged. "But nothing I've seen on active duty is as bad as what we went through plebe year. Academics were hard, but the hazing was nerve-wracking. If it weren't for the basketball team and you guys, I wouldn't have graduated."

"Ya," Lori agreed. "I thought we'd get a fair shake, but most of the guys just wanted us gone and were dumb enough to think we'd cry and go home if they hazed us enough."

Trish responded first. "They never considered that the more they hazed us, the more determined we were to graduate."

"Some considered all women as pleasure toys and airheads… well not their mothers of course," Lori remarked sarcastically. "Remember the women from the local colleges being bussed in for the monthly dances?"

"You got that right…" Julie said, "I still remember the cattle cars bringing the college gals to all the hops on Saturday nights. The guys were quietly mooing when the girls got off the busses but they couldn't get enough of them."

Lori recalled dryly, "I remember going to only one dance our plebe year at Cullum Hall and that was enough for me. It was so humiliating and besides, I had way more fun hanging out with you."

"Same here," Trish said as she looked at her empty glass and asked, "Anyone else need a refill?"

"We sure did have some fun times playing sports together. I would've quit plebe year if it weren't for you guys," Reggie said nostalgically as she handed Trish her glass for a refill. "I realize some of you had it harder than me, but all I really remember is screaming my plebe poop as loud as I could. Even after we were recognized, the guys in my company made my life miserable and I never felt like I belonged."

"You weren't alone…my company never included the female cadets in their activities, but made sure we pulled our fair share on the duty roster," Trish said.

"The cows were the worst," Lori thoughtfully remarked. "They were mad their *all boys club* had come to an end and took it out on us. We survived by trying not to stand out."

Julie smiled and said, "Well, I remember a few good times. How about our basketball trip to Indiana and all the road trips and team parties?"

"Don't forget our road trip to Florida. I had the best time on Spring break with you all," Reggie added.

"Oh ya! I loved the ocean and the beach, even if it was too cold to swim in," Lori said. "Remember all the drunk college kids getting wild and getting naked? That was so weird. I did like the pickup beach volleyball the last day we were there."

"I'll never get the Cat Stevens soundtrack out of my head. We must have played that 8-track 10 times on the way home," Trish added.

"Yeah, it was a great week. How 'bout we start a new great week here in Vegas? I wanna check out all these cool hotels," Julie said as the group finished their drinks and left the room.

★ ★ ★

THE VEGAS VACATION FLEW by for Lori and her West Point teammates. Despite losing all the money they'd set aside for gambling, they enjoyed touring the large hotels, eating at the lavish and inexpensive buffets, and seeing Wayne Newton's show on their last night together. After the show, Julie asked, "Everyone up for a few last drinks together? We still have the 2 for 1 drink coupons at the Flamingo. I thought we may as well use them before we fly back tomorrow."

"Good idea Julie. I could use a few more laughs before I go back to my hell-hole," Trish said.

Arriving at one of the casino piano bars, they sat down in a round booth and ordered their drinks. Lori asked Trish, "So what's going on besides your crappy boss? It can't all be bad."

"Well, that's true. I joined a community softball team and I love the gals on that team. The problem is sometimes I can't make the games or practices due to my hellacious work schedule. We're in a tough Seattle league but we should make it to the state championship and possibly nationals if we win state. That team really helps me keep my sanity."

"That's cool. I wish we had softball leagues, but even if we did, I'm too busy to play. I rarely get out of work before seven or eight at night," Lori said.

Julie added, "That sucks Lori. I usually get out by five or six. My boss believes in family time and recharging after a long day. He says, 'You're mine from 0600-1700 but then I want you to have a life,' I like that philosophy and it makes for better motivated soldiers."

Lori replied, "Yeah. My boss is good, but he's a workaholic and expects his XO to be there with him until he leaves for the day. The good news is he lets his platoon leaders run their platoon how they want to. I loved being a platoon leader with a more flexible schedule."

Reggie added, "My boss is okay. I never know how long we'll be working until that afternoon. Plus, we've been in the field a lot lately getting ready for our ARTEP, so any time off is good to me. This vacation has been really great, it'll be tough to go back to the long hours again."

"I'd love to play on a basketball or softball team but that'll have to wait until I'm a staff officer and have more free time," Lori added.

"I think it's more dependent on who your boss is." Trish said. "Some are idiots and think working long hours proves how loyal you are to your unit. My boss in Korea cared about his soldiers and their quality of life, even though most of us were unaccompanied. He respected us and gave us free time on the weekends when we weren't in the field. I learned so much from him on how to take care of soldiers. The jerk I have now is totally self-absorbed and only cares about his own OER and his own promotion. The soldiers despise him. They would frag him in a minute if we were in a warzone. Unfortunately, I'm learning what not to do from his poor leadership example."

Lori added, "That's a good thing about the Army Trish; wait a while and either you move or your boss moves. We have so many examples to learn from. Theories are one thing, but seeing the theory in action is another."

"Yeah true, but I don't like being part of the social studies science experiment. We get scrutinized every day purely due to our gender. It's not fair!" Julie added.

"True, but life's not fair and neither is the Army. You do your best and hopefully make changes in areas you *can* influence," Lori said.

"Man, Lori, you're too optimistic. I don't see women being accepted in the Army in the near future, if ever. As long as men rule the world, run the politics, and have the money, women will never get a fair shake. That's just the way it is!" Trish said.

Reggie disagreed. "I think we make our own environment. We have the ability to change things, even if the change is small. As a leader in the Army, we influence and reach many soldiers. Our actions and determination will go a long way in making change."

"Maybe you're right," Trish said. "I'm just not willing to wait decades to see the changes. I want change now!"

Lori lifted her glass in a toast, "I hear ya Trish!" and adroitly changed the subject. "So tell us about your new dog."

Trish's face lit up. "Her name is Wookie. She's a mutt; part lab, part poodle, and 100% adorable. I love her curly brown hair, her energy, and that wagging tail. Wookie's super smart and she's already trained. She even goes and retrieves the newspaper for me in the morning. How's that for cool!"

"Sweetness! So who's watching her this week and the weeks you're in the field?" Reggie asked.

"I trade dog-sitting time with my female sergeant and her husband. They have a cocker spaniel named Sammy. Wookie loves playing with Sammy when I'm gone. In two weeks, I'll be watching Sammy when they go on vacation. It's a lot cheaper and more humane than kenneling the dogs."

"That's cool. I'm not responsible enough to care for a dog. I have a fish, but my last fish only lasted a month….I'm hoping this one lasts longer than that!" Julie said as she finished her beer. "What time you guys flying back tomorrow?"

"Lori and I need to be at the airport by nine. How 'bout you?" Reggie asked.

"I'm not leaving 'til noon and Trish leaves at ten. You wanna meet for an early breakfast before you go?" Julie asked.

"Yes! Who knows when we'll be able to meet again? Let's meet at seven at the buffet," Lori said.

"Sounds great. Now how 'bout another round?" Trish said, motioning to the waitress.

29

FORT BRAGG, SEPTEMBER 1982

LORI WATCHED WITH TREPIDATION, as First Sergeant formed up the 82nd MP Company for the change of command ceremony in the field behind the company headquarters. Captain Luster was replacing Captain Archibald, Lori's boss for the last two years. Lieutenant Colonel Martin, the battalion commander, stood between the two captains as the company guidon was passed from the Company First Sergeant to Captain Archibald to LTC Martin, to Captain Luster. The soldiers were wearing their new battle dress uniform (BDUs) with their green and brown camouflaged woodland pattern with matching BDU caps and black spit-shined Cochran boots. The ceremony was uneventful and at the conclusion of the ceremony Captain Luster dismissed the Company. He strode up to Lori, looked her up and down as inspecting an item for purchase, and said, "Nelson, round up the platoon leaders, first sergeant, and platoon sergeants. I want to see all of you in my conference room in 30 minutes and bring your notebooks."

"Yes sir," Lori replied, as she quickly left to notify all the unit key leaders.

Thirty minutes later, the new commander and key leadership were in the unit conference room. "Okay troops. Sorry to take you away from the reception, but I want to hit the ground running. I want to let you know my leadership is much different from your *former* commander. I am not married so I can spend more time in the company area. I have very high standards and demand the same of you. I expect your best effort at all times in support of my priorities, so we will always look good!" scanning the assembled group at the conference table he continued, "After our 0600 PT, we will have our daily meeting here in the conference room at 0800 hours sharp. At the meeting I want you to brief your priorities for the day, suspense's, and any issues that need my attention. I also want a list of all overweight soldiers, soldiers on profile, or soldiers who cannot pass the APFT on my desk before close of business today. Any questions?" Not waiting for a response, he immediately said, "Good! Dismissed."

The first sergeant quickly spoke up, "Sir, most of the soldiers have families and they assumed they had the rest of the day off, like the other change of commands. Is that your intent?"

"No, bad assumption first sergeant. Everyone will work a full day today."

"Yes, Sir," the first sergeant replied and walked out the door to deliver the bad news to the company.

As Lori walked out the door to her office, she overheard SFC Adams talking to another platoon sergeant, "He's gonna be a bitch to work for."

★ ★ ★

LORI KNOCKED ON REGGIE'S bedroom door when she got in from her date with Tom. Reggie had just fallen asleep but opened her door and said, "Hey Lori, what's going on?"

"I really need to talk with you. I got some really shocking news this evening when I was with Tom. I still can't believe it."

"Okay, you got my attention. Spit it out!" Reggie said.

Lori sat down on Reggie's bed, tears started to cascade down her cheeks, she blubbered, "Tom told me. He told me… he has a boyfriend."

"What! You've got to be kidding me. How can that be? He's Special Forces for Pete's sake!"

"I don't know. I had no idea. He told me in the strictest confidence after I asked him why we couldn't be intimate."

"I'm so sorry Lori. I don't know what to say."

"I know....me too....who would have guessed? He's the nicest, toughest guy I know. I really love him. Why does this always happen to me Reggie? First Scott and now Tom."

Reggie walked over and gave Lori a big hug. "I don't know Lori, but I'm here for you."

Sniffling Lori looked at her roommate and said, "Thanks for always being here for me Reggie."

★ ★ ★

LORI HAD LOST 12 POUNDS. One night after work Reggie said, "Lori, don't tell me you're not hungry again. You look terrible. You must have lost 10 pounds in the last month. Your uniform is just hanging on you. You wanna talk about it?"

"Not much to say. I'm bummed Tom broke up with me and my new boss is a true butthole. Yes, you could say I'm a little stressed."

"What about getting some professional help? I wish I could help you get through this tough time but I don't know how to help."

"Naw, I'll be okay. If I can't snap out of this funk soon, I will go see a professional. I'm so busy at work, I don't know if I'm coming or going."

"I know the feeling, but at least my boss is fair. Your boss sounds like the worst captain ever. How does the battalion commander let him get away with his terrible leadership?"

Lori replied, "I don't know....maybe because we get the mission done. The morale is terrible in the company...the worst I've seen it in 2 years. "Sometimes I feel like all I do is try to fix his poisonous leadership style. It's funny. We have a high reenlistment rate because all of the soldiers reenlist for another unit or location to get away from him. He is almost worse than some of the upperclassmen who hated us when I was a plebe."

"Wow, that is bad. You'd think a captain would have his shit together and be a good leader."

"Yeah, you'd think….not in this case. I feel like I'm being torn in half. I try to follow his orders and guidance but he is so self-centered and he doesn't care at all for the soldiers' welfare. The NCOs are going crazy."

"That does suck Lori. I can't help you fix an idiot," Reggie said.

"Yeah, we'll get through it somehow. I just need to keep my head in the game or I'll be transferred to a new job in a heartbeat. He already thinks I'm not loyal and he's told me it's more important to support the commander than to support the subordinates."

Reggie replied, "Quite the dilemma. You are supposed to support your boss, but you're also required to care for your troops. I don't know the answer to this one Lori."

"Yeah, no one does. Until Captain Luster does something illegal or unethical, I'm bound to support him and his stupid orders. Too bad they didn't cover this at West Point."

"Yeah, me too. Well how about going out for some pizza? I don't feel like cooking or zapping something tonight."

"Sounds good Reggie. I'll be changed and ready in 10 minutes."

★ ★ ★

TWO MONTHS LATER, LORI was called into the battalion commander's office. She knocked twice on the door and heard an "Enter." Lori entered through the door stopped two feet away from the Commander's desk and saluted, "Sir, Lieutenant Nelson reports."

Colonel Martin saluted her back and said, "Please have a seat Lieutenant Nelson. Do you know why I called you here?"

"No sir."

"How long have you been in the 82nd?"

"Sir, about a year as a platoon leader and a little over a year as the executive officer."

"You were with Captain Archibald for most of that time is that correct?"

"Yes, sir."

"How was Captain Archibald's leadership style?"

"Sir, he was a good leader who cared about his soldiers and treated everyone fairly and with respect."

"That's what I observed too." Colonel Martin stated. "I'll get right to the heart of the matter; there have been nine IG complaints in your company in the last three months. The first one was filed one week after Captain Luster arrived. I find this very disheartening and I want to get to the bottom of these complaints and fix the problem. I need your help to do that. Do you now understand why you are here?"

Lori slowly nodded, "Yes, sir, I think I do."

"I also understand you are in a precarious position because you are supposed to be loyal and support your company commander. As the company XO, you are the second in command of the unit. Since the change of command, I'm sure you've seen ample evidence of Captain Luster's leadership style. How would you characterize his leadership?"

"Sir, I feel awkward talking about Captain Luster when he's not here."

"Yes, and I think that's a good thing Lori. Tells me you're loyal and don't like to talk about people behind their backs. Well I can assure you that this is different. I need your candid assessment as one of two people who see Captain Luster the most. My Command Sergeant Major is talking with your First Sergeant right now and asking him the same questions. So my question remains, how would you characterize Captain Luster's leadership?"

"Sir, it's awful," Lori blurted out. "I mean, he gives irrational orders with no regard to the soldiers or their families. Most of the soldiers are working 6 or 7 days a week and they often get home very late at night. I've had wives calling me at nine in the evening asking me if their husbands are really still at work."

"Are they?"

"Yes, sir. They are required to stay until Captain Luster releases them for the day."

"Was that an unusual event or does Captain Luster release the soldiers every day?"

"Sir, every weekday they work late. The platoon leaders have the authority to release their soldiers on Saturday and Sunday."

"So what is morale like in the unit?" Colonel Jones asked.

"Sir, it's the worst morale I have seen; especially since Captain Archibald was a fair and trusting leader who mentored and developed his subordinates."

"What kind of professional development is going on in the unit?"

"The first sergeant has weekly meetings with his platoon sergeants and I am trying to mentor the platoon leaders, but Captain Luster is providing no professional development. He holds a daily meeting at 0800 but he does not provide guidance or instructions. He leads by fear and intimidation, by yelling and demeaning the officers and NCOs."

"Hmmm...What's your relationship with your boss?"

"I am fairly confident I will get a terrible OER from him because I try to do the right thing and often that contradicts his guidance. I believe I'm the buffer between the soldiers and the commander, and I've had my share of chewing out sessions."

"You seem to be holding up well under the circumstances, although you do look a little thinner. Have you been losing weight?"

"Yes, sir," Lori replied.

"Hmmm, I see. Well I appreciate your candor Lori and I will be taking your comments, the first sergeant comments, and all of the evidence into consideration when I decide what needs to be done. Rest assured I will take appropriate action pronto!" Leaning back in his chair he continued, "Now I believe Captain Luster will quiz you on what we discussed and if he asks, I want you to tell your commander that I have ordered you not to discuss our privileged conversation. You can tell him that I will be speaking with him in the next few days."

"I can do that sir."

"Yes, I know you can. Thank goodness you are a strong officer. I appreciate your support to our soldiers."

Sensing the session was over, Lori stood up to leave.

Looking up while writing down some notes, Colonel Martin said, "Not so fast lieutenant. After this issue is resolved, I plan on moving you to my battalion 3 shop. I think you will enjoy the change of pace. Any questions or problems with that?"

Smiling, Lori answered, "No sir. That would be great."

"I think for your professional development you need to get a better understanding of MP operations and our training mission. Keep your head up soldier!" Colonel Martin saluted Lori while saying the MP motto, "Of the troops, for the troops!"

Lori stood at attention and returned the salute, executed an about face and walked out the door and slowly returned to her unit. Captain Luster was waiting for her to return. "So Nelson, come on in here," motioning to his office. "I've been waiting for you."

"Yes sir."

Smiling a fake smile, Luster said, "Tell me what your visit with the old man was all about."

"Sir, Colonel Martin ordered me not to discuss our privileged conversation. He said he would be speaking with you in the next few days."

"What the hell? That's bullshit! Tell it to me straight and don't mess with me Nelson. What did old numb-nuts tell you in his office?"

"Sir, I'm being truthful, the Colonel told me to tell you he would have a meeting with you in the next few days."

"God-dammit Nelson! I gave you a direct order! You better tell me what he said or you'll be in deep-shit!" Luster yelled.

"Sir, I am telling you what he told me to tell you. We also discussed a professional development opportunity for me in the future."

Suddenly smiling Luster said, "That's fine with me. I guess he'll be replacing you with a real MP. I need a real kick-ass MP who can hang with the men. Okay, you're dismissed Nelson. Get back to work!"

Lori saluted and said, "Airborne, Sir," and quickly left the room.

★ ★ ★

THAT EVENING LORI TOLD Reggie about her interesting day.

"Wow, Lori, perhaps Colonel Martin will fire Luster and solve everyone's problem."

"That would be the best thing for the soldiers and the unit. I didn't know so many soldiers have lodged IG complaints against him, but I'm not surprised. They get home around eight or nine every night with PT at six the next morning. They have no life."

"Considering the hellish hours you're working in garrison, I'm not surprised. Soldiers expect to work long hours in the field, but not in garrison. The families are affected too," Reggie said.

"The sooner Colonel Martin decides what to do, the better. Morale can't get much lower."

★ ★ ★

TWO DAYS LATER, Captain Luster returned to his office and slammed his door. Ten minutes later Lori picked up her ringing telephone saying, "Lieutenant Nelson. May I help you sir?"

"Nelson, this is Colonel Martin. I have just relieved your company commander and you will be the acting commander for a day or two until I find a suitable replacement to rebuild the unit. I trust your good judgment and I know you can hold down the fort for a few days. Do you understand?"

"Ah, Yes, Sir!"

"By the way, I'd steer clear of his office and don't let anyone go near him. Luster will be

packing up his office and will be out of the building this afternoon. He is not allowed to come back into the building. Do I make myself clear?"

"Yes, Sir. When can I tell the soldiers?" Lori asked.

"Any time you want, but the sooner the better. The first sergeant is getting his call from my sergeant major now, so the troops will know shortly."

"Sir, can I ask where he'll be going?"

"I offered him a deal he couldn't refuse. After the sexual harassment complaints, slapping a private in the motor pool, and confirmed travel fraud, I offered Luster a general discharge out of the Army in lieu of a court-marshal. He gladly accepted it. Of course, that info is between us, and the troops don't need to know that. If you need any advice or have any questions, call me. I know you're not school-trained on how to be a commander, but you served under Archibald, who was as good a Commander as they come. I know you'll do fine," and then he abruptly hung up the phone.

Lori sat for a few minutes and processed the phone call before she got up and walked into the first sergeants office. He was smiling from ear to ear. "I guess you heard the news?" he asked.

"Yes, Colonel Martin just called me and told me he relieved Luster and I'm the acting commander for a few days. I'm happy it turned out this way," Lori said.

"Happy? I'm so God-damned happy I could dance a jig right now. That boy was a self-centered, egomaniac, slimeball! All he did was ruin a good company. Let me know what you need ma'am, and I'll help you."

"Thanks Top. How about rounding up the soldiers for a very brief formation and we'll give them the news and then we'll dismiss them early. I think they'll enjoy that for a change."

Smiling for the second time in over three months, the first sergeant said, "Sounds great ma'am. I'll have the troops ready in 30 minutes."

30

FORT BRAGG, FEBRUARY 1983

"I'M SO HAPPY FOR you Roni," Lori commented as they walked in the park. "You know you don't have to get out. Many women have a baby and stay in the Army nowadays."

"I know. George and I discussed this. We haven't made a decision yet, but I'm leaning toward getting out. I'm only 12 weeks and haven't even told my mother yet. She's gonna freak out."

"How can you even think about getting out? You're a natural leader Roni. Your soldiers love you and you love them."

"I dunno. I think it's tough to have both parents on a FAD1 deployment cycle. What if George and I both get deployed at the same time?"

Lori said, "I've got a single mom who has a family care plan that gives temporary custody to her parents in the event she's deployed. Would your parents or George's parents be willing to have custody for a few months?"

"I don't know. There's so much to consider. I think they'd love to do it. But, I don't think I'd like to be away from my baby for a really long time either, but do I really want to give up my career because I'm having a baby?

I guess I could ask for a job and post that has units that are more stable and don't deploy at all, after I PCS from here."

"George and I talked about going to Fort Jackson or the Engineer school at Fort Leonard Wood. I'm due to rotate to my advanced course this fall and that would work out well for the baby timing. We'll figure it out." Roni abruptly changed the subject and asked, "So what's new with you Lori?"

"Same old stuff. I really like being a staff officer. I thought I wouldn't but I can influence so many people with thought-out planning and detailed training schedules. Plus, now that we're captains, I get so much more respect from the other units when I coordinate ranges and training areas."

"Yeah, amazing what doors open when you have a little rank," Roni added. "Enough about work; how's your love life after the gay SF guy?"

Smiling, Lori said, "Still as blunt as ever I see. Does George like your candid style?"

"Oh yeah! He loves my spunk and sass. He wouldn't have married me if he didn't love my attitude and frankness." Looking Lori in the eye, "So? How goes it?"

"I'm hanging in there but it's been tough. Every time I really like a guy, they surprise me and I get hurt. I guess I'm afraid to love again. The pain is just too great."

"You've had it rough. Most people have their hearts broken, but not twice in two years. I really liked Tom. I had no idea he was a homosexual."

"Welcome to the club. He seemed like the perfect guy for me. I was totally blindsided by his admission and never saw it coming. We're still friends but it's not the same."

"Shit, no kidding?" Roni asked as she changed subject again. "So what's next for you Lori?"

"Well, Reggie and I keep busy on the weekends when we're not in the field. We just found out the 503rd's going to Syracuse, New York in two weeks to help a community reign in some women who are protesting the nuclear energy plant. I don't know how long we'll be up there."

"Okay, but what about your love life?"

"You won't give it up will you? Okay, I think I might be ready to test the waters again, but I don't have anyone in my sights. I'm in no hurry to get burned again."

"I understand Lori. I think you're smart to go slow. Things happen when you least expect it. I mean, look at me and George. I didn't even want to go on the blind date and it was love at first sight...well actually for me it wasn't, but very close. Plus, you should see him in the sack. He makes my toes melt he's so good!"

Lori started blushing, "Ah."

Grinning, Roni said, "Sorry, I can't help myself. I'm pregnant remember?"

"Ya, and you're actually glowing; you look so happy Roni."

★ ★ ★

"SO LORI, YOU WANNA watch the final episode of MASH with me?" Reggie asked.

Lori replied half-heartedly, "I don't have anything else planned."

"Great! I try to catch up with my favorite shows when I'm not in the field. I love Hawkeye and Radar, they're so funny. I ordered pizza and we've got all kinds of beer in the fridge," Reggie added.

"Sure." Lori replied, "What's more fun than laughing with friends?"

31

FORT BRAGG, APRIL 1983

ANNE AND MAURA HUGGED Lori and Reggie, as they walked into their house and Anne held out a bouquet of fresh tulips. "Thanks for inviting us to dinner Lori,"

Lori admired the flowers as she handed them to Reggie. "Thanks, they're beautiful! Now I must admit I'm not a cook; which is why it took so long for me to invite you over for dinner. Reggie did most of the cooking. She makes a mean lasagna. All I did was make the salad, bought desert, and cleaned up the place."

Reggie walked back to the kitchen to put the flowers in a vase and set them on the dining room table. Maura handed Lori a vintage bottle of red wine as they followed behind her and Reggie. Anne said, "It's great to see you Reggie. We haven't seen you since Lori's promotion. I know we've all been so busy with our work schedules, but we really do need to figure out a way to get together more often."

"Great to see you both again! Lori, how 'bout you pour all of us a glass of vino, while I check on the lasagna? I need to take it out of the oven and let it sit for 15 minutes."

Lori got the wine opener out of the drawer, pointed to a nearby cabinet and asked Maura and Anne, "Could one of you get four wine glasses?" As Maura and Anne brought the wine glasses over to the counter, Lori asked, "Would you like some wine before we eat?"

"You know we never turn down a glass of wine. Are you drinking wine now too?" Maura asked.

"As a matter of fact, I started drinking wine on special occasions. It's a little classier." Lori responded and added, "This will be perfect to toast to all of us being captains!"

"Easy for you to say Lori. I've got another six months before I make captain," Reggie groaned as she set the hot lasagna pan on the stove top.

"Sorry Regg, I keep forgetting you haven't pinned on." Lori said apologetically. "But it'll be nice to be the same rank for a while and not have to deal with the rank issues until Maura and Anne pin on their major leafs."

"Hard to believe it's been five years since we were you and Trish's sponsors in Germany," Anne remarked in a reflective tone. "We had so many cool adventures that summer."

"That summer was *so* much fun," Lori remarked wistfully.

Reggie walked over to join the group and picked up her wine glass. "What are your plans after the advanced course?"

"I'm thinking about putting Germany on my dream sheet for my next assignment. I'd love to command an MP Company in Germany."

"That would be cool," Reggie said. "How 'bout you guys? Where will you be heading next?"

Maura replied first, "I'm working with branch. They want me to go to PERSCOM to be an assignments officer."

Anne joined in, "I'm hoping to extend here for another year. I'm really enjoying being the S-3 at the S&T battalion and Derek and I don't want to be split up. But enough about the Army, I thought we were going to toast to friendships and promotions."

Each woman raised her glass as Anne proposed, "To friends, lovers, and more adventures to come! Each woman took a sip of wine and Lori murmured appreciatively. "Very nice, not sure if I can go back to Boone's Farm, after tasting this."

Laughing, Maura asked, "So Lori, what's new on the boyfriend front?"

"I'm doing okay." Lori mused. "I've been dating a few guys off and on, but nothings clicked. I can usually tell after the first 5 minutes, if I want to see them again."

"How do you know?" Maura asked.

"It's a gut-feeling I get. Sometimes it's nonverbal gestures, sometimes it's the self-absorbed, one sided conversation. Can't really explain it, just know it when I feel it and the few times I've ignored the signs, I've regretted it."

"I'm so glad we don't have to deal with the dating scene anymore, not sure I'd even remember how to act, it's been so long since I've even thought about the possibility of having to get in the fray again," Anne remarked thoughtfully.

"Tell me about it." Lori moaned. After my experiences with Scott and Tom, I'm hesitant to even get involved again."

"Oh? What happened with Tom?" Anne asked.

Lori looked over at Reggie and hesitated before replying. "Roni and Reggie are the only friends I've talked to about this," adding, "I know I can trust both of you, but have to ask that you keep this strictly between us."

"Of course you can trust us; but please don't tell us he's an ax murder!" Anne remarked sarcastically before Maura could reply.

Irritated by Anne's comment, Lori replied curtly, "This information could damage and end Tom's career."

Equally irritated by the unexpected request and drama, Maura snapped, "Out with it Lori. You have our word that this will stay between us."

"Tom admitted he's a homosexual," Lori blurted out.

"Well shit, who would'a guessed such a hunk liked boys…what a waste," Anne mournfully replied.

Lori nodded. "I was totally unprepared for that. We're still friends, but I'd really started to care for him and wanted more than just a platonic relationship."

"You've just had a run of bad luck Lori. You're still young, you'll find the right guy. How old are you anyway?" Maura asked.

"I'm 25, but I feel older than that sometimes."

"You've had some pretty serious and traumatic experiences not to mention your work problems in your unit last year," Maura said sympathetically. "But don't let that jade or destroy your spirit. There's someone special out there for you, you just need to keep looking."

"True enough. I just met two new guys at the gym last week and one of them asked me out. We're going out for a burger and a movie tomorrow night. Who knows, this could be the one for me." Lori countered hopefully.

"Drink some more wine and cheer up Lori." Anne said as she refilled Lori's glass. You never know when the love bug will bite….and like Maura said, sometimes it takes longer than you'd like." Looking at Reggie Anne walked over, filled her wine glass and asked mischievously, "So Reggie, what's new with you?"

"Well, As far as my new job, I just started as the Traffic OIC in the XVIIth Airborne Corps, provost marshal's office this week. I really don't know if I like it yet or not. I was hoping to be selected as XO, but that didn't work out and I'm really going to miss being a platoon leader. On the personal front, I've been dating a nice guy named Doug for the past 6 months. I think our relationship is going well but we're not in a hurry to get serious."

"What company were you in?" Maura asked.

"I was in the 65th MP Company, 503rd MP Battalion. You know, as a leg, I couldn't get to the 82nd MP Company with Lori and because she was the company XO, when I got to Bragg, it would've been a conflict of interest to work for her."

"Yeah, that could have been difficult," Maura said. "There's also politics to deal with and there's no way they would have assigned two women to that company. Lori coming here from West Point and jump school, is what got her assigned to the 82nd MP company rather than the 65th, 21st, or 108th."

Lori chimed in, "Well, I have it on good authority that my second commander had a cow when he found out he had a female XO. The troops hated him because he was just plain mean and he messed with them and their families all the time. Thank God he was relieved when he was or there might have been a mutiny in the unit."

"I know it wasn't easy for you Lori," Anne said sympathetically.

"You can say that again. I hated going to work. I felt like I was a buffer between the soldiers and the commander. Every morning at our staff meeting he belittled someone for a minor issue. He was arrogant, focused on the negatives, and always picked on someone. I learned more about poor leadership and what not to do from observing him in action. The sad part is many good soldiers got out of the Army because of their experience with him."

"That's terrible. We've all seen commanders who shouldn't be in the job; but we also know there are a lot of good commanders too," Anne said finishing the last sip of her wine. "Speaking of which, how's my favorite Fort Lewis captain doing?"

Lori replied, "Reggie and I saw Trish last summer in Vegas. She's doing much better now that she's on I Corps staff. When she arrived at Fort Lewis, she got another platoon because they were short quartermaster lieutenants. Her commander made her life miserable because of her sex, but because she was a 1LT and had been a platoon leader in 2ID, she only stayed in the position for 4 months before moving to Corps staff. I talked to her last week. She's happy with her job and she's playing basketball on the post women's team."

"That's great!" Anne said. "I know she's not much of a letter writer, but I was worried because I hadn't heard from her in months. Thanks for the update and tell her I said hi."

"I only got 3 letters the whole time she was in Korea. But she's doing great at Lewis and her mom is happy she's back in country," Lori replied. I'll tell her you said hi."

"I think the lasagna should be ready now," Reggie replied eagerly. "Don't know 'bout anyone else, but I'm hungry. How about we move to the dining room?"

"Sounds good. It smells delicious," Anne said as they all reached for something to carry and moved into the dining area just off the kitchen.

32

FORT BRAGG NC, JUNE 1983

AMELIA AND MAURA ADJUSTED the simple two layer elbow length bridal veil around Anne's bare shoulders. Amelia stepped back to look at her friend. "It's perfect."

Anne turned to look in the mirror. Seeing her mother's veil on her for the first time brought a lump to her throat as she looked upward, trying not to cry. In a grief stricken rage shortly after her mother was killed in a car accident, her father gave all her mother's belongings to the Salvation Army. It was not until her 16th birthday, that she discovered her oldest brother had secretly hidden the veil from their father and kept it for Anne. She smiled at the memory of her brother taking her to her bedroom, pointing to the white rectangular box on her bed, and telling her it was a special birthday surprise from their mom.

Turning back to her two best friends, Anne announced, "It's time ladies, are you ready?" Both Maura and Amelia nodded yes. Anne pulled the upper tier of the veil down over her face as Amelia opened the door of the bridal party prep room at the Fort Bragg post chapel.

With both parents dead, Anne had originally decided to walk down the aisle alone; but when Derek's dad had offered to walk her down the aisle shortly after they had told his parents they were engaged, Anne, took him up on the offer. As they entered the chapel foyer, Anne smiled at the sight of her about to be father-in-law. He had complained that he'd had to give up his nightly martinis for the past month, so he could fit in his mess dress uniform. As he turned to greet her, he let out a quiet whistle and winked at her as he extended his bent arm for her to take hold of. Being a retired two star general, his uniform was quite impressive. His white dress mess jacket was adorned with five rows of miniature medals, including the combat marksmanship badge and master blaster airborne wings. Below the medals were Army and Joint Staff badges.

"You're looking quite magnificent yourself, Sir." Anne whispered as she gave him a wink and locked her arm in his. Anne turned her head and nodded to the two captains serving as ushers, standing by the closed wooden doors that lead to the chapel. Looking extremely handsome in their dress blues with bloused pants tucked into their Corcoran airborne boots, the ushers opened the doors, which was the cue for the organist to start the bridal procession march, which started with six commissioned officer saber bearers.

Having worked together at JSOC for over a year, Derek and Eric had become close friends and Derek asked Eric to be his best man. Derek and Eric had their eyes glued to the open chapel doors, waiting for their first glimpse of the woman each of them loved. Eric got his first glance of Maura waiting in the door arch, as the sword bearers took their place at the chancel with the chaplain, groom, and best man. He beamed with pride as she walked down the aisle in a strapless, purple bridesmaid dress with a lavender waistband. Amelia, who was the matron of honor, followed in the same strapless gown, but it was lavender with a dark purple waistband. Anne came into view shortly after and Derek couldn't take his eyes off of her. Her simple dress with the veil reaching below her shoulders and covering her face, gave her a wraithlike appearance. Derek had never given up on the possibility that if he were patient, Anne would eventually trust him enough to lower the emotionally protective wall she'd entombed herself in. As Anne walked down the aisle, she was glad she'd chosen to wear her mother's veil, not only because it helped her feel like her parents were there with her in spirit; but because she knew she might shed a tear or two during the ceremony and the veil would hide the emotions she was feeling. The ceremony was a blur for both of them until it was time for her and Derek to exchange vows.

Anne put the ring on Derek's finger and quietly recited, "I give you this ring as a symbol of my vows and with all that I am and that I have, I honor you in the name of the Father, and of the Son, and of the Holy Spirit."

Derek then lifted Anne's veil and their eyes locked on each other as Derek placed the ring on Anne's finger, never releasing his gaze on her as he recited the same vow.

The military priest had barely declared them man and wife when Derek gently kissed Anne on the lips. The electricity that ran through both of their bodies was palpable and it was with great reluctance, that Derek ended the kiss. At the priest's introduction of them as man and wife, they turned to face the small, but loving crowd of friends and family. It seemed like an eternity as they watched the rest of the bridal party and all their guests depart, before they walked down the aisle behind them. Standing at the outer door of the chapel, Derek quietly asked, "You ready for this?" Looking straight ahead, she whispered "Yes." They walked down the steps of the chapel to the portico where the six saber bearers, in dress uniform, bloused pants tucked inside highly polished Corcoran jump boots, green berets, with flash insignia were waiting for them to proceed through the arch of raised swords. Even though she knew it was coming, Anne gave a slight gasp, as the outer saber bearer swished her backside with his sword and instead of yelling the traditional greeting he would to a nonmilitary bride, he yelled, "Airborne ma'am!" which elicited laughter from the waiting guests, who immediately started pelting the couple with rice, as they made their way to the waiting horse drawn carriage that Derek had insisted on.

With all the guests headed to the chapel parking lot to drive to the reception at the officers club, Amelia, Maura, Eric, and Charles, along with Derek and Amelia's parents posed for pictures in front of the white with gold trim, open horse drawn carriage.

As the carriage pulled away from the chapel, Derek wrapped his arm protectively around Anne's shoulders as she rested her head on his shoulder. She couldn't remember any time in her life when she was as happy and content as she was now. As they apporached the first intersection, she looked out at the cars queued up by the military police, waiting for them to pass. She waved to them and quietly said to Derek, "I sure hope no one we know well is in one of those waiting cars. People don't expect to be held up on a Sunday afternoon for a horse drawn wedding carriage." Derek just squeezed her closer to him and replied, "This is gonna happen once in our life and when you showed me the picture of your parents wedding with them in a white horse drawn carriage, I decided this was a way for you to feel like they were here with us."

Her voice quivering with emotion, Anne turned her head to look at Derek. "Was this the wedding day surprise you mentioned you had for me at our rehearsal dinner last night?"

Derek responded with a nod of his head and a big grin. "Happy?"

Unable to talk, Anne just reached up to kiss him and nodded back, before burying her face in his chest, so he wouldn't see the tears of joy welling up in her eyes.

★ ★ ★

DEREK HELPED ANNE OUT of the carriage in front of the officers club and they walked into the entry foyer, where Eric, Maura, Amelia, and Charles were waiting for them.

"Do you guys need a few minutes before we do the reception line?" Eric asked.

Derek shook his head. "Nah, we're good. I want to get the formal stuff over with, so everyone can just relax and have a good time." With that, everyone except Amelia and Charles walked toward the ballroom where the guests were waiting for the reception to begin.

Amelia took Charles aside. "Thanks for being such a good sport. Why don't you go to the bar, get a drink and chat with my parents, while we do the receiving line. Once we're done, I'll come get you and we can go to our seats at the head table."

"Sure." Charles responded amiably, as he kissed Amelia and walked away.

The reception line finally finished, Maura exhaled loudly as they prepared for the wedding party to enter the hall for the cake cutting ceremony. Pulling Eric aside, Maura whispered into his ear. "When we get married, you can wear your uniform, but we are not getting married at Bragg and doing all this military stuff!"

Eric chuckled, "Yes ma'am, WILCO; which elicited a grin and nod of approval from Maura. The command for the saber bearers to enter the reception hall had just been given and once they were lined up facing each other, Derek and Anne made their way to the wedding cake passing under the final saber arch. Derek removed his ceremonial saber from its sheath, put it in Anne's hand, put his hand over hers and they cut the wedding cake. They had agreed beforehand not to smash wedding cake in each other's face, much to the disappointment of some of their guests, who expressed their displeasure by hooting and yelling. Smiling, both of them made their way to the head table, followed by the bridal party and Charles, who Anne had insisted on breaking with tradition by having him at the head table, because while it would not have been appropriate for him to be included in the wedding party, it would also be inappropriate and awkward for everyone if Amelia could not be seated with her husband. As soon as Eric was certain everyone was seated at their tables and had their champagne glasses filled, he put the microphone in his hand, and tapped his glass with a fork, to get everyone's attention.

"Ladies and Gentlemen, I propose a toast to the newly married, Captains Williams!" A loud cheer of "Hear, hear!" arose as the guests lifted their glasses and took a drink of champagne. Eric sat down and shortly thereafter, the wait staff arrived with a shrimp cocktail appetizer, and silver baskets filled with bread. This was followed by the seafood entrée of Coquilles san Jacques, which was Anne's favorite dish. Anne noticed the confused look on some peoples' faces when the small salad of mixed greens with alight vinaigrette arrived after the entrée. Standing up, she retrieved the microphone Eric had used for his toast and tapped it, to get everyone's attention. "Ladies and gentlemen, for those of you who are not familiar with French formal dining, while I have abbreviated and deleted some of the courses, unlike American eating customs, the French eat their salad after the entrée. If you will look at the menu card in the middle of each of your tables, you will see that a small meat course with a side of vegetables will follow the salad and a small scoop of lemon sorbet will be served to cleanse your palate. Lastly, you will be served the wedding cake and by that time, with all the bread, food, and liquor you've consumed, if you are still capable of dancing, we hope you'll stay to party 'til you drop, or the staff tells us it's midnight and they are closing." This elicited more laughter as Anne returned to her seat.

★ ★ ★

HAVING FINISHED THEIR SLICE of wedding cake, Derek leaned over and whispered in Anne's ear. "Are you ready for our first dance as man and wife?" Anne smiled and nodded 'yes' which prompted Derek to turn and nod to Eric, who knew that was his cue to have the DJ start the musical portion of the evening.

The lights flickered and then dimmed, as the DJ's deep baritone announced, "Ladies and Gentlemen, Derek and Anne have chosen Elton John's *Your Song* for their first dance as man and wife. Derek and Anne motioned the head table to join them, followed by his parents. At the end of the song, the DJ announced, "Let's give the happy couple a big shout out and join them on the dance floor" as *Then Came You* started playing.

After the second dance ended, Anne told Derek, "I'm going to take Maura and Amelia aside for a few minutes. Can you get Eric and Charles and have a drink together until we get back?" As soon as Derek said, "Sure." Anne motioned to Maura and Amelia to join her, as she started walking away and Derek simultaneously motioned to Eric and Charles to join him.

"What's up?" Maura asked, surprised by Anne's summons. "I want a few minutes with both of you. I need to get something I had the staff put under the table at my feet. I'll meet you in the hallway." Anne entered the hallway with two small rectangular packages wrapped in lavender colored foil with a dark purple satin ribbon and bow. Pointing to a door just down the hall, Anne said, "Let's go in there." Anne opened the door and turned the light on, revealing a small private dining room used for VIP meetings. Turning to her best friends, she handed the packages to them. "You guys are too funny. I wasn't sure how I'd deal with you asking me if I'd forgotten to give you your presents from me." Anne looked at Maura and chuckled, "I knew Amelia would never ask; but I figured the two of you would discuss it and she would convince you to ask the question. But noooo, you both just soldiered on and never brought up the subject. Pausing, Anne gave them a loving gaze. "Thank you to both of you or always being there for me. The reason you didn't get your gifts until now, is because I was at a loss about what to give each of you, after the beautiful pearl necklace and earrings Amelia gave us, which matched the set she wore on her wedding day. But when we agreed on the colors and style of dresses you'd each wear, Amelia's suggestion that we all wear the pearl necklace and earrings we'd worn the day she'd gotten married, provided the inspiration for your gifts." Anne pointed to the still unopened presents they were holding. "Open them please and I hope you like it."

Amelia's gasp of surprise was quickly followed by Maura's grin as both of them exclaimed, "This is perfect." Anne's face glowed as she murmured, "I'm so glad. I want you to know that I gave myself one as well and it'll be prominently displayed in our home, wherever that ends up being." The gift Anne had given them was a Waterford crystal frame of the close up, head and shoulders picture of the three of them at Amelia's reception, smiling, wearing the matching pearl necklaces and earrings. As the three women hugged each other, Maura grinned ruefully and announced, "I obviously should have gotten married before Anne. I'll never be able to come up with a present for the two of you that beats this!" Maura hugged Anne, "Good job."

"I hate to break this up," Amelia said apologetically. "But if you and Derek are going to walk around and mingle with your other guests and still get out of here in time to get to Raleigh tonight, so you can catch your flight to Atlanta and Key West in the morning, you need to get back to the reception soon. But before you do that, Charles and I need to talk to you and Derek. You say your good-byes to Maura, while I go fetch the guys." Without waiting for an answer, Amelia walked out of the room."

Maura laughed. "And to think we worried that Amelia would be taken advantage of and mentally abused by Charles."

"I told Amelia years ago, she was stronger than she gave herself credit for." Anne remarked musingly. "I guess being in the Army, spending three years with us and going back to Charles on her terms, has helped her blossom."

Maura sat down. "Maybe Charles has changed too. I've spent a bit of time the past few days trying to get to know him better. He seems to genuinely care for her, is protective of her, and is actually nice."

Anne started to respond, but didn't because Amelia returned with the three guys in tow. As she closed the door behind her, Amelia walked over to Charles, gave him a kiss and turned to her friends. "We promise not to keep you guys long, but Charles and I have some news that we want to share with you privately, before all of us go our separate ways." She turned and quietly said, "Charles…"

Charles nodded and addressed the group of friends who were both intrigued and curious. Charles took Amelia's hand and walked over to Anne. "Derek, could you join us?" When Derek came over to stand by Anne, Charles continued. "Almost a year ago, we asked both of you to consider being godparents to our yet unborn child. As you know, a few months later, Amelia miscarried. We discovered last week that Amelia is pregnant again and would like to ask you again to be our first child's godparents."

Stunned into silence initially, Anne was the first to respond as she hugged Amelia, exclaiming, "Of course we will, we'd be honored." Then realizing her oversight, she turned to Derek, "Right Derek?"

Everyone laughed as hugs and congratulations were exchanged. After several minutes, Derek announced, "Okay, I hate to break this up, but we have to spend a bit of time with my parents and other guests before we head to Raleigh." Turning to Eric, he said, "Brother, we need the limo here in an hour. Got that covered?" Eric nodded affirmation as Derek and Anne walked out headed back to the reception.

33

FORT BRAGG, N.C. MONDAY, 24 OCTOBER 1983

THE PREVIOUS THURSDAY EVENING, Anne had called Maura to see if Eric had come home. Maura resignedly replied, "No, have you heard from Derek?"

"No," Anne replied. "How about we agree to calling each other if one of us hears from our strays?"

Maura and Anne had gotten quite accustomed to the unexplained disappearance and reappearance of their Special Forces husbands, so Maura agreed with Anne's plan to talk on Friday, before hanging up the phone.

Early Saturday morning, after receiving a telephone call using a code word alerting them to a possible deployment, Maura, Anne and Lori received a briefing similar to the one that Eric and Derek had gotten the previous Thursday. The briefing included the details of their units deploying in support of a top secret mission to rescue American medical students being held hostage on the Caribbean island of Grenada, which later became public and was given the code name, *Operation Urgent Fury.*

CPSIA information can be obtained
at www.ICGtesting.com
Printed in the USA
FFOW02n1633200318
45759681-46620FF

9 781457 560774